CHRISTMAS MOUSE
© 2022 BY RACHEL SPANGLER

THIS TRADE PAPERBACK ORIGINAL IS PUBL_____ ⌐Y BRISK PRESS,
WAPPINGERS FALLS, NY 12590

SUBSTANTIVE EDIT BY: LYNDA SANDOVAL
COPY EDIT BY: AVERY BROOKS
COVER DESIGN BY: KEVIN @ BOOKCOVERS ONLINE
AUTHOR PHOTO BY: ANNA BURKE
BOOK LAYOUT AND TYPESETTING BY: SUSAN SPANGLER

FIRST PRINTING:

ISBN: 978-1-7343038-8-9

Christmas Mouse

Rachel Spangler

To Susie:
In every place, and every season, it's all your fault.

Chapter One

"Well done, friend." Bex snapped off her gloves as the door to the OR closed behind her. Then she turned to give Howie a fist bump. "Still the steadiest hand in the game."

He laughed as he knocked his knuckles on hers and threw his arm around her shoulders in an off-centered half hug. "You're one to talk. She didn't even flinch when you inserted the epidural."

Bex shrugged. "Some are easier than others."

"You always make it look easier than anyone else on staff, and I never worry about anesthesia when you're beside me. I want to buy you a drink after every single surgery we do together."

"I'm free tonight," Bex offered, never one to turn down an evening out. "Want to start at Puffy's around eight and see where the night takes us?"

Howie removed his scrub hat, revealing short-cropped dark hair with flecks of gray near the temples. "I'd love to, but I need to pack. I'm catching the train to Vermont tomorrow."

"Ugh, you're seriously going to spend the day before Thanksgiving on a train to the boonies?"

He laughed, a deep rumbling sound. "Don't start this again. My family's less than thirty minutes from Burlington and fifteen minutes from Montpelier. It's not the middle of nowhere. Vermont is kind of the home of your people."

Bex shook her head. "My people are all New Yorkers."

"You know what I mean."

"Lesbians?"

"Exactly. I always see them hiking and cross-country skiing and walking their dogs through the farmers' markets with their organic produce and fleece vests."

She laughed. "Hard no. I'm not that kind of queer. These are country lesbians you speak of. We're a distantly related species, but our customs and norms are entirely different. I'm an urban gay. I'm suspenders to their functional footwear. I'm the Michelin star to their Tofurky. I'm *The L Word* to their Indigo Girls."

He stared at her a few seconds before saying, "I didn't understand half of that."

"You're not meant to. The point is, I live in New York City because this is where I belong, and I don't understand why you'd want to leave the greatest place in the world for someplace that's, well, not."

"You're such a snob. Vermont is beautiful, always, but especially in autumn. It's been a warm fall. There's still vibrant color on the trees in the lower elevations and snow on the mountaintops. It's the best of both worlds. You're going to pass it up to stand in the wind and rain to go to the parade ... again?"

She folded her arms across her chest as he landed a legitimate point. She loved attending the Macy's Thanksgiving Day Parade every year, but the forecast for this week made the word "dreary" seem understated. There'd been some speculation that the big balloons might not fly.

"You're wavering." Howie rocked forward as if he could hardly contain his excitement. "Come with me. It'll be good for you."

She rolled her eyes. "I'm a doctor. I don't buy all the fresh mountain air propaganda."

"The air is fine, but some home cooking would be a nice break from restaurants, and a few days away from work would do a world of good for your stress levels."

She held up one finger. "If you give me statistics about anesthesiologists and mental breakdowns, I'll punch you."

He tightened his arm around her shoulder, having to angle up slightly to do so. "I wouldn't dare, but I hate the idea of you eating takeout all alone on a holiday."

"I'm never alone in a city of eight million people."

"You know what I mean. You're a part of my family here. Come meet my family back home."

"Wait, aren't they kind of conservative?"

"No," he said quickly. "We're from Vermont. Everyone's super liberal, well, except for one great-uncle, but he's just a button pusher who's never even met a person of color and thinks feminism is the real f-word."

She pushed back. "Great. I can hear the banjos already."

"Come on. He's one guy. Everyone else is abundantly awesome and smart and fun. One of my cousins is bringing an organic heirloom turkey. Another one is doing a master's in sustainability at UVM with an interest in medical-grade plastics, which is right up your alley."

She nodded grudgingly.

"Plus, I saved the best for last. The cousin who still lives in town is gay, so you won't even be the only out person there."

"Oh yay, one gay in the whole village."

"No," he corrected. "With you there, we'll have two!"

As they pushed out into the waiting room of the surgical center, she caught a glimpse of sideways rain hitting the front windows and shivered. She didn't have any desire to leave New York, but the prospect of being cooped up on a long weekend didn't sit right either. She looked forward to this time of year for months, and she wanted to kick off her holiday season on the right foot. If she couldn't go to the parade, maybe a home-cooked meal, a mountain retreat, and time with a good friend's big family wouldn't be a terrible backup plan.

"Come on," Howie prodded as they headed toward the recovery wing. "I need to check on a couple more patients, but then, what do you say we bust out of here together and head north?"

She sighed heavily. "I suppose a country Thanksgiving sounds like it might be kind of charming once in my life."

"It will be. Don't overthink it. I'll call my grandma right now and tell her you're coming." He grinned like a kid who'd just been told he could have a puppy, and slapped her on the shoulder. "Trust me. You're going to love it so much you'll want to come every year."

She opened her mouth to argue or at least set a more reasonable expectation, but before she got the chance, he jogged off down the hall. She might've even heard him whisper, "Tribeca's taking a country vacation," to one of the nurses as he passed.

She wished she could share some of his enthusiasm, but as she pushed open the door to the locker room, she couldn't help but wonder what she'd gotten herself into.

A country holiday wasn't her style. Would Howie's family even know how to cook a turkey? Would their mashed potatoes come from a box? What if they deep-fried everything or yelled at football games through dinner, or smoked, or … she shook her head. She should've asked more questions. In fact, she wasn't sure she'd actually even agreed all the way. She should call Howie back and say she changed

4

her mind, but as he skipped off out of view, the thought of wrecking his joy made her even sadder than the prospect of a botched Thanksgiving. He was a good colleague and an even better friend. She ground her teeth and resolved to take one for the team, even if it did feel a little awkward.

Besides, as much as she didn't want to miss a holiday in the city, at least it was just Thanksgiving and not Christmas.

"Ava, love, will you get the seat covers from the basement?" Gram called from the kitchen. "I'm trying to limit the number of times I have to go up and down stairs today."

"Of course." She hopped up from the dining room table where she'd been snapping the ends off green beans. "That's what I'm here for."

"I do appreciate your enthusiasm." Gram chuckled. "And your young knees."

"You want me to get anything else while I'm down there?"

"Not that I can think of. Your brother already came by yesterday and hauled up all the folding chairs. I should've had him look for the covers then, but you know my mind these days."

"Your mind's fine. Don't think I haven't noticed you pulled out your recipe book last night and haven't even cracked it open yet."

"I may've peeked at the pie filling ratios, but I suppose I've made the rest of it enough times by now to know."

Ava knew what she meant. In her younger years, cooking seemed almost magical. There were potions and measurements and movements to be perfectly timed, but after thirty years of Thanksgivings spent at her grandmother's

5

side, she too found she could make many of the recipes from memory. She felt a little prick of pride as she flipped on the basement light and descended the stairs.

She didn't have to search long for the seat covers, as she'd been the one to put them away last year, but still she glanced around to see if she should snag anything else. She spotted a few old cornhusk turkeys they'd made when she and Howie were little and grabbed them to use as a centerpiece for the kids' table, then gave a fleeting glance to the Christmas decorations on her way back up. Their time would come soon enough, but just the thought of pulling them up when she took all of these things back down tomorrow gave her a thrill of anticipation.

"Tomorrow," she chided herself in a whisper and climbed back toward the main floor of the old farmhouse. She headed for the dining room when the television caught her eye, and she paused to watch the Macy's Thanksgiving Day Parade kick off with a great swirl of music and flashy logos, but as soon as they faded, the picture turned gray and hazy around two announcers in rain ponchos and hoods.

"I'm glad you spent the night here," Gram said. "You were right about getting an early start ..." Her voice trailed off as she came in and saw what had caught Ava's attention. "Those poor people."

"I don't get it," she said. "All those crowds pushing around those slick city streets in the rain and the cold. They look flipping miserable."

Gram elbowed her in the ribs. "Since when are you one to mind the cold?"

"I'm not, but I'd take snow over a fifty-degree drizzle any day. Besides, the best part of cold weather is coming in to get warm by the fire with hot cocoa and melting marshmallows and your favorite quilt. Those people are headed

6

back to sterile hotels and impersonal restaurants. No, thank you."

Gram waved her hand. "To each their own."

She couldn't argue. Everyone was welcome to enjoy whatever holiday activities they wanted, but maybe some of them didn't even know any better. Not everybody had been raised in paradise like she had. She wandered over to the big picture window in the front of the house and stared past the spacious wraparound porch to the vast natural masterpiece before her.

Gram's house sat midway on a hill that rolled down to a cascading creek, then rose steeply up the other bank through a grove of thickly crowded maple trees. The last hints of autumn color stuck stubbornly to the lowest branches, but the frost line had crept ever closer for weeks, and even as the early sun shone brightly over the small apple orchard and down to the narrow road running into town, she could make out gray wisps of clouds bringing welcome snow to Stowe and Killington. Without thinking too much, she cracked open the front door, exhaling the indoor air and taking a long, slow breath laden with the scent of crisp leaves and wood smoke rising from her neighbor's chimney.

"Now you stop right now!" Gram scolded. "Trying to heat the whole outdoors just to smell nature when you have a whole house full of cooking food to enjoy."

She grinned and shut the door. Gram wasn't wrong. Then again, she rarely was. "The turkey's starting to take over the aromas now."

"And it ought to for all the fuss Ethan made over the damn bird. It probably should've cooked itself."

She shook her head and wandered back into the kitchen. Gram loved having her grandkids take pride in helping keep family traditions alive or create new ones. She pretended not to understand their return to organic farming.

Or maybe she enjoyed ribbing them as a reminder that the younger generation wasn't doing anything she didn't already know how to do. "I know. Back in your day, you used to shoot the birds out in the woods."

She shrugged. "We didn't know what they ate. We just intended to eat them, but I'll admit, those new apples you and Howie planted when he graduated sure do have more flavor than the old ones. I mixed some into the pie, and it gives it more ... I don't know what."

"Complexity," Ava offered as she started pulling potatoes from a bin and tossing them into the sink to rinse.

"That's a good word for it. I've got two of those, two pumpkin pies, and two maple pecan. Your mom's bringing cookies and the rolls." Gram ran through the list for the fifth time as she grabbed a potato peeler and took a seat at the table. "Ethan brought the bird. Mel's bringing both green bean and sweet potato casseroles. Your uncle Clay's bringing beer."

"Shocking," she deadpanned.

Gram ignored her tone. "And your Aunt Helen's bringing roasted Brussels sprouts. She wanted to bring the cranberry sauce, but she lost those privileges the year she put oranges in it."

Ava snorted softly, not wanting to relive the trauma. "And we've got the mashed potatoes, the noodles, gravy, and stuffing. Wait, you forgot Howie. What's he bringing?"

"Howie's bringing some wine," Gram said, then quickly added, "and I don't want to hear you fuss about how he never helps. He's taking time off from work to come all the way up from New York. Also, he's bringing a friend with him this year."

"I didn't know Howie had any friends." She took the last of the potatoes to the table.

8

Gram slapped her arm but laughed anyway. "You two should've been siblings the way you dig at each other. You need to be nice to his friend too."

"I'm never rude to any guest, but if this friend happens to sit down next to Uncle Clay, he's on his own."

Gram clucked disapprovingly.

"What? If someone has to fall on that sword, it might as well be someone we don't know. The poor city guy won't know what he's in for until it's too late."

Gram finally laughed. "That's a fair enough plan, but just so you know, it's not a he, it's a she."

Ava raised her eyebrows. "Howie's bringing a woman to Thanksgiving dinner?"

Gram shrugged. "Don't ask me anything else. I have no idea where this is headed."

"Wow," Howie said as soon as Bex met him outside her hotel. "You suited up."

That should've been her first clue something was off, paired with the fact that he wore jeans and a brown, cabled sweater, but Howie always dressed down. He'd worn sneakers to a wedding they'd both attended once. He was not to be trusted on matters of attire, but as they pulled off a country lane onto a gravel driveway leading to a large, old farmhouse, she noticed two men standing outside in jeans as well.

"I'm overdressed, aren't I?" she asked as he killed the engine.

"Totally, but it's okay. I'll tell everyone you're from the city and I told you to wear whatever you usually wear on Thanksgiving."

She gestured to her suit. "And how did you not see this coming? I don't normally spend holidays dressed like a peasant."

He laughed. "It's fine. Maybe lose the tie and pop open the collar."

"So, you do need me to dress like a mechanic?" she grumbled but did as instructed. "Will I fit in now?"

"Nope, but you'll be welcomed all the same. Seriously, relax. I'm really glad you're here, and you will be, too by the end of the day."

She sighed, not sure she believed the second part, but the guy was so damn earnest, she couldn't feel much anxiety as they climbed out of the car. She glanced around and had to admit the vista projected an almost postcard quality beauty, and the warmth hit her before she'd even fully stepped onto the wraparound porch.

A whole cadre of people met them at the door. Kids ran past, dogs jumped excitedly, women hugged Howie and patted his cheek as he struggled to make introductions. Bex couldn't even begin to learn all the names as everyone completely overwhelmed them in a sea of denim and flannel. And vests. It looked as though maybe fleece or down vests might be a sort of requirement for women in this group. If she'd known, she might've tried to purchase one, but then again, maybe not.

"Let them through the door," an older woman called from the back of the pack, and the people parted, allowing Bex to step across the threshold.

"Hello, Gram." Howie hugged her tightly, then turned. "This is my friend and colleague, Bex."

"Welcome Bex." She shook her hand. "Aren't you a tall drink of water?"

She smiled genuinely. "Thank you for having me, Ms. ..."

The woman waved her off. "Call me Gram. Everyone else does."

"Then thank you for having me, Gram. You have a lovely home."

"It's cozy enough. Come in and have a snoop around if you like."

"Thank you." She didn't feel the need to snoop, but she did edge deeper into the house, no longer worried about trying to remember all the names. She felt relatively certain she'd just met the most important member of the family until a younger woman exited the kitchen.

She stood out immediately on every level. Even though she wore an apron, it was abundantly clear she'd forgone the jeans and fleece in favor of black leggings under a burnt orange sweater dress. She wore her long, brunette hair pulled back loosely and flashed the most heartachingly pretty smile at Howie before turning to include Bex in the expression, causing Bex's pulse to drum a little louder in her ears. She stared, unsure she'd ever seen such a naturally beautiful woman before. Even with no trace of makeup or heels or high fashion, she was still utterly captivating.

Howie's voice held a hint of amusement as he said, "There's my cousin Ava. The one I told you about."

She racked her brain to remember the cousin rundown he'd offered, but all the details had gone fuzzy, or maybe her whole brain had. "The one who goes to UVM?"

"Nope," Howie said, "the one who lives here."

Bex finally tore her eyes off the woman long enough to arch an eyebrow at him, and he gave her a smug smile, confirming Ava was the lesbian cousin. This time her heart didn't beat so much as kick her, hard, but she managed to school her expression and turn to Ava, extending her hand and saying a sincere, "Happy Thanksgiving."

11

Chapter Two

Ava's mother passed her two baskets of still-warm yeast rolls. "You can take the big one to the big table and the smaller basket to the kids' area."

She nodded and took a few steps toward the porch but stopped when she caught sight of her father talking to Howie's friend.

Bex.

She mulled the name over in her mind, wishing she had more opportunity to say it out loud. She imagined it would sound as cool as the woman who stood several inches taller than any other woman there, looking most of the men in the eyes even without heels. Not that heels would've flattered her the way the suit did. She wasn't sure she'd ever seen a woman wear a suit like that in real life, lush and tailored with the silk shirt open at her throat, showing the elegant hollow there. Blond hair wisped over a smooth forehead before swooping back to feather along one side.

She was so lost in the discordant sight of something so refined amid her everyday existence, she barely noticed Gram sidling up beside her until she poked her in the ribs. "Are you going to stand here and serve those personally or put them on the tables?"

"What?"

Gram nodded to the rolls. "Your mother sent you out to help, not gawk at our guest."

She shook the haze from her head and dropped the basket onto the table unceremoniously. "I'm not gawking."

"Are too," Gram singsonged, then said, "and I don't blame you a bit. That's not what I pictured when Howie said he was bringing home a girl from work. I thought he'd picked up a cute little nurse or some such, but I'm not sure I've ever seen such a handsome woman outside of movies."

"Right?" Ava finally dropped her pretense. "I can't seem to process that she's real."

"And don't get me wrong, you know my grandson the surgeon is quite a catch, but those two are not dating."

"Not if there's any sense in the world."

"You think she's your type?" Gram whispered conspiratorially.

Ava's burst of laughter caught her off guard, and people turned to look, forcing her to pretend to busy herself with the place settings. When she finally looked up, Gram's eyes sparkled with mischief.

"No," she said firmly. She was not about to catch feelings for Howie's model-good-looking coworker. "Not my type at all."

"Why not?"

She snuck another peek. She normally went for masculine-of-center women, but Bex was more androgynous than traditional butch, and entirely too polished. She dated lesbians who drove SUVs and walked their dogs in the woods and shopped at the Lands' End Outlet and had rough hands. Nothing about Bex was rough. Her skin was flawless, and as she gestured in response to something Howie said, Ava couldn't help but notice her long, elegant fingers. "She's a bit refined for my taste."

"Refined, yes," Gram admitted, "but not soft."

"No. She cuts an imposing figure."

"Sure stands out in this crowd," Gram said with enough admiration in her voice that Ava didn't feel nearly as bad about the sensations stirring low in her own stomach.

14

She didn't need to say it aloud, but she suspected Bex would stand out in any room, anywhere.

"Hey, what's the holdup out there?" her mom called from the kitchen. "Are we ready for the bird?"

"Yes," Ava said, grateful for the distraction, then turned to the larger group and reasserted her voice by yelling, "All right everybody, get to the table!"

Whoops of celebration went up from the kids, and the adults may've possessed a little extra zip as they moved toward the main event of the day. There was a rush of excitement and bodies clamoring for their favorite spots, either in the dining room or on the porch for the young or young at heart. Ava gave a fleeting thought to joining the kids but didn't want to stray too far from Gram or the kitchen, so she stood back and waited to see who landed where.

Her parents took up spots next to each other, and the cousins filled in the far end of the long table. Then, Aunt Helen and Uncle Clay sat in the middle, and no one rushed to take the seat next to him. Like a reverse game of musical chairs, no one wanted the last one. Someone was going to waver eventually because none of them would dare take Gram's post at the head of the table, but as the final crew came in from the deck, her heart nearly seized. Bex headed straight for the seat no one else wanted.

She kicked herself internally as she remembered discussing this exact scenario with Gram a few hours earlier. She'd been so eager then to throw Bex under the bus before she actually knew her. Well, she still didn't know her, but despite what she'd told Gram about not being her type, the woman exuded a sort of magnetism Ava wasn't immune to.

She was being silly. Bex would be gone in a day's time, and they'd probably never see her again. Letting her take the fall was clearly the better choice, and yet as she scooted past her and placed a hand on the back of the chair

15

next to Uncle Clay, Ava's arm shot out seemingly of its own accord. She caught Bex by the sleeve of her expensive suit coat.

The woman froze and glanced up, hitting Ava with the sharpest blue eyes she'd ever been this close to. For a moment, she lost all power to process words and managed only to squeak out, "Hello."

She smiled brightly, if a little amused, and said, "Hello. We didn't get formally introduced. I'm Bex."

"Ava." She managed to spit out her own name while subtly pulling her another step or two away from Uncle Clay. "Is this your first Thanksgiving in Vermont?"

"My first time in Vermont, period."

"Wow, you've missed out on so much."

"Oh?" Bex raised her eyebrows. "Do tell."

"Sure, come sit down here."

A couple of other people groaned as if they'd clearly been listening in to see if Ava would throw the newcomer to the lion, but Bex smiled again, this time more broadly, making the sacrifice more than worthwhile. Then again, as Howie frowned and sat down next to Clay, she had to admit it wasn't exactly her sacrifice.

She pointed Bex to the spot next to Gram, and then, indicating the one on the other side, whispered, "Save this one for me while I go get the turkey."

"I'll guard it with my life," Bex vowed solemnly, and even though she understood she was playing, Ava's cheeks warmed. She turned away to hide her blush, but in doing so made eye contact with Gram, who shot her a knowing look, which she still preferred to the hint of smugness in Howie's expression.

While she did look forward to chatting with Bex over dinner, the last thing she wanted to do was give those two any ideas.

"That went well," Howie said to Gram as they settled in.

"For who?" Gram asked with a pointed nod. Bex craned her neck a little to see the man she indicated but couldn't remember which uncle he was since several of them all looked the same, with barrel chests and three-day stubble.

He laughed. "A small price to pay."

"You're meddling, Howard."

He lifted his glass of iced tea. "I learned from the best."

Bex wasn't at all sure what she'd missed, but it seemed important, or at least it had until Ava stepped in from the kitchen carrying a huge, golden brown turkey on a silver platter.

Oohs and aahs went up from around the room, and even she agreed it was one of the prettiest meals she'd ever seen.

The aroma hit her two seconds later and she nearly swooned. "Wow."

"Right?" Howie asked. "I told you top-notch food exists outside the five boroughs."

She suspected she was about to eat her words, and in this case, didn't find the prospect unpleasant at all.

Ava slid in beside her, but instead of digging into the food, everyone around the table bowed their heads in unison and lifted their hands. It took entirely too many surprised seconds for Bex to realize they intended to pray before eating, but when Ava slid her hand into her own, she didn't mind at all. Hers was much softer than Howie's, but she found she didn't mind holding his either. Honestly, she couldn't remember the last time she'd held anyone's hand for any length of time, and while the ritual felt foreign, simple

17

contact had its charm, as a small child stood on a chair and recited a simple prayer.

"Lord, we are thankful for the food and our family and our dogs and no school for five whole days in a row, and please let me have pie *and* a turkey cookie for dessert. Amen."

"Amen," everyone echoed enthusiastically, even Bex.

Gram rose from the table and addressed her assembled group. "Thank you for that lovely grace, Marley. I'm thankful to have my family here today. I love how many of you contributed to this feast before us. You make a feisty old woman proud of her legacy, and on that note, I want to hand off one more tradition today."

She picked up a large carving set and held it out to Ava. "You do the honors this year, my love."

The murmurs and presentation helped Bex discern this was a big moment. The younger people seemed quite pleased, several of them smiling and nodding, but a couple of the old men frowned until the one next to Howie released what she could only describe as a harrumph.

Gram held up a hand. "I don't want to hear it, Clay. She's been beside me since last night. She trimmed it. She stuffed it. She seasoned it and cooked it. She's earned the right to carve it."

Ava smiled adoringly and rose to accept the tools of her new trade with a steady, sure hand. She went about the job with easy confidence, cutting even, thick slices that showed off the magnificence of the preparation so much, Bex's mouth began to water in anticipation.

"Nice," Howie said as she finished. "I couldn't have done a better job myself, and I have a lot of practice cutting flesh."

"Ew," someone called from down the table.

"We can't all be vegetarians, Mel," he called.

18

"You all could be," she shot back.

"Ew," someone else said, causing several people to laugh as they passed plates, but the uncle Gram had shot down cleared his throat.

"Don't mind her, Howie. Women don't have the stomach for doctor talk, too squeamish."

Bex stiffened slightly, but he wasn't done.

"Most of them would probably faint if they tried to do what you do."

"Come on," Howie said quickly. "Could we have one holiday without the sexism?"

The uncle laughed as if he found the idea absurd. "It's just the order of things. I'm sure you know some real pretty nurses, but they don't have the constitution to keep their hands steady enough amid all that blood."

Bex finally leaned forward. "I manage to hold my own."

He winked at her. "Are you one of his surgical nurses, hon? I'm sure you look real cute in those candy striper out-fits."

Her vision flashed red as her brain short-circuited from the myriad of offensive implications in those two sentences. She didn't know which one to address first, the over-sexualization of nurses, the idea that a woman couldn't be a doctor, the flippant assessments based on judging anyone by their looks rather than their qualifications. She could've eviscerated him on any count, but in her indecision, Howie jumped back into the void with a bite to his words Bex had never heard before.

"Uncle Clay, I love you, but if you don't stop talking right now, I won't be held responsible for the things I say next. Bex is a guest, a colleague, and the finest anesthesiologist I've ever had the honor of working with. She has a cooler head and a steadier hand than any man in the field, and if

19

you ever need to have surgery, you should pray you have a woman like her at the helm." He picked up the basket of bread and nearly chucked it down the table before adding, "Now here are the rolls. Please put one in your mouth and let the rest of us enjoy our meals."

The man accepted the rolls with a little chuckle and a mumble sounding slightly like "too sensitive," but didn't push any further.

"I'm sorry," Howie turned and whispered as conversation picked up around the table.

"No, that was epic," Bex said. "I take it he's the one you mentioned being outweighed by your cousins."

He grinned. "The one and only, but Ava, you better start talking fast, or I'm about to be made a liar here."

Bex turned to her. "Really, it's fine."

"No, Howie's right." Ava jumped in. "You're a guest, and what's more, you're a human being here to celebrate a holiday. I hope you won't let his comments make you feel unwelcome. He's cranky and old."

Gram grunted. "I'm two years older than he is. Doesn't mean I'm idiot enough to think women can't be good doctors."

"Good point." Bex gave her a nod. "You're right. Those attitudes have less to do with age and more to do with life experiences. We're all products of how we're raised until we encounter something to make us question those assumptions."

"Still, I'm sorry if it put a damper on your meal." Ava pointed to her plate. "You haven't even tasted a bite of food yet."

Bex took the hint and began spooning turkey and stuffing off the platter. "No need to apologize. I've heard worse, both in med school and since I began to practice, though admittedly probably less so in New York City than it might come up in rural areas."

Howie groaned. "Don't get this one started on New York. I'll have to shove food in her mouth too."

Bex grinned and tried a bite of turkey delicious enough to distract her, not just from the previous conversation, but from the one Howie was warning them against. She may've even made a little yummy noise as she chewed, and she certainly closed her eyes to savor all the flavors. "Wow."

When she opened her eyes, she met Ava's. "Wow?"

"This is the best turkey I've ever tasted, hands down."

Ava's smile crinkled the corners of her hazel eyes. "I'm thrilled to hear it, but I'm a bit curious as to what Howie didn't want you to say about the city."

"Everything." Howie laughed. "Once you get her waxing poetic about the Big Apple, we'll be here until at least Christmas. This one is a city mouse through and through."

Bex speared another piece of turkey onto her fork, running it through the mashed potatoes and gravy before lifting it to her lips. For once, she had something in front of her worthy of keeping this particular answer short and to the point, so she simply said, "Guilty as charged."

Ava pushed the plate of iced sugar cookies shaped like turkeys, leaves, and acorns farther down the table so she wouldn't be quite as tempted to pick up another one. She was so stuffed she couldn't have possibly swallowed anything more, but that didn't keep the little kid in the recesses of her mind from reaching for more sweets when someone set them right in front of her.

Bex shook her head and tried to pass them back. "Don't push your temptation off on me."

She laughed. "Send them the other way then. I have no impulse control."

Bex smirked but did as instructed and sent them on down the table. "No impulse control sounds awfully fun."

"Now that's not the kind of thing someone wants to hear from an anesthesiologist. You're supposed to be the one with steady hands."

"No one could ever question my hands in a crisis, but I'm not on call this weekend, which is a rarity. Maybe I have some pent-up impulses to work out."

The comment was delivered casually enough, but it still caused Ava's stomach to tighten disconcertingly. And she didn't quite know how to respond, "Oh?"

"The question is which impulse to indulge," Bex said conspiratorially, her voice rich and smooth as she angled a little closer. "Pumpkin or apple?"

Ava blinked a few times as the last words sank in. "Pie?"

"Of course. What better way to end this magnificent meal?"

"Right. Pie." They were talking about pie. Which made sense as everyone else was already finishing up their dessert, only Ava's mind had gone somewhere else.

"Which do you recommend?" Bex asked.

"Both," she said quickly.

"Perfect solution."

"Really?"

"Sure, if we're surrendering to impulses, moderation seems counterproductive." She stretched her long frame across the seat Howie had recently vacated and snagged both pie plates from in front of Uncle Clay, who'd wisely kept to neutral topics through the rest of the meal.

Ava watched her cut a slice of each, exactly the same size, and lift them gently onto her plate. Such a mundane

22

movement to note, but ever since Howie made the comment about Bex's hands, she couldn't stop noticing them.

She added a liberal amount of whipped cream to each slice, then did what appeared to be an almost scientific-style taste test before sitting back and declaring, "It's official."

"What is?"

"Best Thanksgiving meal I've ever had, which is saying a lot. Last year I spent the holiday in a Michelin-starred restaurant."

Pride welled in Ava's chest, and she felt certain it radiated through her smile.

"Seriously," Bex continued, "ask your cousin. I don't give compliments lightly, and I'm a serious foodie. Was everything made from scratch?"

She nodded. "Gram's spent her whole life perfecting the recipes."

"A worthy legacy, but be honest, you had a hand in all of it too."

She nodded. "I love to cook, and I think of these holiday meals as, I don't know, more than just tradition, kind of a connection on a lot of levels."

"Absolutely," Bex said emphatically. "Food is stories. Food is conversation. Food conveys and inspires mood and place. Food is art and meaning and comfort."

"Yes. Thank you."

"Thank me? What for?"

"For not making me feel silly."

Bex met her eyes and held them as she asked, "What sort of terrible person would make you feel silly after a meal like that?"

Right on cue, Uncle Clay pushed back from the table and declared, "It's football time, boys. Let's move to the living room so the ladies can get to doing the dishes."

Ava pinched the bridge of her nose but held her tongue as he and several of the older men shuffled away. Once they were out of earshot she said, "If I didn't think it would be such a disaster, I'd tell him the ladies he's referring to did almost 100 percent of the cooking and perhaps the men should show their appreciation by offering to do the cleaning."

"Where'd Howie go?" Bex glanced around. "He doesn't seem to have much trouble saying it."

She shook her head. "No, Gram wouldn't want them in her kitchen anyway. We have a system they'd only muck up, but the assumption still irks me."

"Would I muck it up? Because I didn't cook, and I wouldn't have even known where to start if I'd been asked to. I'm more than happy to scrub in for dish duty as a sign of my appreciation."

"No." Ava laid a hand on her arm. "You're a guest. Stay and chat with me while you finish your pie, and then you're free to join the others."

"Please don't throw me to the Patriots fans. I'm a New Yorker, and what's more, I've seen too many brain surgeries to have any interest in a game where people hit each other with their heads. I'd rather help with the dishes."

The answer surprised Ava. "I see your reasoning, but I would've pegged you for a sports person."

Bex shook her head. "Sorry, not that kind of lesbian, which is a statement I seem to be making a lot lately. What about you?"

"I haven't had to make that statement at all lately, or ever."

"Sorry, I meant are you a sports lesbian?"

"I've never given any thought to the classification, but I do have an affinity for the Red Sox."

24

Bex grimaced slightly. "I suppose you can be forgiven because of where you live, but what do you do now that October has ended and we're a long way from spring?"

"Honestly?" She lowered her voice. "My answer will probably horrify you."

"Please don't hold out on me."

She leaned forward. "Starting tomorrow, I'll put my television on a steady diet of nothing but Christmas movies until at least December 25."

"No," Bex said. "Did Howie tell you to say that?"

"Howie? No. He makes fun of me, or at least the level of my obsession, and you can, too, because I don't care. I love what I love."

"Why do you keep expecting me to make fun of you for things like food and Christmas movies? I love both. I have spreadsheets to make sure I get all my favorites in every year."

Ava noted a twinkle in those blue eyes, but she still didn't know this woman well enough to tell if it stemmed from joy or teasing. "All right, if I'm to believe you, which films top the list?"

"Wow, do you want to narrow it down a bit?"

"No."

"Fine. I hear the challenge, but I feel confident in my ability to meet it. For classics, my tops are *Miracle on 34th Street*, *It's a Wonderful Life*, and *A Charlie Brown Christmas*. More modern, I'm partial to *Scrooged* and *Love Actually* and *Elf*. I could go on and on."

"Those are some top tier picks!" Ava's excitement bubbled over. "I'd add *White Christmas* to the classics, and *The Holiday* to the modern ones."

"Worthy additions, both." Bex nodded appreciatively and stuck out her hand. "It is a pleasure to meet a kindred spirit."

Ava enjoyed the chance to feel Bex's soft skin against hers, but her enthusiasm kept her from fixating too much, as she felt the need to issue another disclaimer. "You may regret opening this particular topic, though, as it's not just movies with me. I'm super obsessed with all things Christmas."

"No one is a bigger Christmas fiend than me. I start scheduling my entire yearly work hours around this time in January. I cover all the anesthesiologists' vacations, especially the Jewish ones, because they don't need time off for Christmas, and I front-load my shifts in October and November at the surgical center, so I have enough days off to do all the things."

"All the things?" Ava slapped Bex on the shoulder. "I love how you say that. I do all the things every year. I have a list. It's like a full-time job."

"Shut. Up." Bex laughed. "I have an elaborate taxonomy and routines to make sure I fit everything in. The food, the festivals, light shows, and that doesn't even cover all the entertainment items, plays, music, the aforementioned movies."

"Seriously," Ava sat back, her grin stretching until her cheeks ached. "The only channel on my TV for the next four weeks is the Hallmark Channel."

"Wait." Bex held up a hand. "Full stop. Hallmark? I call foul."

"Foul? How can you call foul on Christmas movies? You said you love them."

"I do love Christmas movies," Bex's expression turned grave, "but Hallmark doesn't make real Christmas movies. They make counterfeit Christmas movies to perpetuate harmful stereotypes and lead people away from the real and true joy of Christmas."

That didn't make any sense, and Ava glanced over her shoulder, half expecting her family to be holding up a

26

camera to capture her reaction, but none of them were even in the room anymore. She glanced back to Bex, who continued to scowl. "Maybe you get a different Hallmark channel in New York than we get in Vermont? The one I watch is all about the Christmas spirit, and they make such cute little romances where people transform their lives."

"The lives they live working important jobs in the big city?"

She nodded. "Those are the ones."

"And they leave those cities to live in some small town with like fifty people and no theater and no four-star restaurants and no ballet, because the only way to celebrate Christmas is to hole up in a cabin far away from all the things that make the holiday amazing?"

"I'm sorry?" Ava shook her head. "Who goes to restaurants on Christmas when there are roaring fires and local markets and snowy nights and hot cocoa in your pj's?"

Bex rolled her eyes. "They've got you."

"Who has me?"

"The Hallmark marketing team. They've sucked you into their myth machine. Poor woman, have you ever even experienced a real Christmas?"

"Excuse me? This will be my thirty-first real Christmas here in Vermont, which is a literal winter wonderland." Ava scoffed. "Oh no, are you one of those city slickers who doesn't know a real holiday when it hits her in the face with a big fluffy snowball?"

Bex pushed back from the table. "What a terrible stereotype. I already told you, I plan my whole career year around this time. I'm not some soulless workaholic in need of saving. I live in the greatest Christmas city in the whole world."

"Christmas and city don't even go together."

"Oh yeah? Where do you think all those great Christmas movies take place? *Miracle on 34th Street*? New York City. *Scrooged*? New York City. *Elf*? New York City. And the entire series of *Lily and Dash*, all eight episodes take place in ... you guessed it ... New York City."

Ava folded her arms across her chest. "Where does *White Christmas* take place?"

"Vermont, big deal. You have one movie about how some old general's business in Vermont is going under because no one wants to go there, so Bing Crosby has to go to New York City and get people from there to go visit him out of the kindness of their hearts, which your Hallmark movies say we don't even have. Oh, and spoiler alert," Bex warned triumphantly. "They filmed the whole movie in Southern California. None of Vermont was actually in the film."

Ava's face flamed. She hadn't known that, but she didn't want Bex to know she hadn't known, so she simply stammered, "So what?"

Bex laughed. "I win."

"Win what?"

"The Christmas-off."

"Christmas isn't a competition," Ava found her voice again, "and if you weren't some city-driven egomaniac, you'd know that."

Bex clutched her chest. "Ouch. Why do you keep dealing in these harmful tropes? Have you ever even spent a Christmas season in the city?"

"Have you ever spent one in the country?"

"Why would I?" Bex shuddered. "New York is the greatest place in the world, and Christmas is the greatest season to live there."

"How do you know for sure if you don't have anything to compare it to?"

"That's the same thing straight guys ask me about being gay."

"Ugh," Ava grimaced. "Talk about harmful stereotypes. Look, I didn't mean to imply you've never had a nice Christmas."

"You just meant to imply mine aren't as nice as yours," Bex shot back.

"Has anyone ever told you you're maddening?"

She laughed and crossed one long leg over the other, looking awfully sure of herself. "Every woman I've ever dated."

Ava pressed her lips together to keep from smiling. She didn't want to add to the hint of smugness Bex oozed, but she did wonder what was behind it. It wasn't every day she met someone who riled her up so quickly and thoroughly. They were clearly on opposite ends of a variety of worldviews, and yet the fact was that Bex cared enough about Christmas to get into such a passionate argument with a near stranger. Ava preferred this reaction to the dismissiveness or apathy she usually got when the subject arose. Still, Bex was wrong. Painfully, almost comically wrong, and as someone who truly understood the deeper meaning of Christmas, didn't she have an obligation to share it?

"What's the look for?" Bex asked.

"What look?"

"The one like you're hatching some sort of plan?"

"Not a plan so much as making peace with my responsibility to the less fortunate," she reasoned.

"I don't like the sound of that."

"No, I don't suppose you would, given how tenuous your position is."

"Hey now," Bex warned in a low tone, "am I the less fortunate in this scenario?"

"Yes, and since it's the season for charity, I'd like to formally extend an invitation for you to spend as much of the Christmas season here as possible. I'll devote myself to showing you a real holiday experience as free tutoring of sorts, to help bring you up to speed."

Now, it was apparently Bex's turn to sputter. "Speed? Seriously? What do you know about coming up to speed? If anything, I should tutor you."

Ava laughed at the absurdity of the idea.

"No, no." Bex held up a finger. "I like this."

"Like what?"

"A conversion bet."

"A what? Don't gays get a little twitchy around conversions?"

Bex shook her head. "Maybe out here in the backwoods, but it's a new millennium in New York City, which is why a visit would do you good. I propose a contest of sorts."

"Ew, again with the competitive Christmasing."

"Competition is healthy. What are you, a socialist?"

Ava shrugged. "I believe health care, education, and clean water are human rights."

Bex smiled at her, bright and genuine. "So do I, which is why I don't think this plan of yours will be a hardship."

"The plan where I tutor you?"

"The plan where we each put our best holiday foot forward in an attempt to decide once and for all who has the better Christmas, the city mouse or the country mouse."

"That's not exactly what I had in mind," Ava said slowly, but as the idea sank in, she didn't hate it. "We'd split time?"

30

Bex nodded. "As much as it pains me, I'd be willing to compromise some of my holiday traditions as long as you keep your mind open too."

"Compromise doesn't come easily to me."

"Something else we have in common," Bex said, "but I like to win more than I hate to compromise, and I wouldn't make this bet if I wasn't sure I'd bring you around."

"What if I bring you around?"

Bex laughed again, a sharp, bold sound. "Then, I guess people in hell can have some ice water, but don't worry, once you see what I have up the sleeves of my Santa coat, I feel confident you'll see the error of your ways."

"And what if I'm right, but you're too stubborn to admit it?" Ava began to suspect the probability of such an outcome.

"Then, we'll shake hands and wish each other a Merry Christmas before we go our separate ways." Bex shrugged. "The upside is one of us could walk away knowing we're the purveyor of the true holiday experience. The only downside is we'd have to give the other person a chance to win us over. Aside from time spent away from our home territory, I don't really see what we have to lose."

Ava eyed her seriously for a few seconds. While she didn't relish rearranging her Christmas schedule, she supposed spending the next few weeks reveling in her favorite time of year with someone who looked like Bex wouldn't exactly be a hardship. She lifted her glass. "Then, here's to a Christmas with nothing to lose."

Chapter Three

Bex pushed open the door of the little coffee shop at 8:00 sharp after waking up genuinely excited to see Ava again. The two of them had agreed to table their discussion on the details of their bet until after Thanksgiving, as was right and proper, so as not to blend holidays. However, neither one of them wanted to wait too long, so they made plans to meet ahead of Bex's train back to the city on Friday, and she couldn't remember the last time she'd been this excited to prove someone wrong.

She started toward the counter planning to place two orders for hot chocolate, but as she wound between tables, a hand caught the sleeve of her gray peacoat, and she glanced down to see Ava smiling up at her, two steaming mugs topped with whipped cream in front of her. "You beat me."

"Get used to it."

"Touché." Bex slipped off her supple leather gloves and draped her jacket over the back of the chair before sitting down, then pointed to Ava's stocking cap. "I didn't recognize you with the pom-pom."

"Another thing you should get used to." Ava slid one of the mugs across to her. "Do you have good snow gear?"

"Um, I have several nice coats and scarves."

"What about boots? Hats? Mittens? All-weather pants?"

"Wow, getting right down to my pants. You're not one to fuss around."

Ava shrugged. "If I'm going to show you the error of your cold-hearted city ways, you can't be frozen solid, but I'll take that as a no and rustle you up some proper attire."

"I'm not sure I want to wear something that's been rustled up. Why don't you send me a list and I'll purchase my own? Then, when I'm done here, I'll donate them to charities for less fortunate country queers."

Ava snorted. "What makes you think you won't want to keep them for when you come back next year?"

Bex shook her head. The woman was sharp, no doubt about it, and it had been a while since anyone had pushed her in such an amusing way. She lifted the mug to her lips and took a sip, intending to check the temperature, but as soon as the hint of chocolate hit her tongue, she closed her eyes and moaned. "Is there peppermint in here?"

"Of course," Ava said as if the answer should've been self-evident. "It's the day after Thanksgiving. Adios pumpkin spice, hello peppermint."

For a second, it seemed like she might add a "duh" to the statement, and Bex suffered an overwhelming urge to grab her face and plant a kiss on her smooth forehead. "God, you really could be the perfect woman if we get you into the city."

Ava laughed. "Then I guess I'll always come up short, and you'll have to live with the disappointment of knowing you were so close to perfection and failed to seal the deal."

Bex took another sip, closing her eyes to savor the flavor she'd waited nearly a year to relish again, but when she opened them once more, she added, "I never come up short. Not at work, not with women, and never, ever at Christmas."

Ava's cheeks flushed as she took a sip of her own drink before setting her mug down gently. "I'm not ashamed to admit I'm a little interested to see what you've got up your

34

sleeve to inspire such confidence, but I have to remind you, you only have two weeks and one of them will be mine."

"Right, presumably you'll want to spend half the time in your futile attempt to sway me."

"Presumably?"

"You might come to New York and have such a transformative experience you'll decide to spend the rest of the holiday there."

"You're delusional," Ava said with more than a little amusement in her voice, and while Bex hadn't exactly meant the comment as a full-on joke, she didn't hate the humor of her response.

"Then I guess it's time to set some ground rules?"

Ava pulled out a phone from her puffy-vest pocket and pulled up a calendar, so Bex followed suit. "Let's just start with one weekend in New York, and one here."

"I call dibs on next weekend," Bex said before she even looked at the dates.

"I suppose it's only fair since you came here this weekend."

"And I need you to get there before Wednesday night."

"Wednesday's not the weekend."

"No, but it's the official kickoff of the holiday entertainment season in the city, and you cannot possibly miss the big event if you intend to get the full experience."

"Which big event?"

Bex placed a hand over her heart and clutched at her shirt as if she might be having a heart attack. "You can't be serious. Actually, wait, if you don't know, then I have to preserve this innocence at all costs. Protect it like a conservative father guards his daughter's virginity. I'll get a shotgun and a purity ring, but whatever you do, don't Google 'New York City at Christmas.'"

Ava laughed. "That's a horrifying analogy, but your enthusiasm is compelling. I promise not to do any research that might endanger what little Christmas magic the city may possess."

Bex shook her head and took another healthy swallow of the hot chocolate. "I'll pick you up at Penn Station, and we'll hit the ground running. Dress warm … or you know, sort of like you are right now, but pack something a little more upscale for later in the weekend."

"How upscale?" Ava asked with a hint of nervousness.

Bex waved off her concern. "No ballgowns or anything this trip."

Ava's eyes went wide. "This trip? How about no ballgowns ever? Unless you're the one wearing it."

She laughed. "Point taken. Honestly, the dress you wore yesterday was lovely."

"Really?"

She nodded at the memory of the way it cut in at Ava's waist, then flared at her hips. "Truly. Something along those lines will more than suffice for any itinerary I'd like to pursue with you."

Ava's cheeks turned a little pink, and Bex did nothing to correct the double entendre. She enjoyed how easily she blushed, and while the stakes around their time together remained her top priority, she didn't hate the idea of getting to know Ava a little better along the way.

"I'll take a train down Wednesday afternoon," Ava forged on, "and head out Sunday morning so I can be back in time to meet my Monday responsibilities."

She noted the vagueness of the comment but didn't push for more information yet. "Then I'll head up here for the next weekend."

"And you'd better arrive on Wednesday night, because I want equal time on my investment."

Bex nodded. "Fair. Wednesday night to Sunday morning for the next two weeks. I think that will be enough for you to declare me the winner, but it also still leaves us two more weeks in case we need wiggle room after we see how things go."

"I like that plan, and don't get me wrong, I understand you still suspect I'll fall in love with your way of life and concede quickly and want to spend all my remaining time in the city."

She shrugged. "Just keeping the possibility open."

"Then stay all the way open because you might love my weekend so much you decide to stay here."

"It is the season of miracles," Bex deadpanned, "but I get first crack at the plate, and I want you to know I'll accept your surrender at any time."

"Go on." Ava grinned. "Keep talking trash now. It's only going to make it all the sweeter when you crack."

She bit her lip to keep from escalating that line of conversation yet again. She enjoyed the competitive banter and the coyness of Ava's smile, but she had a train to catch, and in the end, talk was cheap. This bet wouldn't be won with words. She'd have to bring her A game next week, but thankfully she'd scored the first point the moment she convinced Ava to start on her turf, and New York provided the greatest home court advantage in the entire world.

Ava had brought a book to read with her on the train, but she'd spent much of the ride utterly captivated by the scenery outside the window. It was as if Mother Nature bowed to her own personal holiday calendar, unleashing a winter wonderland right on cue. The snow arrived in the lower elevations a day after Bex returned to New York, coating everything in a fluffy white blanket, then graciously applied a light new layer each morning to keep the scenery fresh and bright.

A part of her hadn't wanted to even board the train this morning. The first weekend in full snow always carried an electric energy, which only compounded its beauty. She didn't doubt the city would carry a buzz of its own, but her heart ached knowing it wouldn't be the same as at home. As the mountains gave way to barely frosted hills outside, she couldn't help but ask herself again why she was leaving her favorite place during her favorite season. However, every time Bex's memory flashed through her mind, she had her answer.

There was something unquantifiable about the woman. Ava didn't have any trouble admitting the physical appeal, and perhaps she could even cop to the fact that having someone so stunning and polished pay her enough attention to want to convince her of something felt sort of flattering. Then, there was her own competitive spirit to account for. She didn't care much for sports or games, or even keeping up with the Joneses, but she did possess a stubborn streak and the courage of her convictions. When she was right about something, she stuck to her guns, and Bex triggered her tenacity in a big way. City holidays were better than country holidays?

She snorted softly at the absurdity of it all, causing the man next to her to glance up from the phone he'd stared at unblinkingly for the last two hours. She offered a chagrined shrug and angled her body back toward the window, where even the hills had given way to forests and then ramshackle towns. She tried to tell herself no place put its best face toward the railroad tracks, but her chest tightened as pretty scenery gave way to suburbs. She closed her eyes and tried to picture Bex in those moments when her smug smile surrendered to more genuine excitement. She had a magnetism when she spoke about her love of Christmas that pulled at Ava's core. No one who exuded such yuletide joy could be completely off base, and when Ava refused to focus on the graffiti-covered warehouses springing up around her now, her natural curiosity took hold once more.

If nothing else, she'd at least be able to tell people she'd seen the big city at Christmas, and while she'd never made a big bucket list, she suspected such an item was probably on a lot of them. She tried to anchor herself to a sense of adventure and the connection she'd felt with Bex last weekend as the first glimpses of the city skyline rose ahead of her in the fading light of a winter evening.

Her heart beat a little faster as the lights glittered like tinsel before the train snaked underground and people began to rustle around in anticipation of their arrival. By the time they slid to a stop, her regrets had already begun to fade amid the hustle and bustle. As the mass of bodies flowed toward the exits, she had no choice but to get swept away.

She had no plan from here. It hadn't occurred to her she'd need one. Train stations back home were generally small, squat buildings, but as she crested the escalator into Penn Station, she realized she might be in over her head. Hundreds of people rushed about, and Christmas music played over the din of the garland-strung hall. She had enough wherewithal to step out of the press of human traffic behind her, then stalled, her feet rooted to the tile floor as she let her eyes wander up to the massive glass ceiling and the buildings towering high above the translucent barrier.

She must've gotten transfixed by the enormity of it all because she wasn't sure how long she'd stood anchored to the same spot before she became keenly aware of someone watching her. It shouldn't have been possible to feel a single set of eyes amid such teeming masses of humanity, but she turned her head and met Bex's gaze without a hint of searching.

The woman stood mere feet away, dressed in charcoal slacks and a crisp white dress shirt under a hunter green V-neck sweater, but the sheer fashionable appeal of the ensemble paled in comparison to the sparkle in her eyes as she surveyed Ava.

Wordlessly, they threaded their way around frazzled commuters, then paused inches apart, smiling sillily in that awkward dance of greeting. Ava briefly considered shaking hands, but dismissed the prospect as too formal, and yet she didn't know if Bex was a hugger, so she did a hesitating sort of lean in and half hug. Mercifully, Bex not only took things from there, she clutched her shoulders warmly and kissed her cheek with a soft sort of suave Ava certainly couldn't have pulled off on her own.

"Welcome to the greatest city in the world." Bex beamed as she stepped back. "Here, let me take your bag."

"I can get it," she offered.

"Nonsense, we can't let you think the country is the only place where people have manners anymore. I assure you, chivalry is alive and well here." Then, without waiting for an argument, Bex took her carry-on and nodded for her to follow.

Out on the street, she stuck close to Bex, trying not to gawk or crane her neck at all the sights flashing around and above them, and she must've done an okay job because before she knew it, they were ensconced in a taxi zipping through city traffic.

"How was your trip?" Bex asked.

"Uneventful enough, but I'm glad to be off the train for a bit."

"Then I'm glad I chose the cab. Normally, I'd catch the two train from Penn Station to my place, but we're close enough to the evening rush, I didn't want to overwhelm you right away. We can drop your bag off at my apartment before we head back out for the big event."

Her curiosity swelled again. "Do I get to know what we're doing now?"

Bex shook her head so her blond hair shimmered a bit in the dim light. "I won't be able to keep it a secret right up to the moment due to the size of it all, but a bit longer."

"Size? As in big?"

Bex winked playfully. "Despite Texas's marketing machine, everything is actually bigger in the Big Apple."

She relaxed a bit at the first hint of banter. "Promises, promises."

"No," Bex said, her voice low and knowing, "I made my promises last weekend. Tonight, I start delivering on them."

Chapter Four

Bex pushed open the door to her apartment but didn't flip on the lights right away because she loved the way the city sparkled through her large floor-to-ceiling windows. She wasn't in the penthouse, but in this southeast corner of Tribeca, twelve floors up was enough to offer a relatively expansive view of the Brooklyn Bridge and parts of the Financial District. Sometimes, she'd sit in the dark all night to watch it shine. Still, she wasn't here to linger, so she stepped aside for Ava to enter and activated the dimmer switches for the kitchen.

"Wow." Ava glanced around. "Color me impressed."

"Thanks. I won't lie and say it's nothing. I like where I live."

"Do I even want to know what a place like this costs?"

"Probably not. The cost of living here would likely make your head spin, but then again, so would the cost of a good anesthesiologist. It all evens out."

"Okay, then I'll just say I like your tree there." She pointed to the ten-foot faux spruce strung with white lights in the corner by the windows. "The twinkling complements the city lights in the background."

"Thank you. There are not many things I'd allow to block any part of that view, but it's not Christmas without a tree." She glanced at the clock over the stove and confirmed they didn't have a ton of time. "Here, let me show you your room and give you the thirty-second tour. Kitchen, dining room, living room."

Ava looked around the open space. "And don't forget the view."

"Not a chance, and when we have more time, I'll take you up to the rooftop to see the whole panorama, but for now, you can put your bag in the bedroom and get freshened up before we head out."

"The bedroom? As in singular?"

"I'm a doctor, not a tycoon." Bex laughed as she pushed open the door to her room to peek in. "So, yes, there's just one bed. Isn't that what happens in those cheesy holiday knockoffs you like to watch?"

She turned back to Ava, whose brow furrowed as she bit her lower lip in consternation while she surveyed the lush queen mattress stacked high with pillows and a down comforter. A part of her wanted to drag this out, maybe make her squirm a little, but she looked so earnest, Bex laughed.

"I'm teasing. The couch folds out, and I'm not talking old-school metal springs. It's got a full-size memory foam pullout. Sometimes, I sleep on it even when I don't have guests because I enjoy the view."

"Sounds great." Relief flooded her voice. "I'm happy to couch surf or stay with Howie even."

The idea of Ava going somewhere else made her jaw tighten in ways she didn't want to examine. "I won't hear of it. You'll take the bed, for privacy. I'll sleep out here. I'm an early riser, so I'll probably be up before you, and I'll use the time to get some work done."

"I thought you had time off from work?"

"I'm off tomorrow and all weekend, but I have a few cases to review before Monday. It's boring stuff I can work around our busy Christmasing schedule, but if you want your big surprise, we'd better bundle up and hit the road."

"How much bundling?"

"Jeans, comfortable shoes, top layers, mittens, and a hat."

"Now, that I can do," Ava said, and then, unlike the other women Bex had scheduled outings with of late, she did so in a matter of minutes, emerging from the bedroom adorably dressed in a red and white Christmas sweater under an open wool coat and topped off with a pom-pom stocking cap.

"Be honest," Bex grinned as she scanned her up and down, "how many of those hats do you own?"

"I couldn't even begin to guess, but I packed four. You'll get a different one each day."

"Lucky me." Bex held open the door, and as they headed back toward the elevator, she realized she was actually looking forward to seeing them all, or at least spending enough time with Ava to see them all.

"When do I get to know where we're going?" Ava asked as Bex led her down into the Fulton Street subway station.

"You might figure it out when you see which station we get out at." Bex flashed her card and then handed one to Ava before saying, "Here's your first Christmas present."

"A MetroCard?"

"Yes, it's a gift that keeps on giving." She expected Ava to roll her eyes or maybe gloss over the gesture, but instead she took it in her gloved hands and held it up proudly.

"Thank you. I appreciate you offering me something with so much meaning for you, so I can share in your world."

Bex's heart expanded at the genuine and well-spoken response. She hadn't been sure how much each of them would stick to their own sense of superiority during this little experiment, but she wasn't too stubborn to understand they'd both have more fun if they stayed open to the experiences, and Ava had set the bar pretty high.

They rode the subway up the middle of Manhattan before switching to a new line for a couple more stops. She navigated quickly and intuitively, a sort of tunnel vision taking over, the natural byproduct of both her city upbringing and a desire to get to the main event. She was a goer and a doer even in her downtime, but those instincts compounded a desire to show off the city she loved to Ava. She didn't just want to make a point, she wanted to impress this woman more than she'd wanted to impress anyone in ages.

The thought gave her some pause as they neared their stop. There was no legitimate reason to care about Ava's opinion as much as she did. They hadn't spent more than a few hours in each other's company, and aside from an abiding love of Christmas, they hadn't found a lot of common ground. After the next few weeks, they likely wouldn't have much occasion to cross paths. She supposed their bet could account for this newfound drive to win her over, but as she remembered the sight of Ava standing in the train station looking small and staring up at the ceiling with eyes full of wonder, Bex suspected she would've been drawn to her no matter what other plans or priorities they'd set. Ava stood out amid the crowd of hundreds swirling around her, so few of them barely having enough interest to glance up, much less stop and marvel.

The train slowed, and a garbled announcement came over the speakers, pulling Bex out of her own head. "This is our stop."

"Which one is it?" Ava asked excitedly. "I couldn't hear."

As the door slid open, she pointed to a sign on the wall reading "Rockefeller Center."

Ava clutched her arm through the thick sleeve of her coat as she seemed to realize where they were. "Are we going to see the big tree?"

"More than that," Bex said proudly, "we're going to the lighting ceremony!"

🌲 🌲 🌲

"Okay." Ava turned on Bex as soon as they dropped into the front-row seats overlooking the plaza. "How rich are you?"

She laughed, a low rumble. "Not rich enough to score these on my own."

"What do you mean? Did you steal them?"

She laughed. "No, I worked a breast reconstruction for an NBC executive two months ago. I can't say which one, obviously, but when she woke up after the surgery, she said it was the first time in her life she didn't vomit when coming out of anesthesia, and even though I told her I was just doing my job, she insisted if I ever wanted to take part in anything the network had a hand in, I should call her."

"Wow, that's really special."

"Yeah, not a bad time to call in a favor, right?"

"That too, obviously, but I meant it must be really meaningful to offer someone such a positive experience during what's probably a scary time."

Bex's smile morphed into a more reflective kind of happiness. "You know, it honestly is."

"And now, since I'm doubly impressed, both with your connections and with how you scored them, the evening will be even more meaningful. You do seem to have a flare for the opulent."

"It's Christmas. If there's any time to go all in, this is it, right?"

Ava nodded. Though she didn't usually lean toward flash and pizzazz, she couldn't argue with Bex's enthusiasm. She let her eyes wander about their surroundings, from the

47

tree, to the famous gold sculpture of Prometheus, to the outer rim of the iconic ice-skating rink that had been all but covered by a large stage decked out in Christmas décor. She'd seen these sights on her television many times over the years, and she found herself more excited than she would've imagined to be a part of the event as she stared up in awe at the mammoth Norway spruce Christmas tree rising into the night sky. She couldn't even make out the top branches from this angle since they blended into the night sky, but it had to be at least ten stories high, if not fifteen. She may've seen trees that big in the woods back home, but the sheer scope of witnessing such a gargantuan chunk of nature amid all the city bustle and buildings nearly boggled her mind.

"How'd they even get it in here?"

"Carefully," Bex said, with a little smirk. "It comes in early November, and they take weeks to decorate it with thousands of lights. I heard someone this year say that if you strung them all out in a row, it would stretch five miles."

She shook her head in disbelief, but didn't question the stat. "The star on top would be big enough to signal an incoming aircraft."

"And it's made of Swarovski crystal."

"I wonder how much that costs."

"I'm definitely not rich enough to know."

"What about—" A sharp blare of music flooded through the sound system, and the words died on her lips as the crowd noise settled to a low murmur. She and Bex turned toward the show, attention rapt, as several people took the stage in a flurry of activity.

"There's the mayor." Bex pointed to people on the stage. "And there's Bon Jovi. Oh, and there's the whole team from *The Today Show*."

48

Ava swiveled her head from one side to the other, trying to take it all in as a choir flooded the stage in bright red robes. "We're in for a whole production, aren't we?"

"If there's anything this city understands, it's putting on a show."

And within fifteen minutes, Ava could verify the truth of those words. They weren't even on Broadway, but aside from the chilly outdoor air, she would've never known. A star-studded lineup put on a concert to rival some of the best music festivals in the world. She tapped her toes and sang along to Christmas carols with some of the biggest names in every musical genre from country to jazz to rock, each performer seeming bigger and more impressive than the last. It went for nearly two hours before the Rockettes took the stage in all their shimmery shimmying glory.

She could hardly believe she was seeing something so iconic in person as they high-kicked into their famous formation. She turned to Bex as a blur of bare legs all moved in unison, but instead of focusing on the exposed skin, she was watching her.

"What do you think?"

"I think you've fired quite the opening salvo here, and they haven't even lit the tree yet." She thought for a second. "I wasn't expecting the full concert, but the best part is how excited everyone else is to be here, like we're all showing up for the same reason, and with the same energy and hope. I don't know how to explain it."

"No, you just did," Bex said. "I love the communal spirit around a city holiday, and this is where everything coalesces. All year long, we go about our own lives, surviving our own traumas, working toward our own goals, and tomorrow, we'll branch off and celebrate the holidays in a million different ways, but for a couple of hours tonight, we all focus on one shining spark together."

Ava let the idea curl through her. She was used to celebrating on her own timetable, with, at most, a small group of close friends and family, but her chest expanded with the sense she'd joined with this city of millions, all collectively holding their breath in anticipation of one bright moment.

The sensation only grew as the mayor stepped toward the mic and told a story about the first Rockefeller tree, which was purchased with pooled money from the workers who were building the plaza. It became a sign of hope and unity during the Depression, and the gesture so moved a destitute city, they'd kept the tradition through wars, after terrorist attacks, even during the pandemic. If the tree still stood, so did all the ideals it represented. Ava's eyes misted at the emotion of it all, but the mood quickly turned exuberant once more as they began the final countdown to the official holiday season.

The crowd's excitement reached fever pitch immediately, and Ava's heart rate spiked. Mere hours ago, she didn't even know what they were doing tonight, and yet in this moment, she felt certain much of her season had been part of this larger countdown.

"Five. Four." She and Bex counted with the crowd, but seconds before the big moment arrived, the anticipation overwhelmed her. She wanted, or maybe even needed, to anchor herself and the momentum coursing through her. Without thinking, she slipped Bex's hand into her own.

"Three. Two."

Their fingers intertwined.

"One."

A cheer went up as bright light flashed through the night sky and thousands of bulbs cast colored rays across the scene. The choir burst into song, strains of "Joy to the World" reverberating off skyscrapers and rattling out into the night. The breath she'd held left her lungs in a rush as she stared up at the brilliant sight.

Bex gave her hand a squeeze and leaned close enough to be heard over the exuberant Christmas carol. "Not a bad way to start our shared celebrations."

She turned away from the tree only long enough to see its light reflected in her eyes. "Thank you for sharing it with me."

Chapter Five

Bex had already been up for several hours when movement on the other side of the bedroom wall finally gave her the excuse to stop reviewing work files and press "brew" on the coffee machine. She hadn't planned anything for early this morning since Ava had had a big day of travel followed by a late night, but that didn't lessen her excitement for their time together in the city.

"Good morning," Ava said, a hint of sleepiness scratching at her voice as she padded in from the bedroom.

"Good morning." She didn't even hide her amusement at the sight of her in Christmas jammies with red flannel bottoms and a long-sleeve white shirt featuring a llama dressed like a reindeer. "Coffee will be ready in a few minutes. I hope you take yours with creamer."

"I do." She yawned.

"Good, because I stocked up on peppermint, gingerbread, and holiday hazelnut flavors."

"Nice. Which one did you have?"

Bex shook her head. "I don't drink coffee."

"What?" That seemed to wake her up all the way. "How's that possible? You're already up and dressed even after not getting to bed until after midnight. How can you accomplish so much without caffeine?"

She laughed. "I didn't think of it as a bold accomplishment. Normally, I've done at least one surgery, maybe two, by this point in the day, and caffeine makes me jittery."

"Oh jeez, no one wants the person slipping the needle into their spine to shake."

"Right? Besides, you've seen me on my natural Christmas high. No need to add any uppers to my natural buzz, but I still keep some in the house for when I have guests."

Ava arched an eyebrow coyly. "Do you often have early morning guests?"

Bex shrugged. "Not as often as some people like to imagine, but it happens from time to time, and I like to be a good host, which is also why I picked up some fresh *pain au chocolat* and bagels from a shop down the block before you woke up."

"You're not a coffee person, but you do support morning carbo-loading?"

"Very much, and we'll need both complex and simple sugars to sustain us this weekend, so if you tell me which creamer is best, I may be tempted to add some to a mid-morning hot chocolate."

"If that's what the doctor recommends, who am I to argue? Lay 'em on me."

Bex obliged, pouring coffee for Ava and setting all three options on the counter between them before heating a mug of milk for herself.

"They all have potential." Ava sniffed each one. "But I'm feeling hazelnutty this morning."

"Good call. I think I'll join you."

Ava poured some in her cup, then passed it to Bex. "What's on our agenda today?"

"I'm sure it won't surprise you to learn I took the liberty of making some plans."

"I would've been disappointed if you hadn't."

"Good, because the first item on my list is to go over the list."

"Of course it is." Ava snagged one of the chocolate croissants and began to pull it apart. "Do I get to know all the things, or will there be more surprises?"

"You'll get a general picture, but don't expect me to lay all the cards on the table."

"Gimme the highlights then."

"Starting with today, when we'll have a leisurely morning."

Ava pointed to her pajamas. "Look at me already doing the thing you planned."

"You're advanced, for sure." Bex went on. "Then I thought we might take a stroll around the neighborhood. There are some nice trees and storefronts worth seeing nearby. Then we'll come back and dress up a bit for an early dinner."

"Where?"

"That's not a card I'm showing yet, but let's say if you wear something Christmasy cute, you'll be good."

"So, the ballgown's still off the table?"

"Only for tonight, but after dinner, we're going to take in a show."

"The title of which is also on a need-to-know basis?"

"No, because I feel like you had to see this one coming. We're going to the Radio City Music Hall Holiday Spectacular."

"More Rockettes?"

"Wouldn't be Christmas without a full helping of scantily clad Amazons."

Ava cocked her head to the side and opened her mouth as if she might argue with the assessment, but Bex didn't give her the chance before forging on.

"Then, after the show, I booked us a little treat for our nightcap."

"You do nightcaps here? Fancy."

"What, you only day drink in Vermont?"

"No, I've just only heard it called a nightcap in classic movies."

"Well, this weekend is reminiscent of some classic movies because tomorrow we're going to Central Park. Think strolls through the grounds, ice skating on the Wollman Rink, and I invited Howie to join us for drinks at Tavern on the Green."

"Really?" She sounded rather impressed.

"You've heard of it?"

"No, but I've met Howie, and the idea of him going someplace trendy for drinks makes me happy."

"He and I go out a couple of times a month. He'll probably wear a jacket with elbow patches or something not quite hipster."

"Glad to hear he's not just a nerd at home."

"No, no, all the time, which is why I didn't invite him to come with us at all on Saturday."

"No nerd Saturday? Do I get to know more?"

Bex opened her mouth, then got caught up in the sparkle in Ava's eyes and suddenly wanted more than anything to hold onto her anticipation. "Actually, no. Saturday's still a surprise. All I'll say is it's the closest you'll get to ballgown territory."

"Hmm." She tapped her chin playfully as if trying to suss out a mystery. "Saturday night in the big city at Christmas, and ballgown adjacent."

"No guesses." Bex hopped up. "We have plenty to do between now and then, and while I want you to relax and enjoy the weekend, I don't want you to ever quite forget I'm winning our bet."

"You are, are you?" Ava shook her head. "After a whole, what, seventeen hours?"

Bex pushed back from the counter. "I didn't say I'd won yet, but if the Mets scored runs in the first and the Red Sox scored none, you'd still say the Mets were winning, right?"

Ava pursed her lips together. "I may, but I'd also be quick to note the Red Sox hadn't had a chance to bat yet."

"Look, I told you I'm not really a sports lesbian, but don't you have to get some outs before the other team can come to the plate? I wonder what would happen if the Mets kept getting hits and they kept batting and never made a mistake."

"You're funny," Ava said as she rose.

"Funny as in 'ha ha,' or funny as in 'strange'?"

"I don't see why I have to choose, but how about I think about it while I take a shower and get ready to roll?"

"You do that, and then I'll keep hitting home runs all day."

Ava snorted softly as she walked away, but when she reached the bedroom door, she paused and turned around. "Hey Bex?"

"Yeah?"

"I'm not going to let you bat around for the entire game, but I did have a really good time last night, and country mouse or not, I'm looking forward to the next few days."

Bex grinned so hard it stretched her cheeks. "Me too."

Ava disappeared into the bedroom once more, and a few minutes later, the sound of running water came faintly through the wall while Bex hummed along to the echoes of "Joy to the World" in the arrangement the choir used the night before. She stared out at the view of traffic coming across the Brooklyn Bridge and tried not to bounce her feet in anticipation. Today wasn't even the best day she'd planned, but she had to admit, it wasn't just the itinerary that

57

had her amped up. She did many of the same things every year around Christmas, and while they never got old, there was a new sort of buzz surging through her at the prospect of sharing them with Ava this time around.

🎄 🎄 🎄

Ava thought her eyes might bug right out of her head when Bex opened the door to Rolf's restaurant. "What?"

"Merry Christmas." Amusement coated Bex's voice.

Ava blinked a few times, then leaned back enough to look at the outside façade. "It seems so unassuming from the sidewalk."

"New York is full of hidden gems, but this is one of my favorites."

"I can see why. It looks like Christmas vomited all over the walls."

"What a lovely image." Bex laughed before telling the maître d' they had a reservation for two.

"Sorry, maybe vomit is the wrong analogy," Ava admitted as she struggled to take in the ornaments covering every surface, and garland draped over everything. Even the ceiling dripped with silver, red, and green ornaments until they bubbled downward like yuletide stalactites. She had to duck out of the way of one as they were shown to their table. "It's more like Christmas swallowed us, and we're modern-day Jonahs inside the belly of some holiday whale."

Bex's eyes danced as she and Ava slid into a bright red booth. "I would've gone with something less intestinal, but you're not wrong. It's like being ensconced in some Christmas cavern where they use every inch of space to hang decorations."

"And then, when they ran out of space, they stacked another layer on top of the first one. It's so extra, I can see why you'd be drawn to it."

"Thanks?"

She grinned. "You know what I mean. You're all in for the glitz and glamour."

"Guilty as charged." Bex picked up a menu. "Though, despite the décor, this will likely be the least fancy meal you eat in the city."

"Ah, are we paying for the ambiance?"

"No, the food's fantastic and the serving sizes are relatively huge, but it's not avant-garde cuisine, and instead features traditionally hearty German fare."

"Sounds amazing."

"Also, this is a big spot for Instagrammers and tourists, so we're on the clock. We have one hour to eat."

"Are you saying we have to eat a homestyle meal with gusto? Because if so, then you absolutely picked the right woman for this particular outing."

"I saw you down three servings of turkey and mashed potatoes at Thanksgiving. I knew right then and there you were made for Rolf's."

Ava didn't even have it in her to pretend to be offended. "You're not wrong, but now I'm starting to wonder about you. I was so busy stuffing my own face last week, I didn't know I needed to check your speed-eating chops. You're not going to embarrass me here, are you, city mouse?"

"Are you kidding? I've eaten here every year since I was a kid." As if to prove her point, when the waiter arrived, she ordered the chicken schnitzel and potato pancakes without glancing at the menu.

Ava had to read fast to catch up, but thankfully she didn't see a bad option, and her stomach actually growled as she reached the pork tenderloin, so she took the hint.

"Good choice." Bex nodded approvingly.

"You've had it?"

"My mom loved it."

"She's the one who brought you here as a kid?"

Bex nodded. "She was a foodie too."

"Was?"

"Yeah." Bex's voice stayed steady, but her eyes roamed over the ornate distractions all around them as she continued. "She died about five years ago. Aneurysm. She was in a hospital when it happened, but there was nothing anyone could do. I was in my residency at the time. I've reviewed all the files."

Ava nodded as if she understood, but she didn't. She couldn't imagine losing a parent suddenly, so she didn't judge the urge to make sense of it in any way possible, but for a young doctor to sit down and pore over medical documents searching for answers when there clearly wasn't any rhyme or reason to such a thing seemed lonely and sterile. She had the urge to take Bex's hand the way she had in her excitement last night, but doing so here and now felt much more intimate. Instead, she said, "I'm so sorry."

Bex shrugged. "She's the one who taught me to love Christmas. She was an ENT, and nobody wants to have their five-year-old's tonsils out right before the holidays, so she always took time off in December."

"Sounds like someone else I know."

Her smile returned. "You can make all the apple-and-tree jokes. I welcome them with her."

"Yes, but can I work in something about the Big Apple too? Is she the one who taught you to love the city?"

Bex scrunched up her forehead as if thinking hard. "In a less clear way."

"Don't hold out on me. We've still got like fifty minutes left on our dinner clock."

60

"Ah, ironically, that's the same amount of time as my therapist gives me to talk about such things."

"You don't have to tell me if you don't want."

"No, it's fine. I don't mind talking about it or talking about therapy either for that matter. I'm a big mental health advocate. My upbringing's just more complicated than my relationship to Christmas."

"Whose isn't?"

"Fair." Bex took a sip of her water. "My dad was a filmmaker. He was eleven years younger than my mom and a total Bohemian. They met at the Tribeca Film Festival, which is where I get my name."

"Bex is short for Tribeca?"

"Beca morphed into Becs, and then, when I was in high school, I started using an 'x' instead of 'cs' because I thought it made me sound edgier."

"High-school-you was not wrong. Bex suits you."

"Thanks, and I have my father to thank for that. He loved the city. He grew up as a bridge-and-tunnel kid in the burbs and always wanted to live in the heart of it all, or at least that's what my mom told me, since he wasn't around for much of my childhood. She never resented him, always said he wasn't the stick-around type, and she knew as much going in."

Ava couldn't imagine, but Bex didn't seem nearly as bothered as she would've been. "Did you have any sort of relationship with him?"

Bex shook her head. "I have some vague memories of him living with us until I was about five, and then he popped in a couple of times in my youth, but most of the things I got from him came from stories my mom told. She'd always point out things in the city and tell me about memories they'd made. She talked about how much he loved Central Park at night, and his ability to find secret bars and restaurants, or scale fire escapes to get the perfect shot of a city scene. I think she wanted me to view him as a dynamic person instead of some deadbeat."

"Magnanimous of her."

Their food arrived quickly, and Bex glanced at her watch as she picked up a fork and knife. "We've got thirty-eight minutes. No problem."

Ava stared at her large portion of meat and potatoes with doubt, but the aroma of the gravy alone suggested she'd at least *want* to finish the meal in time. "Let's give it a go."

They both tucked in, taking several minutes to enjoy the rich food and the sounds of Christmas music playing softly from a speaker she couldn't see through all the globes and tinsel dwarfing them in their booth.

"She was," Bex finally said.

"What?"

"My mom. She was magnanimous. She accepted people without trying to change them." Bex smiled wistfully. "She never said a bad word about my dad. When I came out, she kissed my cheek and told me the only thing she was sorry about was all the boys' hearts I'd break."

Ava's chest ached in the best way.

"And she's totally responsible for my bedside manner, or at least my aspirations of it anyway. I never once heard her complain about a patient even though I know some of them broke her heart with the choices they made. She always said talking down to them only taught people to feel ashamed about needing help, and any doctor who did that missed the whole point of healing."

"She sounds amazing," Ava said, "and honestly, as do you."

Bex shook her head. "I told you that's aspirational as far as I'm concerned."

"Not just the bedside manner, all of it. The under-standing of where you came from, the realization your parents were real people, your ability to hold onto the joy of the city and wonder of the holiday without them. You cling to the very best of what they loved instead of the sad parts."

"Thank you," Bex said sincerely, "but it's not hard when you have so much to be thankful for. I live in paradise, I'm eating amazing food in a place literally overflowing with holiday cheer, and I'm about to take a fellow Christmas aficionado to her first Radio City Christmas Spectacular. If you can't find joy in that scenario, you're doing life the wrong way."

Ava marveled even more at the woman in front of her than she had at the sea of ornaments overhead. She raised her glass and echoed the sentiment. "Then, here's to joy in abundance."

Chapter Six

The Spectacular was, well, spectacular. There was a reason this show had been a staple of the New York City Christmas essential experience for almost a hundred years, but even as the finale raged in all its sparkly glory, Bex kept sneaking peeks away from the stage and toward Ava.

There was something about the way the light sparkled in her eyes that made the production all the more dazzling. She had the most expressive eyes, deep and reflective as she took everything in. Or maybe it was the way her lips moved as she mouthed the words to all the Christmas carols. Then again, perhaps it was how her chest rose and fell with each held breath or gush of excitement. Bex would've said Ava watched the show like a kid waiting to see Santa, except the only thing childlike about her was her sense of wonder. Every other characteristic showcased a smart, beautiful, engaging woman. Bex had gone into the day expecting to enjoy all the activities, but she hadn't anticipated how much she'd enjoy Ava's enjoyment.

She smiled at every little detail from the way the ceiling of the theater became part of the show via projection and fake snow to the way the dynamics of the stage allowed the orchestra to be in different positions during different numbers. She thrilled at the young ballerina who got to dance an abbreviated version of *The Nutcracker* and held her breath during a number featuring actual figure skaters doing jumps and lifts.

Best of all, Ava gasped and clutched at Bex's arm when the live animals filed on stage during the nativity scene. She managed to squeak out, "Camels!"

Bex chuckled.

"Seriously?" she whispered. "Where did they get live camels in the city?"

"You can get anything in the greatest city in the world."

Ava shook her head, apparently too overcome with awe to offer a rebuttal as the Rockettes launched into another musical number. Bex had seen a lot of theater over the years, but she didn't know if she'd ever witnessed a harder working cast. They all went nonstop for ninety minutes, then reset and did it again for four shows a day.

"Wow." Ava sighed as the final note faded into the applause of the crowd. She clapped along as the large cast took their bows, then turned to Bex and grinned. "I know this technically isn't Broadway, but it's pretty much how I always imagined it."

"Wait." Bex clutched her chest. "Are you implying you've never seen a Broadway show?"

Ava threw back her head and laughed, her long hair shaking out in shimmering waves. "Don't have a heart attack, and don't get any ideas. Focus on Christmas first, and then you can work me over about the city's many charms during the rest of the year."

"That's a given. Christmas is a powerful gateway drug to city life." Bex held up Ava's coat for her to slip into. "And it's a beautiful night to wander a bit on our way to our next event."

"I'll follow your lead."

"Nah, we can do this part side by side." Bex held out her arm and then held her breath, feeling suddenly cheesy until Ava accepted the gesture and looped her own through before tucking her hand into her pocket.

Together they strolled out through the jam-packed lobby and under the massive crystal chandelier shaped like a shimmery Christmas tree.

"Did you enjoy the show?" a doorman asked as they passed.

"Very much," Ava gushed. "Thank you!"

He tipped his hat. "Have a wonderful evening."

Ava turned to Bex. "Everyone's nice here even though it's crowded."

"Don't let the propaganda fool you. We might be a busy breed in the city, but we're not angry or hostile people. New Yorkers love where we live, and we generally love to show it off," she explained as they stepped into the chilly evening and ambled to the end of the block. "For instance, there's St. Patrick's Cathedral."

"Beautiful," Ava murmured. "I love the simplicity of the golden lights."

"I'm not an overly religious person," Bex admitted, "but it's hard not to feel a sense of the divine hovering when you stand in the candlelit sanctuary."

Ava nodded. "I know what you mean. We have a church back home, nothing so grandiose, but when all the candles are lit and the choir starts to sing, I feel something holy."

Bex sighed, both at the mental image and in relief that Ava understood the sentiment.

"What's up there?" Ava pointed to a spot down the block where people gathered on the sidewalk.

"That's why I wanted to point out the church first, because while the subtle sense of the Holy Spirit is much more profound, we're about to be blinded by the light in a different way."

"Oh?"

Bex pointed to the storefront. "We timed it well. All the retailers up and down Fifth Avenue have amazing holiday window displays, but Saks goes a step further and does a whole light show every ten minutes for the entire season."

As if on cue, the entire building burst to life in a flash of silvery white. Oohs and aahs went up through the gathered people, and Ava tightened her grip on Bex's arm. Then the music kicked on, a cheery instrumental version of Mariah Carey's "Christmas," and when the bells kicked in, the lights climbed the entire eight-story storefront, revealing the façade of a winter castle.

For the next few minutes, the soundtrack ran through a medley of upbeat holiday standards while lights flashed in time, illuminating banners and bells and snow-lined trees, all dancing in time to the beat. Bex and Ava bopped along with the crowd. So many others pulled out phones and cameras, but just like at the show, Ava seemed more than content to stare up, wide-eyed, imprinting the memories in her mind. She smiled and bobbed her head or mouthed along the words until the entire show flashed in a full-color grand finale. Then she burst into applause before turning back to Bex excitedly.

"They do this every ten minutes?"

"Yup."

"For free? And anyone can stand here all night watching it as many times as they want?"

"I suppose you could."

"No wonder people are happy around here. Anytime they get down or tired or grumpy, they can come get a holiday pick-me-up!"

"In theory, yes, but there's so much to see and do to bring joy, there's no need to limit yourself to one."

Ava's eyes narrowed. "Why do I feel like you're building up to something?"

"Always." Bex tugged on her arm. "Come and see. The place we're going next is about a mile up Fifth. If you're cold or tired of all the walking, we could catch a cab."

"No." Ava shook her head quickly. "I'm hearty, north country farmstock, remember? I can walk all day. Besides, you said there were a ton of decorated storefronts. I want to see them all."

"Right answer." She turned them south as they started to stroll again.

"Were you testing me?"

Bex shrugged. "Maybe a little. I would've been fine with whatever you chose, but I'm a walker too. I don't even own a car."

"Really?"

"Honest. I have a license, and I rent cars when I need to, but I don't need to much, and when I'm here, who wants to traverse this city with their eyes on the taillights in front of them? I like to look up at the architecture and down alleys and into the doors I pass along the way. I've taken the same walk to work almost every single day for nearly two years, and I still notice new things at least once a week."

"I like that about you," Ava said. "I mean, I know you were raised here, but you know all the little things like the schedule for the light show. I would've thought someone in your line of work would get tunnel vision."

"The harmful Hallmark movies you watch keep filtering into your worldview."

"Don't start again."

"It's true. Those things poison your brain against surgeons and bankers and executives. Just because we have jobs we believe in doesn't mean we can't have other nice things, too. In fact, I believe the same attention to detail that makes me a great anesthesiologist also helps me notice and commit to memory other tidbits that add up to something miraculous."

Ava seemed to consider the point. "I'll admit, I don't know what an anesthesiologist does other than put people to sleep."

"There's a little more to it, and I'm not going to lie, it carries stressors a lot of people can't imagine, but it takes many of the same skills I'm using this weekend. I have to read people, and I have to make elaborate plans. I have to check in on my patient in a multitude of ways, and I need to always be attuned to both the forest and the trees."

"Then, I'm lucky you're not one of those Hallmark doctors while we're in the city, but I reserve judgment on the total package until I see how you do in the country next weekend."

"What if the problem isn't me? What if it's the country? Why do people always assume I must be some soulless workaholic if I don't want to sit around and watch paint dry in my free time?"

"Paint dry?" Ava gave her a little shove, breaking the easy contact between them. "Is that what you think my life is? I mean, I do occasionally have to wait on paint to dry, but I don't sit around staring at it, and besides, I have friends and a family and a small farm with chores and upkeep, none of which pays for itself."

"Oh, so you're the workaholic then?"

"No!" Ava pursed her lips. "Are you baiting me?"

Bex laughed. "Maybe a little, but come on, we're here."

"Here?"

She opened a gold-framed glass door and led her through the lobby to an elevator, then pushed the button for the top floor.

Ava folded her arms across her chest. "Is this the nightcap you promised?"

"Yes, and I swear it'll be worth the walk. We'll get a drink and some small plates, and once we get settled in, I want to hear more about your real life to help combat the defensiveness I feel every time I think of those movies you like."

She clearly tried to hide the smile that still managed to quirk her lips, but she abandoned the effort entirely as they stepped out onto the rooftop deck. "Damn it, Bex."

"What?"

"It's not fair. You can't keep annoying me minutes before you show me something like … are those igloos?"

She grinned and turned to survey the transparent plastic igloo alcoves dotting the open space, each one of them lit up with festive lights and offering expansive views of the city skyline. "Why, yes, yes they are. They're heated and come with plush robes, and there's one with your name on it."

Ava pushed her in the shoulder without any force. "You know it's impossible to stay peeved when you're in an igloo, right?"

She laughed. "I didn't, actually, but let's go find ours, and I won't test the theory anymore tonight."

🌲 🌲 🌲

Ava accepted a mug of something called boozy hot chocolate, piled high with whipped cream, and scooted over to let Bex slide in next to her so they both faced the Empire State Building in all its red and green glory. They'd both snuggled into their red robes as soon as they'd entered their transparent cocoon, and with a mini heater styled like a

71

fireplace, the chill that started to seep in during their walk faded away. "This place is pretty amazing."

"I'm glad you think so," Bex said, "but in case I hadn't won you over completely yet, I also ordered us truffle fries."

"Fries? I'm still waddling from Rolf's."

"A solid four hours ago? You've walked several miles since then. Besides, the salty fries with the sweetness of the drink are just ..." Seemingly lost for words, Bex pinched all her fingertips together and kissed them like a cartoon chef.

"You haven't steered me wrong yet."

"Good. I'm glad I got you in an igloo so quickly after pinging your defenses with my own, but I do want to hear more about your life up north."

She shook her head. "You don't have to. We're on your turf now."

"Yes, but I'm genuinely interested in you. Are you going to make me guess what you do for a living? I know you sometimes have to wait for paint to dry, but you don't sit around, and you still make enough money to keep a small farm afloat?"

"It's nothing so exciting or steady as surgery. I have a grove of maple trees, so during the spring, I get a good bit of production out of them."

"Production of what?"

"Maple."

Bex's eyes went wide. "You make maple syrup? Are you fucking with me?"

"No. Why?"

"Because you're from Vermont and you make maple syrup for a living! I mean, I don't want to open the Hallmark movie wound again, but you have to admit that's like something they'd write into existence."

She had to laugh. "Probably, but it's not like a full-time job, and I don't bottle the syrup myself. I collect it, and then we have a co-op to sell it, though I do keep small batches for myself because I make a mean maple sugar candy."

Bex stared at her skeptically as if she still didn't quite buy it.

"I also have a small apple orchard with a contract to sell to a cider co-op."

"Of course you do," Bex said as if trying hard to be serious.

"There's a small, one-room cottage on my property I rent out to skiers, and for a couple of weeks in the winter, I lease duck-hunting rights to a pond on my property."

"So, let me get this right? Maple in the spring, apples in the fall, rental and hunting income in winter. This is quite a series of hustles you have going on here. Anything else?"

Ava didn't quite want to say the rest, not with the early comments about paint drying still hanging heavy over her, but unlike those characters in the Hallmark movies Bex liked to tease her about, she didn't want to keep silly secrets. "I do a little bit of art."

Bex leaned a little closer. "Cryptic. What kind of art?"

"The cheesy kind you'll make fun of."

Bex put her hand over her heart. "I promise I won't."

"I do signs for people."

"Signs?"

She nodded.

Bex's expression turned grave. "Like from the great beyond?"

She burst out laughing, "No. Like for their mailboxes or businesses or ski cabins."

"I'm sorry. I'm still not coming up with a good picture for this line of employment."

"I design and cut, then either paint or engrave signs that say, like, people's last names accompanied by a painting of their dog, or a nature scene, or … here." She grabbed her phone and pulled up an image of a wooden board featuring two snowboarders in bright gear under the words LaCroix Boards and Bindings. "Here's a sign I made for a local snowboarding shop."

"Wow, that's really good, and an actual, literal sign. Okay." Bex rubbed her face with her hands as if trying to scrub some other image from her head. "Wait, why would I make fun of you for this?"

"I don't know, because it's the kind of job someone would have in a Hallmark movie?" Ava swiped through a few more pictures of her work.

"For sure. And I'm starting to see a pattern of why you might like those things, but your work's impressive." She pointed to one with a golden retriever on it. "The puppy is freaking adorable. Where did you learn to do this?"

She pocketed the phone and picked up her hot cocoa. "My grandparents used to make them. My grandpa would plane the boards and contour the shapes and then router the edges before handing them over to Gram, who'd do the engraving and the painting. After he passed, she was going to give it up. She said it wouldn't feel right to outsource his half to a stranger, so I learned to do the woodworking."

"What a great way to honor him and help her at the same time."

"It made me feel like a part of his legacy. I loved working with his tools, and if I'm honest, I felt like pretty hot stuff taking over a traditionally boy's job. This was right around the time I came out, and I think part of me was trying to figure out where I fell on various spectrums, but even when that settled down, I loved the woodworking aspect of the job. It's satisfying to watch something beautiful take shape, literally."

"I can only imagine. Even though I pride myself on having good hands, I don't have an artistic bone in my body. Does Gram still do the painting?"

"No, she retired a couple of years ago. I still consult her occasionally, but she's got too much arthritis in her fingers these days, though it turns out she passed her creative genes on to me too. At first, she had me fill in things she'd sketched, like the letters or the shading, but it didn't take long to figure out I had her eye for the rest of it as well. Now I've got her art supplies in my studio and Grandpa's shop moved over to my little barn."

"Color me impressed," Bex said. "I didn't even know people still crafted handmade signs, much less with such flare and personality."

"They might not be common around here, but wooden signs carry the kind of charm folks expect around ski chalets, hardware stores, and farm stands. I'm certainly never going to have enough business to afford a high-rise apartment with skyline views, but I stay busy enough to turn away jobs I don't want."

"Fantastic." Sincerity filled Bex's voice. "I bet Gram is proud."

Ava's heart swelled. "Yeah. She and I are super close. She's a big reason I am who I am."

"Were your parents not around when you were growing up?"

"Oh no, they were. I mean, they still are. I have a great relationship with them. I have a good relationship with pretty much all my family, except for Uncle Clay." She gave a shudder for emphasis. "But Gram's special. I grew up about a mile from her house, and as soon as I was old enough to be let out on my own, I started running right to her. She taught me how to cook and can vegetables and garden. At home, I had to stay out of the mud and keep my feet off the couch and not touch my parents' work stuff. You know, all those normal household rules?"

Bex nodded.

"Gram never had any of them. And she never talked down to me. There was never a job I couldn't help with even though, looking back, I must've slowed her down. And we could talk about anything. No subject was too big or too small. Anything that mattered to me mattered to her, from dolls to colleges to girls. I still run everything past Gram before I let it settle across my heart."

"I love that," Bex said. "I never knew my grandparents on my dad's side, and both my mom's parents passed before I was a teenager."

"I'm so sorry."

Bex waved her off as she stared out over the expanse of the city she loved. "It's okay. Even if they'd been around, I doubt either of them could've taught me to can vegetables."

The thought made Ava's chest ache. Bex had so little family in her life. While her exuberance for the holiday and the city and, well, everything, made it clear she wasn't lacking for fulfillment or passion, she couldn't help but wonder, even in this city of things she adored, did she sometimes feel lonely.

Chapter Seven

"There you go," Bex encouraged as Ava zipped around a toddler who'd taken a spill. "You're getting the hang of it."

Ava laughed. "You make it sound like I need skating practice. I've been skating since I was two and a half."

"I believe you," she said with a grin, then threw out her arms wide to encompass the mammoth Wollman rink, "but have you ever skated here?"

They were in the thumping heart of Central Park as the city hummed around them. Bex had intended to get there a little earlier in the day, but they'd lost track of time in their igloo the night before and hadn't made it home until after midnight, so they'd both allowed themselves to sleep in until breakfast turned into brunch, and brunch turned into afternoon, but she couldn't complain, because while they were losing track of time, Mother Nature had blown up a little ambiance in the form of a light dusting of snow.

"I've never skated anywhere like this," Ava admitted.

"Because there's no place quite like it in the world." Bex gave a little twirl on her ice skates. "I mean, there are ice rinks all over the city, and in some cool places. Rockefeller is iconic, and the one in the middle of Bryant Park's Winter Village is steeped in Christmas. Oh, and there's an awesome rooftop rink at Pier 17, but this one is the big fish in a diverse sea for me."

"Why?" Ava asked as they split apart to circle around a struggling newbie.

"First of all, it's huge, and though I'm not a size queen, when it comes to ice skating, bigger really can be better. Beyond that, what more ambiance could there be than a fresh snowfall across Central Park?"

"I'll admit, the views are pretty impressive." Ava skated closer to the wall and ran the fingers of her glove along the edge, leaving a trail in the thin layer of snow.

"Right? You've got this lush, green space full of tall trees and lookouts and scenic vistas, but towering above it all are skyscrapers and stunning architecture. If the city were an urban desert, Central Park would be its oasis, but this time of year, instead of a shimmering pool of water, you find an icy playground at its core."

"I like the way you talk about this place." She shifted her weight to bring their trajectories together again. "You see it all in such poetics."

"I do now, but when I was little, I used to think of the trees around the rink as sort of a secret circle, and the buildings spiking up around them as trying to sneak a peek. I knew they might be able to peer over the top, but they couldn't come in because the trees held them out and protected this paradise for me to play in."

Ava smiled at her sweetly. "I love that image."

"Really?"

"Yeah, it makes this place feel more personal."

"How so?"

Ava shrugged. "Don't get me wrong. I'm impressed, both with the rink and the scenery, and its place in pop culture."

"Did you know it's in the movie *Serendipity*?"

"Yes, it's insanely impressive, but also kind of immense. I feel a little bit like everything here's so big I can't possibly take it in, especially while trying not to skate into or over anyone I don't know."

78

Bex heard the early edge of anxiety creeping in and reached for Ava instinctually. "We can stop if you want."

"No." She shook her head but folded Bex's gloved hand into her own. "I like it. I do, but I like it most of all because you like it. Ugh, that was ineloquent, so many 'likes,' did I even make sense?"

She smiled. "I think so."

"Your joy is contagious, and the more I feel a part of it, the easier it is for me to get swept away. Picturing you, young and playful, imagining a whole world inside and around this place, helps anchor me to something other than the crowd or the enormity or the frenetic pace."

"I don't even notice those things." Bex slowed so as not to cross paths with an aspiring figure skater who wobbled into their way.

"I know." Ava laughed. "You exude total chill. You bob and weave like it's a dance and you knew the steps in advance."

"Thank you?"

"You're welcome, but don't you ever get tired?"

"I was tired this morning," Bex admitted. "I'm used to being an early riser. Surgeries start predawn, and I'm always in before the surgeons, so staying out late last night threw me off, but once we started moving, I got invigorated by pretty much everything. The city's my drug of choice, and I soak up the energy around me."

"I admire that about you," Ava said, then reflected on it all a little more before squeezing her hand. "You're much more dynamic than I imagined."

Bex squared her shoulders. "I won't bring up the reasons why you might've pictured city dwellers as flat or static, but I'm glad I've exceeded expectations. I hope you've been able to have some fun along the way."

"So much fun," Ava gushed. "I honestly can't remember the last time I had such a great trip anywhere or with anyone. And while I feel like I'll have to sleep for a week to recover, I wouldn't trade these days for anything. I just don't know how you do it all the time."

"I have a job and paperwork and mundane chores. It's not like I'm a full-time igloo-dwelling, show-seeing, brunch-eating, ice skater day in and day out."

"What?" Ava feigned disbelief. "You're not a professional ambassador for the NYC Board of Tourism, or some sort of fun city social media influencer?"

"Sadly, no. They didn't have a booth for such occupations on career day at my high school, so I settled for med school."

Ava bumped her shoulder. "You poor baby."

Bex laughed as they settled into a skating rhythm. "You're pretty dynamic yourself."

"Well yeah, people from small towns are always multifaceted and layered with intriguing back stories, right?"

She laughed. "You and I must be watching different movies. I always thought people from small towns were small-minded."

"Not in Vermont. We're like comically liberal."

"Except for Uncle Clay."

"There's one in every bunch, but every other person in my family has a rainbow flag *and* a Black Lives Matter flag."

"I didn't mean small-minded like bigoted. Howie told me you're all cool on that front, or I would've never gone to Thanksgiving, but I thought you'd be more stuck in your ways, not as open to new experiences."

"What gave you that idea?"

"You mean aside from your fervent assertions that Vermont holidays were the best and everyone who disagreed

80

must be a soulless movie villain or a sad sack who didn't understand the true meaning of Christmas?"

Ava laughed. "Don't make me sound judgy when you made some similar assertions. Do we have to brawl again, right here in the middle of this rink full of children? Because I grew up in hockey territory, and I'm not afraid to toss off these gloves."

Bex held on tighter to her hand to prevent her from doing so. "Leave them on for now. I was giving you a compliment. You've jumped in completely for everything I planned for us this weekend. You haven't picked anything apart or complained or tried to find fault or remind me your own traditions are superior."

"Don't get me wrong. I'm still going to beat you, and don't think I haven't already begun planning your time on my turf next week, but I've got no interest in ruining these days here for either of us," Ava said seriously. "Besides, even if I wanted to nitpick, you've made it hard for me. Virtually everything's been amazing."

"Virtually everything?" Bex's voice pitched up, but she couldn't manage to throw any side-eye, as some dude commanded her attention by crashing into the wall directly ahead of them.

Ava laughed. "Now who's being picky?"

"It's this, isn't it?" Bex knew the answer. Ava had been kind and engaged, but her eyes hadn't projected their usual sparkle since they'd arrived at the rink. "You're not loving this particular activity."

"I'm fine."

Bex laughed. "Fine. Okay, here's the thing. You're being super polite, and I just complimented you on jumping in wholeheartedly, but we're becoming friends, right?"

Ava nodded. "I hope so."

"Friends tell friends, okay?"

She sighed. "I've never needed to skate around so many people. It makes me nervous and a bit tense."

Bex nodded. "Makes sense."

"Does it?"

"Sure. You're out of your element, and honestly, you have been for a few days. There might be a bit of a cumulative effect with crowds too."

"Maybe, because they haven't bothered me anywhere else."

"Got it," Bex said. "Small doses are doable."

"I feel kind of silly because this is a uniquely cool experience."

"Literally and figuratively," Bex joked.

"Yes, both, but I'm feeling overwhelmed by the magnitude of everything."

Bex's heart gave a dull kick at the admission, but she forced a smile. "Thank you for telling me, and I have good news."

"What?"

"We're in Central Park, which is exactly the place to be if you need a break from the hustle and crowds. It's kind of the whole point of Central Park."

Ava smiled. "I hadn't thought of that."

"Why would you? You're not a New Yorker, but you're with a pro, and what's more, this pro is about to serve up a little dose of home to help you."

"How?"

"No, not how," Bex grinned. "Howie."

Ava rolled her eyes. "Am I supposed to be happy to see that nerd?"

"You don't have to be. I could call and tell him to scram."

She shook her head as a bit of mirth returned to her eyes. "No. I actually really love him, but we can't let him know because his head is big enough as it is."

Bex tapped the side of her nose with her index finger and gave her a little wink, glad to hear some of the playfulness return to Ava's voice. "Your secret's safe with me. Come on, let's get out of this traffic jam on skates."

"Are you sure?"

She thought about the question just a second before answering with surprising honesty. "Actually, I don't mind at all."

Ava's heart rate had dropped significantly after fifteen minutes of walking arm-in-arm with Bex through Central Park. The place didn't exactly offer the quiet solitude of the forest around her own home, but Bex seemed to know which tree-lined paths would offer them the most seclusion, so it did feel a bit like a walk in the woods. The gathering dusk didn't hurt to settle her senses either. It was only a little after four o'clock, but evening came early this time of year, and she enjoyed the soothing sense of classically styled lampposts flickering on like fireflies.

"Thank you," she finally whispered.

"What for?"

"Taking things down a notch."

"Walking through Central Park with a beautiful woman after a fresh dusting of snow is never a hardship for me."

Her cheeks grew warm at the description of her as beautiful. She suspected Bex was just being nice, but the idea that this amazing, cool, good-looking doctor, who could undoubtedly find a great number of women to spend a Friday night with, actually cared enough about her comfort and enjoyment to offer a bit of reassuring flattery made her feel special. "You're really good."

"At what?"

"Not *at* anything. I mean, probably you're good at *a lot of* things, but I meant in general. You have a good heart. You're a good person."

"Wow, what a nice thing to decide about me after a few days."

She shrugged. "I reserve the right to change my mind if you decide to start kicking puppies or pinching babies tomorrow, but I'm usually a solid judge of character."

"And your initial impression is favorable?"

"Very." She tightened her arm around Bex's, feeling the slight flex of muscle through the wool of her coat. "I thought you might be upset at me for wanting to leave the ice rink early."

"Nope. I'm sorry you didn't love it, but that's one of the great things about this city. If you're not enjoying a particular activity, you have a million other options."

"I love how you manage to turn every single conversation back around to the awesomeness of New York. I was trying to compliment you, not your hometown."

"First of all, you can't separate the two, but second, I'll take any compliments I can get," Bex said as they neared the end of the park path. Brighter lights shone just ahead.

Ava scoffed. "Are they hard to come by? Do people not often say nice things to you?"

"I don't know. I haven't given my compliment-to-complaint ratio any consideration, or even the compliment-to-indifference ratio, which is probably a lot higher. Most people don't take note of me at all amid the conflicts and concerns of their own busy lives."

Ava stopped walking and tugged on Bex's arm so she turned to face her, suddenly feeling infinitely closer than a second ago as their eyes met. "Hey, you've spent days doing a pretty good job of convincing me New York is a great place, but if we're existing in a world where you're not appreciated for the truly spectacular human you seem to be, then you need to tell me now so I can tap out."

Bex laughed. "Wow."

Ava's cheeks burned in full as she realized how forward that sounded, but she didn't want to take any of it back, instead she rushed forward. "You're smart and attentive and thoughtful, and you believe in Christmas magic, not to mention you're rich with impeccable taste and style."

"I'm not rich by New York standards."

"Shut up, is that seriously the hair you want to split from my entire list?"

"I guess not." Her smile softened.

"I've had a great time on this trip so far," Ava continued with more seriousness, "and not because of the city. Because of you."

Bex's lips parted, the warmth of her breath caressing Ava's skin. "Thank you."

"Thank *you*," she whispered, holding Bex's sharp blue gaze with her own.

Suddenly her lips felt dry, and she used her tongue to wet them. Bex's eyes tracked the movement, then lingered on her mouth. The world pitched forward, as did she, but before either of them could close the distance between them completely, Howie's voice rang out through the cold stillness of the evening.

"There you two are!" her cousin called. "I thought maybe you got lost in the park."

In that moment, she wanted to take back her earlier comment about loving him.

The two of them stepped apart, and Bex cleared her throat. "No. We were right where we wanted to be."

"Yeah? How was ice skating?"

"Busy." Bex's voice held a slight tremor. "We didn't last too long, but we've been strolling for a bit, chatting and enjoying the snowfall."

"Snowfall." He shook his head. "This barely even counts as flurries. Hasn't Ava been telling you what to expect in Vermont next weekend?"

"Um, no. We hadn't gotten that far yet."

"Really?" Howie chuckled. "You went three days without talking about Vermont? Be honest, Ava, you've at least been thinking about it the whole time."

"No." She finally found her voice, though it sounded a little raspy to her own ears. "I haven't."

She blinked a few times to clear her memory of Bex's eyes falling to her lips before she turned to face him. "Bex has just given me so many wonderful experiences to focus on, I haven't had any inclination to worry about what I might be missing at home."

🎄 🎄 🎄

Howie made a joke that was only mildly funny, but Bex laughed so hard she snorted, which in turn sent Ava into near hysterics. They laughed until they clutched at each other to keep from falling off their bar stools.

The three of them had been together for several hours without the conversation lagging once. What started as drinks outdoors under a canopy of Christmas lights turned into dinner in the famed Tavern on the Green dining room, followed by a return to the bar. Bex wasn't naive enough not to realize some of her giddiness likely stemmed from the

86

buzz of alcohol, but at least an equal measure came from spending time in such wonderful company.

"When he was little, he was always playing doctor on everyone, me, the dog, toy dolls. By the time he was, like, 10, the whole family was calling him Doogie Howie." Ava laughed.

"Perfect. I'm going to start using it at work."

Howie groaned but couldn't hide his smile. "I don't think anyone there will find it fitting, not with all these flecks of gray sneaking into my hair."

"Is there really?" Ava grabbed his face and pulled his head down to inspect it. "Yay! I always hoped you'd age before me."

"Of course I'm aging before you." He sat back. "You're barely thirty, and I'm edging closer to forty. Besides, the stress of my job was bound to take a toll on my boyish features eventually."

"Boyish features." Ava scoffed and turned to Bex. "You're not going gray, too, are you? What with the same stresses of the job?"

"Similar job," Bex corrected, "but honestly, I haven't checked."

Ava reached forward and cupped her face the same way she had Howie's, pulling her closer before running her fingers softly through her hair. It took everything she had not to lean more fully into the touch the same way she'd wanted to lean into a kiss earlier, but before she even got the chance, Ava released her. "I don't see any gray. I'm going to call BS on the job argument. You're just an old man, Howie."

He pretend-pouted. "Gee, way to make me insecure."

"Don't worry." Bex slapped him on the shoulder. "Gray hair is one of many double standards that condemns women while marking men as distinguished. I bet if you get some chic glasses and always find a way to work in the fact you're a surgeon—"

"Which he always does," Ava cut in.

"Then I think it'll be a nice one-two punch with the ladies."

"Honestly, I'm surprised it hasn't worked for you sooner," Ava admitted, swirling the last bit of red wine in her glass. "You're cute enough, and you more than hurdle the very low bar straight women set for men's personal hygiene. Plus, you're liberal, and I know you were raised with manners. I would've thought some woman would look past your nerdiness and terrible dance moves by now."

"Me too." He shrugged. "Last time I went to the Village with Bex, I got hit on by at least three guys, but no women. My work schedule makes it hard for me to plan regular dates. I don't have enough time for my own social life, much less to coordinate with someone else's."

Ava and Bex locked eyes as an unspoken understanding passed between them, and they both began to speak at once.

"He's ripe for one of your Hallmark movies."

"The city got to him."

"He's not from the city. He's from Vermont."

"But he lives and works here. The job is here."

"He basically has the same job I have."

"Hey!" Howie raised his voice to be heard over their sparring. "I'm sitting right here."

They looked at him and then back at each other before they burst out laughing again.

"Oy, I didn't expect you two to start ganging up on me so quickly. I've known you both for years, and you've known each other only like a week," Howie continued. "What's more, I suspect you've forgotten something critical in all your crazy Christmas movie projections."

"What?" Bex took a sip of her drink and watched him over the rim of her glass.

"You're both single too!"

"Ouch." Ava flattened a hand across her chest as if he'd landed a blow to the heart.

"Yeah." Bex turned to her with more focus now. "Why is that?"

Ava shrugged. "I don't know."

"When was the last time you even went on a date?" Howie asked.

"Hey, now who's getting ganged up on? I went skiing with a woman not too long ago."

"Unless you went skiing this past week, it was a long time ago," Howie pointed out. "The slopes haven't been open since April."

"Okay, fine. Probably April."

"Then why are you busting my chops? I went on several dates over the summer." He turned to Bex for backup. "Right?"

She nodded while still trying to wrap her head around the shocking news that Ava hadn't gone out with anyone in more than six months. "I can verify he had several first dates this summer."

"And there's the rub," Ava shot back. "I don't want several first dates. I want one and then a second and third and fourth date."

"You know you can't have a second date until you have a first one though, yes?" Howie pushed

She pursed her lips. "I do have at least a rudimentary understanding of math, thank you, but I don't want to date for dating's sake."

"She's picky," Howie interjected.

"No. Well, I would've gone with 'discerning.' I don't see the point of testing out random people in the hopes that if we have enough small talk, something might spark. I'd rather go about my life until I meet someone I hit it off with, then let things evolve naturally."

"Yeah, but you never actually meet any new people," Howie argued. "You live in the same town you always have and interact with your family or, like, four straight friends you've known since grade school. You hardly go out of the house farther than your own barn most weeks. You're in a rut."

"Not true." She sounded a little defensive and turned back to Bex. "You said yourself, I'm open to new experiences. Just because I don't want to uproot my entire life and move away from everything and everyone I love doesn't make me insular."

Bex nodded, though now she wondered how someone like Ava would even go about meeting new lesbians. "But you work alone, right?"

"I do."

"And you don't travel often?"

"Aren't you the one who said you love New York so much you don't feel the need to visit anywhere else?"

"There are eight million people in New York. You have to admit it's a bigger pool."

Ava drained her wine glass and set it on the bar emphatically. "I don't need millions. I just need one."

"No no." Bex held up her hands. "I'm only saying, you get on Howie and me for being busy all the time, but if you aren't at least a little busy, how do you meet new people who you might find a spark with?"

She sighed. "I met you, didn't I?"

Bex sat back from the impact of the statement. It wasn't like she could argue. Ava met her without leaving her own small circle, either geographically or socially, but there also seemed to be larger implications relating to that

90

unquantifiable spark. Is that what she felt each time Ava reached for her hand, or in the moment when it seemed inevitable their lips would meet? She smiled at the thought and all the feelings it inspired. "Yeah, you did."

"Seriously?" Howie asked. "You're going to let that stand? She only met you because I brought you home from the city."

Ava rolled her eyes, but her grin turned coy as if she and Bex understood something he didn't. The little connection only bolstered the new lightness spreading through her.

Bex never took her eyes off hers, even as she clasped Howie on the shoulder and simply said, "Read the room, friend."

🌲 🌲 🌲

"I had so much fun," Ava gushed after they pushed Howie into a cab just after ten o'clock. "I mean, he's still a dufus, but he might be more amusing here than he is at home."

"The city brings out the best in people," Bex said.

"No." She slapped her on the shoulder. "You cannot credit New York for literally everything up to and including my cousin's sense of humor."

Bex laughed. "Why not? You're you, and he's himself in Vermont. I don't see what the variable is if not location."

"What if it's you?"

Bex's smile softened. "I mean, I think it's the city, but if you want to credit me, I won't argue."

"Good." Ava looped an arm through hers, not quite sure when they'd decided to start walking everywhere like that, but it felt as natural as everything else between them. "Because I do believe it's you, and don't get me wrong, your love of this place is one of the things that makes you you, but

I wouldn't have agreed to visit in the first place if you hadn't been awfully convincing in your own right."

"I can be pretty persuasive when I set my mind on something."

"Something like proving small-town women wrong about how to spend their holidays? Seems like a weird hill to make your stand on."

Bex chuckled as she steered them down one of the more well-lit park paths. The crowds had certainly thinned out by this time of night, but the place wasn't exactly deserted. "Honestly, I'm not sure what came over me. I've met plenty of people who believe all kinds of stereotypes about the city, and you're certainly not the first woman in my world who bought into the whole Hallmark marketing empire, but for some reason, I couldn't let it go."

"For what it's worth, I still think you're wrong about the whole *best* part, but these last few days exceeded my expectations, so I'm glad you didn't let it go."

"Didn't and won't," Bex said as they turned out of the park and onto a city sidewalk. "But what about you? In the grand scheme of this bet, you were much crazier."

"Crazier? That sounds judgy."

"Sorry, I didn't mean 'crazy' as a pejorative mental health term. I mean as in 'wild.' You're a small-town Vermont woodsy lesbian who admitted she doesn't get out much and isn't actively trying to meet new people."

"Way to paint me a hermit," Ava teased. Even though she saw where Bex was headed, she couldn't resist the chance to rile her up a bit.

"You did the work yourself, which makes it all the more unbelievable you'd agree to train down here alone and spend four nights in the big bad city with a woman you'd known all of twenty hours with only minimal goading."

"No, that's fair," she admitted. "This sort of thing is more than a bit out of my comfort zone, but I generally believe I'm a strong judge of character, and you didn't give off any creeper vibes."

"Good to know I keep those well-hidden, but you still didn't know what else I might've been into. You could've found me living in a hovel or a frat house."

"I knew you worked with Howie, and you dressed too nice for a ramshackle existence. You made it through med school—"

"I know a lot of doctors who are real assholes."

She laughed. "I bet you do, but honestly, that was sort of the worst-case scenario."

"That I'd be a jerk?"

She nodded. "You did give off some snobbery red flags. It occurred to me you might be too self-absorbed to be fun in large doses."

"Don't hold back."

"But," Ava pushed on, "you had a sense of humor, and most egomaniacs don't. They also don't love Christmas as much as you do, so I figured I'd take my chances. Also, I left the return on my train ticket open in case I wanted to call uncle before Sunday."

"Way to hedge your bets, but now, you tell me the truth. How many times have you actually thought about leaving early?"

"Absolutely zero," she said quickly, "not even when you and Howie ganged up on me for being single."

"I'm not sure that's what we actually ganged up on you about, but let's not go there again."

"Deal." They paused at a crosswalk as a horse-drawn carriage rolled by on its way into Central Park. It was white and strung with garland and red bows, pulled by a dapple gray, the driver in a festive top hat.

93

"There's one Christmas tradition you won't see me take part in." Bex's voice held a hint of harshness Ava had never heard before.

"Why not? Seems pretty classic."

"It is for a lot of people, and when I was little, I always dreamed of the whole one-horse open sleigh thing, but when I got older, my mom explained how those carriage horses are treated. They often work long hours under terrible conditions around city streets without breaks or proper care well into their old age."

Ava glanced up at the next one who passed, this time focusing less on the picturesque decorations and more closely on the horse, whose back sagged under its thin, dull coat. Sadness settled over her, and she leaned her head on Bex's shoulder. She'd known and loved a lot of horses. They all lived good lives, and she couldn't imagine being the one to take them away from warm barns or playful romps to drive across concrete and asphalt. It also made her sad to imagine young Bex, dreaming of going for a ride but refusing to take joy at the expense of one of those beautiful animals.

"Sorry. I didn't mean to burst your bubble or end the evening on a depressing note," Bex said.

"You didn't. I was actually thinking you made the right decision. And for what it's worth, I'm glad you're not an asshole."

Chapter Eight

"I may've overdone it," Bex groaned.

"You're such a lightweight." Ava reached across the table and speared a bite of croque madame topped with fried egg and popped it into her own mouth before covering it with her hand and mumbling, "God, that's fantastic."

"Help yourself," Bex said dryly.

"You want to try some of mine?"

"I don't know how I could possibly," Bex said even while she cut off a chunk of Ava's pancake and dragged it through the berry compote before eating. "Ugh, so decadent. Why don't I have any impulse control?"

"Impulse control is overrated. This is my favorite meal we've eaten the whole time I've been here."

"Seriously?"

"Yes, and that's saying a lot, because I haven't had a bad meal, but this was exactly what I needed after last night, and I love the ambiance." Ava gestured around generally at the dark wood bar full of booths strung with garland and holly. "Don't get me wrong, Rolf's was quite an experience, but this is more my style."

"I'm not surprised," Bex admitted. "I do love an over-the-top Christmas explosion this time of year, but Lillie's is always one of my go-to places."

"Is that how you managed to get us the best seat in the house and comped mimosas?"

"You noticed?" Bex asked coyly.

"How could I not? The bartender has been buttering you up since we walked in."

"I may've given him some free medical advice to clear up a little situation a few months ago."

Ava scrunched up her face in a skeeved-out expression.

"Don't worry. It wasn't contagious, at least not in any way we'd have to worry about. I can't say anything more."

"I don't want to know any more."

Bex laughed. "It's one of the perks of the job. People hear I'm a doctor, and they don't care which kind. They pour out all sorts of personal stuff."

"I can't imagine."

"What, you mean your sign clients don't ask you to take a look at their irregular moles or bunions?"

"Nope, though once a couple did ask me to paint a nude portrait of them together."

"To put on a sign?" Bex asked incredulously.

"No, they wanted to hang it in their bedroom. I told them I didn't work on canvas, and I wasn't sure hardwood was the right medium for nudes."

"Ironically," Bex snickered.

Ava shook her head. "Ew, another unpleasant image. Thanks."

"Sorry, you said 'nudes,' 'hard,' and 'wood' in the same sentence." Bex refused to be held responsible when someone teed up something like that. "You don't have to be a fourteen-year-old boy to summon those images."

"How about you give me a rundown on this afternoon to help me think about something more pleasant?"

"Gladly." She checked her watch to confirm they'd lingered the morning away. "Since brunch has now officially lasted past lunch, I think we should walk it off on our way to Macy's."

"Macy's? I thought you New Yorkers went there on Thanksgiving."

"Just the parade, which I missed this year."

"'Cause you spent it warm and cozy in superior company?"

Bex opened her mouth to argue on reflex, but she couldn't dispute any of those points. Ava hadn't exactly said Vermont was better, just the comfort and company, so Bex conceded. "Actually, yes. But after you agreed to come play city mouse for a bit, I knew I needed to wait and share Santaland with you."

"Santaland? He has his own land, like Disney?"

"Of course. You can't have Santa come sit in the middle of a regular department store. You have to make him feel at home. We roll out the red carpet and deck out a whole— you know what? I'm not going to spoil it. I want to surprise you."

"Like tonight?"

"Yes, tonight's the big one."

"Right. Ballgown adjacent," Ava teased.

"You got it, so we'll walk down to Santaland and spend a couple of hours there, along with more window shopping on the way, then head back to my place to rest up a bit and get changed for the evening. What do you think?"

"A full stomach, a few hours with Santa, and a night of fancy dress sounds like a perfect way to spend my last day in the city."

"For now," Bex corrected.

"What?"

"Your last day in the city *for now*. You'll be back."

"We haven't worked out the details beyond next weekend."

"No, but you already want to come back, don't you?"

Ave pursed her lips for a few seconds of holdout, but then smiled. "I think I probably do, which is far from an admission you've won anything, because after you spend next weekend with me, you'll want to come back to Vermont too."

"That remains to be seen." Bex raised her hand to get the bartender's attention and indicated they were ready for the check. "You've got a lot of work to do to top this weekend, and you haven't even seen what magic I have in store for today."

🌲 🌲 🌲

"Wow," Ava said for the twentieth time in the last hour and probably the fiftieth time in the last four days. "It really is like a Disney-level attraction."

Bex nodded. "The whole eighth floor of a store that takes up the better part of a city block."

"You could get lost in here for hours."

"Let's do," Bex said in the tone she always used when accepting some exuberant challenge. "Hey, look at those penguins."

It was impossible not to get swept up in her enthusiasm. Even though the constant motion had begun to weigh on Ava's muscles and the aches in her feet had grown increasingly more insistent on the mile-long walk, all those little exhaustions dulled and dimmed with each detail Bex excitedly pointed out. And she saw all of them, from the lacy snowflakes down to the tiny sweater on an adorable dormouse. Ava had heard of people decluttering their lives by tossing out anything that didn't spark joy, but such a method would never work for someone like Bex, who found joy in almost everything. What would've likely come across as overwhelming if Ava had visited a place like this on her own felt magical with Bex as her tour guide.

98

Together, they wandered through a succession of worlds, one after the other, each one more elaborate and engaging than the last. They wandered for long enough that Ava lost track of time until it became clear they were nearing the natural crescendo of their journey.

Up ahead in the distance, she caught her first glimpse of a red hat and the upper tips of an ornate throne.

Bex leaned closer, her breath warm on Ava's neck as she whispered, "Have you thought about what you're going to ask for yet?"

"I think he knows, right? That's his whole routine, knows when you are sleeping, knows when you're awake, knows what you wish for."

"Maybe technically," Bex admitted, "but you still have to tell him to confirm. Or did you already write a letter?"

"I did not, but I suppose there's still time."

"Not now!" Bex said seriously. "You gotta get those postmarked by December 1. But what good fortune! I got you a direct line right to the big guy, or you might've missed out."

"How generous, but I don't need anything worth mentioning to Santa."

"Then you better think fast, because we're in line to talk to him."

"What?" She glanced around frantically at the guide ropes. "This is the line to see Santa? We're in it?"

Several children turned around to stare at her like she might be daft.

"We have to get out. Where's the exit?"

Bex laughed. "Sorry, you can't come to New York at Christmas without seeing the big guy himself."

"I really shouldn't."

99

"Why?" Bex asked conspiratorially. "Have you been naughty this year?"

"No."

Bex lowered her voice. "It's okay, you can tell me if you have. I can appreciate—"

Ava gave her a playful shove and she tripped over the row of decorative candy canes. "Stop. There are kids around, and I don't want to take one of their slots to see Santa."

"You haven't," Bex explained. "There are reservations. This slot is yours. If you abandon ship, it will go unused. Besides, you and I have been big kids all week. Why stop now?"

Ava wavered slightly. "I don't know if it's appropriate for a grown woman to sit on Santa's lap."

"He won't mind." A little voice behind them piped up.

She turned around to see a little girl who looked to be about six or seven, completely decked out in a red velvet dress, white tights, and black ballet shoes. Even her hair was done up in pigtails with a little red bow atop each one. She stared up at Ava with big, round eyes.

"I'm sorry. What did you say?"

"I said Santa won't mind how big you are. My mom made my brother Ryan sit on his lap last year, and he said he was way too big, but my mom said he had to, and Santa just laughed like 'ho ho ho, you've really grown this year.'" She put her hands on her belly and did her best, deep-voice impression of Kris Kringle. "Ryan said it was embarrassing, but it wasn't. Santa was really nice, and then on Christmas morning, Ryan got exactly what he asked for."

Ava looked from the little girl to Bex, who jammed her hands in her pockets and rocked forward on her toes with a smug smile on her face as if daring her to back out after such an adorable endorsement.

100

Ava shot her a you're-going-to-pay-for-this glare before turning back to the girl. "Thank you so much for telling me that. I feel a lot better now."

"Good." She beamed proudly. "'Cause you're almost up. You better pay attention."

Ava straightened and turned to face the music.

"Have you decided what you're going to ask for?" Bex asked when they were next in line. "If the last week has been any indication, I bet you were good this year."

Ava rolled her eyes.

"I'm serious. He's a good dude. If you tell him what you want most of all, I'm sure he'll find a way to give it to you."

She turned to face Bex, searching for a hint of mocking she didn't quite hear in her tone, but when their eyes met, she saw only sincerity, and she got lost in her gaze for a few seconds before the elf guarding the end of the line said, "You're up."

Ava blinked several times before an idea occurred to her, and she grinned.

"You have it, don't you?" Bex asked.

"Yup. I'm going to tell him what I want most this year is to win our bet."

Bex's eyes went wide and she said, "Wait a second."

Too late. Ava strode right up to Papa Noel and greeted him warmly. "Merry Christmas, Santa."

"Hello, young lady," he said, then looked around her to where Bex rushed to keep up, then grinned in recognition. "If it isn't little Ava all grown up and running around with Dr. Tribeca Leone."

Ava froze, swallowing the request she had perched on her lips. "How did you know my name?"

"Oh, come now, dear. It might've been a few years since you've come to see me in person, but I'd never forget a

101

girl as nice as you. Will I be bringing your presents to the city this year, or up to Vermont as usual?"

Ava's jaw dropped, and she whirled to stare at Bex. "How did you do this?"

"Do what?" Bex maintained a total game face.

"Feed him my info ahead of time. Did you do it when you made reservations?"

She laughed. "No, I'll show you my ticket if you want. It says Leone, today's date, and party of two."

Ava turned back to Santa. "Did she pay you off?"

Santa laughed exactly like the little girl's impression of him. "Don't tell me one of my favorite little bundles of holiday spirit has become a cynic. I thought you were a true believer ever since the year I got you Fuzzy for Christmas."

She gasped as a chill caused goosebumps to rise along her arms.

"What's a Fuzzy?" Bex asked over her shoulder.

"Not what," Ava said. "Who. He was my first puppy, a tiny golden retriever. He came in a stocking."

"Adorable. Wait, you named a dog Fuzzy?"

"Shut up. I was five."

"And you were sweet and kind, so I knew you were up for the responsibility. You took great care of him, didn't you?"

Ava nodded, tears filling her eyes. "For fifteen years."

"I know." Santa winked. "Did you have something special in mind for this year?"

Ava started to shake her head, overcome with the memories of her best Christmas, that most perfect present, and her confusion as to how Bex could've arranged for something this personal. Bex didn't even know Fuzzy—or her, well enough to know about him, at least. She turned to stare at her for a moment, but Bex only shrugged. "Go ahead, tell the man."

102

She nodded and turned back to Santa, no longer wanting to use a Christmas wish that suddenly carried much more weight on something as petty as a bet. So, as she leaned close to his ear, she whispered something she hadn't even let herself want until that very moment.

🎄 🎄 🎄

Bex had called in a favor from one of the orthopedic surgeons she worked with, and still paid a king's ransom to have access to the seat she sat in right now. She'd never actually had a front-row view from the ornate balcony making up the theater's first ring, and they were so close to stage-right that there wasn't even a second row behind them. It felt as if she and Ava had a private box close enough to look directly into the eyes of several ballerinas as they twirled across the stage.

She'd been coming to the New York Ballet's famed productions of *The Nutcracker* every December since she was seven years old, and she'd never noticed all the minute details of the costumes she could see this year. The spectacle was absolutely captivating under any circumstance, but especially from such an exclusive angle, which made it even more powerful that Bex couldn't take her eyes off the woman sitting next to her.

Ava was so beautiful she outshone anything the top performers in the world could do with an utter masterpiece. Bex's heart nearly stopped beating when Ava stepped into her living room wearing that dress. If someone pushed her to describe the red and black ensemble, she might've been able to mumble something about elegant or floor length, or perhaps satin with lace sleeves, but she didn't have anything in her extensive vocabulary to paint an adequate picture. Stunning, breathtaking, radiant, they all fell short of conveying the way the square-cut collar showed off her neck or how the upsweep of her dark hair contrasted with creamy skin.

Ava had arched an eyebrow as she turned slowly before asking, "Ballgown adjacent enough?"

Bex only managed to swallow hard like a freaking cartoon cliché before nodding. "Perfect."

The comment earned a smile, but still felt insufficient hours later. Even the dim light of their surroundings was enough to highlight the outline of her figure and hint at the flush of pleasure in Ava's cheeks, or the way her eyes danced along with the Sugar Plum Fairies.

Bex had been able to keep the evening's main event a secret right up until they arrived in front of Lincoln Center Plaza and Ava saw the mammoth banners advertising the show. She whirled on her as soon as she exited the cab and clutched her by the lapels of her winter suit coat. "Are we going to the ballet?"

For one frantic second, Bex hadn't known if the intensity of the reaction was a good thing or a bad thing, but as soon as she nodded her confirmation, Ava pulled her into a crushing hug.

"I've always wanted to see *The Nutcracker* ever since I was a little girl."

And from there on, she'd been as giddy as any of the tiny aspiring ballerinas all decked out in their little Christmas costumes as they coalesced inside the grand lobby, full of anticipation. As Bex led the way to their seats under the artfully swirled ceiling, Ava clasped her hand the way she had in several other instances, but this time, she didn't release it as they settled in. Instead, she turned to Bex. "How did you know I loved nutcrackers?"

She smiled and shook her head.

"What?"

"I didn't."

Ava eyed her skeptically. "Is this like the Santa thing, and you're not revealing your magical sources?"

She laughed. "I'm not copping to anything about Santa either, but I swear, I had no idea you liked ballet or nutcrackers at all. This is one of my all-time favorite holiday traditions, and I wanted you to be the one who shared it with me this year."

Ava sighed. "I didn't even know to want such a thing, but I'm glad you did."

For the first time in her life, Bex felt something akin to disappointment when the lights dimmed and the show began, because it made Ava turn away from her and toward the stage, but the emotion faded quickly as she realized all the things she loved about this season in this city shone brighter when she saw them reflected in Ava's eyes.

She ended up spending at least half the show that way, and she'd never in her life paid so much money to not actually watch a ballet, but when the final strains of music faded and Ava turned her intense focus to Bex, eyes filled with wonder and gratitude, she knew every penny had been well spent.

"Thank you, Bex, for this perfect end to an amazing weekend."

"You liked it?" she asked, hopeful she already knew the answer.

She nodded, seeming too choked up to speak for a moment. "It was … well … the most wonderful thing I've ever seen. Even as much as I imagined it as a kid, tonight exceeded all my expectations. Honestly, the entire weekend has. I can hardly process it all."

"So, I win?" she asked with as much charisma as she could muster after hearing something so heart-melting.

"No," Ava laughed. "Not by a long shot, but you set the bar pretty high. I'm going to have to bring my A game next weekend."

"I'm looking forward to it."

"Honestly?" A hint of nervousness crept into her voice.

Bex paused to give the question its due, because a week ago, the answer would've been no, and perhaps if the choice were between another weekend with Ava in the city and one with her in the county, she'd have still said she didn't really want to go to Vermont, but she was a little surprised to realize that if the choice was between another weekend with this woman by her side or one without her, she was actually looking forward to her trip north quite a bit. "I honestly am."

Ava's smile was almost enough to buckle her knees, but she took the elation a step further by leaning in and planting a kiss on Bex's cheek. "Me too."

Wednesday couldn't come quickly enough.

Chapter Nine

"There's my intrepid traveler." Gram held out her arms, and Ava stepped into the hug, allowing herself to be completely enveloped. She breathed the scent of Ivory soap and gingerbread as she rested her chin on Gram's shoulder, secure in the knowledge she wouldn't pull away no matter how long Ava held on.

After one more deep inhale to make up for lost time, she finally stepped back. "Did you miss me?"

"So much. The great grandkids came over to help make some sugar cookies, but they got more sugar in their bellies than the dough."

"I remember those days. I was always torn when Howie would steal the dough before it cooked because it tasted delicious, but then again, so did cookies."

Gram chuckled and patted the table in an unspoken invitation for Ava to sit next to her. "At least Howie stole the dough. Ethan always licked his finger and stuck it in the sugar."

"To be fair, he does still say the best foods are the ones you have to do the least to."

"Yes, that's why he keeps bringing me Sugar in the Raw. It tastes fine in coffee, but it's not for dusting spritz cookies." Gram poured Ava a mug of steaming peppermint tea. "But maybe you could explain something to me."

"About Ethan's eating habits?" she asked as she stirred in a little dab of local honey. "I doubt it."

"No, about why you've come in here trying to make small talk instead of bursting with a billion stories about your grand weekend in the big city."

"I'm not sure I can explain that any better than I can account for Ethan's tastes."

Gram shook her head. "I hardly know what to make of you. I thought you'd either come in all smug and satisfied you'd been proven right, then declare the city a mess, or maybe if the opposite were true, you'd be bursting with excitement to tell me about your many adventures."

"I guess it's closer to the latter," she admitted. "I had more fun than I could've possibly imagined. Maybe I'm still too overwhelmed to process it. Everything was amazing, the lights, the food, the shows. Bex went beyond my wildest expectations. She took me to see the lighting of the Rockefeller tree and to Macy's and the Rockettes and even *The Nutcracker.*"

Gram's whole expression lit up. "How did she know you've loved *The Nutcracker* since you were tiny?"

"She didn't. Or at least she swears she didn't, but she also had some inside information with the Santa at Macy's. He knew things there was no way he should have, but then again, Bex shouldn't have known them either." She shook her head, still unable to make sense of it all. "The point is, she hit every note perfectly."

"Sounds like she's as impressive on the inside as on the outside."

Ava smiled wistfully at all the evidence she'd witnessed to support that assertion. "She wore a dark suit to the ballet over a gray vest, and this long black coat, and she held doors and hailed cabs and ordered drinks I'd never heard of. Everywhere we went oozed class, but she was also kind and attentive and considerate. She has every right to be full of herself, but the only thing she's ever smug about is the city,

108

and even that felt more charming than cocky because she was so genuinely eager for me to appreciate it."

"And did you?"

Ava fought the urge to gush, which was both immediate and strong, but also left her unsettled. "I did. Everything was enthralling and engaging and even more amazing in person than the movies, but that might've been the problem."

"I don't know how you managed to find a problem there."

She laughed lightly and took a sip of her tea. "I guess the short answer is it wore me out!"

"Ah, now that makes sense. I got a little tired just listening to you talk about it. I'm not sure how you even walked in here."

"I almost didn't. I left on the first train out Sunday, and even after two nights' sleep, I'm still exhausted and my feet haven't stopped aching." She shook her head. "Bex's strong shoulders never once sagged. She's either locked into some city power source I don't have access to, or she possesses endless supplies of energy on her own. Even in the crowds and rush and constant bustle, her eyes and her brain are constantly moving. She took me skating at this huge rink in Central Park, and I nearly had a panic attack from the claustrophobia of all those people cutting us off and crashing into each other, but she never missed a beat, just kept on chatting nonchalantly."

"There's nothing wrong with being cool and collected."

"And she is, but she's also super active, and she takes everything in with such ease and interest, whereas I never got to fully process one thing before we moved on to the next. My brain was on the verge of overload from the moment I stepped into the teeming anthill of Penn Station right up until the moment I crashed into her bed the last night."

Gram arched an eyebrow.

"Sorry, that sounded bad. She slept on the fold-out couch and gave me her room."

"Good to know she's a gentleman, or rather, a lady." Gram shook her head. "Lady doesn't sound right either, but you know what I mean."

"I do, and she was. Impeccable manners, a gracious host, and much more, but that's just part of the whole picture, right? So much more, always more. Whether it's the bet, or the cuisine, or her grand gestures, she's always extravagant."

"And?"

"And I'm ... not."

Gram patted her hand. "I've always loved that about you. You find joy in simple things, and you don't fall for flash and bang. Even when you were small, you made your own fun. I always believed those attributes would help you be content no matter where you went or what you did."

She smiled softly. "I really am, and I think I'd have a good time hanging out with Bex anywhere, but I'm not sure she feels the same way. What if she's bored here with me?"

"Seems to me there might be two different questions there," Gram said thoughtfully. "Are you worried she won't have a good time while she's here, or are you worried she might be bored with you in a bigger sense beyond a long weekend?"

She sipped her tea to buy some time and stanch the ache pulsing in her chest. Of course Gram would cut straight to the heart of things before Ava was even ready to scratch the surface. She would've preferred to stay in a vague mix between hope and denial, but now that she'd been asked point-blank, she had little choice but to answer. "I want to play as good a host to her as she did for me."

Gram didn't respond. She merely watched her and waited until Ava felt the need to squirm in the silence.

"Honestly, I'm not harboring any fantasies of anything more."

"And why not?" Gram asked without a hint of judgment. "The two of you seem to enjoy each other's company."

"I do, and honestly, I think she does too, but at the end of the day, I'm a country mouse and Bex is a city mouse, and there's a reason that whole scenario became a fable to begin with. There's a warning for both about accounting for tastes and the fundamental truth that none of us are likely to really change how we view the world or where we belong in it."

❧ ❧ ❧

Bex had plenty of case files to review for her Monday surgeries, and she didn't expect to have much time in Vermont, so she'd chosen to travel first class and make use of the train's high-quality Wi-Fi. And she had for at least the first two hours of the trip, but then she began to get distracted by the scenery outside. The snow started light and fluttery before falling in thicker flakes over forests and wooded glens until the tracks began to rise more steadily through hills completely blanketed in white.

By the time she reached anything resembling a mountain, she'd given up on even glancing at her laptop and surrendered to the appeal of staring endlessly at the passing landscape. Much had changed in the two weeks since she'd visited last. She hardly recognized any of the places they passed. Could something similar be said for her internal landscape as well?

At Thanksgiving, she'd been mildly interested at best, and regretful at worst. She'd felt conflicted about everything she was leaving in the city. She hadn't afforded herself any anticipation about where she was headed. Then again, she hadn't known Ava, so maybe the excitement stirring in her now had less to do with the "where" part of the trip, and more to do with the "who."

Last weekend had been the most fun she'd experienced in ages as the two of them explored the city together, and while she tried not to feel too superior in her certainty that little in Vermont could compare to the activities she'd chosen, she found that mattered less to her every day.

A garbled announcement came over the train's overhead speakers telling passengers they'd arrive in Montpelier in approximately fifteen minutes, along with a suggestion they might want to bundle up.

Bex glanced out the window as the snow swirled a little harder, and didn't see any reason to question the advice, not that she needed an extra excuse to break into her travel bag and proudly pull out her new purchases.

She didn't even need to squeeze herself into the tiny train bathroom. She only had to kick off her shoes, because apparently snow pants went on over regular pants. Who knew? Apparently, Howie, who'd been all too happy to help her get "Vermont ready" after work yesterday. They'd gone to several outdoors stores where he'd decked her out completely in the type of clothes he assured her she'd need to both stay warm and appear fashionable.

She snapped the buttons on her khaki-colored outer layer and stepped back into her water-resistant Columbia hiking boots. Then she snagged a long, woolen coat from the overhead rack. She had a waterproof jacket stuffed in her duffle, but she preferred the way she looked in the charcoal trench. She wanted to make a good first impression, which

112

was why she hesitated slightly before pulling on her matching stocking cap, sans pom-pom. It would wreck the way she'd feathered back her short hair, but she was in for a penny, so she might as well go in for a pound. Besides, Ava jumped into city culture with gusto. She didn't want to repay her halfway.

She glanced at her own reflection in the window and adjusted the hat until it slouched back slightly before she noticed a middle-aged woman watching with an amused expression. She turned to grin at her sheepishly before admitting, "It's my first time here in winter."

She nodded. "You look ready. Are you going skiing?"

Bex shrugged. "I honestly have no idea."

She raised an eyebrow.

"I'm at the mercy of my host. I hope she doesn't send me hurtling off any mountains, but it's up to her."

"I hope she's nice."

"I think she is," she smiled as the train slowed substantially, "but I guess I'm about to find out."

She collected her bags, then worked her way to the back of the train car, trying to steal peeks of the snow-covered town, but it wasn't until she reached the door that she caught sight of Ava waiting on the platform.

Bex raised a gloved hand in greeting and thrilled at the smile it sparked. She couldn't remember the last time her arrival anywhere brought such genuine joy.

She'd barely hopped completely down the steps before Ava wrapped her in a hug. Gone was the tentativeness of their meeting in New York, and they held onto each other tightly for several seconds before Ava stepped back to scan her attire.

"You look ready for quite the adventure."

"I think I am."

"I'm surprised you own so much outdoor gear."

113

"I didn't until yesterday," she admitted. "I made Howie take me shopping to prepare."

"Why didn't he let you borrow some of his stuff?"

She laughed. "He offered, but I don't share his aesthetic."

"What a polite way to say he lacks any fashion sense, which is true. I probably could've rustled you up some Carhartts, but this suits you better." Ava tugged on her coat a bit, then wrapped an arm around her waist. "I'm glad you're here."

"Me too," she said genuinely. She made a mental note that she might enjoy leaving the city a little more often if there was always someone so happy to see her somewhere else, then shook off the thought as they headed toward the parking lot.

She didn't need to get ahead of herself or surrender to any blanket sentiments. She wanted to stay in the moment and enjoy the days for what they were, whatever they may entail.

❦ ❦ ❦

Ava pulled her Jeep off I-89 and headed south, grateful to be out of the traffic heading toward Stowe, though she had to turn on her headlights as the last little bit of the gray light faded behind the mountains she curved around. "Things should be less congested from here on out."

"Were things congested?" Bex asked.

She sighed. "Right, City Mouse, probably not by your standards, but I go out of my way to avoid any major roads leading toward the big resorts this time of year. Wednesdays aren't as bad as weekends though."

"Honestly, I'm fixated much more on the weather than other cars. The snow's really coming down."

114

"This?" She gestured at the flakes floating onto her windshield. "This won't even get us a winter weather advisory around here, though between this and the darkness, I did plan to stay indoors for our activities tonight."

"Indoors works for me. Do I get to know what's on the agenda?"

"Some of it. Just like you gave me the bullet points, I'm happy to share a general outline with you, but some activities are weather contingent, and of course I reserve the right to hold back on a few surprises."

"Fair enough. Lay 'em on me."

"Tonight, we'll set a roaring fire and put on our pajamas and some Christmas music while we make an obscene amount of cookies for a major potluck later in the weekend."

"Do we get to eat any of the cookies tonight?"

"We have to taste test them, duh. What kind of neighbors would we be if we gave people gifts without knowing if they were any good?"

"Agreed. It's only considerate, and I'm in."

"Good. Then tomorrow … actually I'm going to hold onto that one until I make sure we get the right kind of day for what I really want to do, but Friday, the local festivities kick into gear, so I'll need you to play one of Santa's elves with me."

"It's because you know I've already got a good connection with the big guy, right?"

"Totally. Since you're close enough to somehow trade insider information with each other, I figure you'll be able to keep up in my own workshop during the day. Then, in the evening, we're getting together with some family and friends for a yearly event we like to call 'Caroling and Cocktails.'"

"Seeing as how those are a few of my favorite things, I'm already excited."

"I see what you did there, and I approve." She pulled onto a smaller road and started to climb the last hill before her own driveway. "Saturday is the local small business holiday festival."

"Will you be one of the featured merchants?"

"I don't have my own booth, but several of my products will be featured by other businesses, so I like to be present. Also, it's good, quaint fun. There will be holiday treats and music, and everyone in town will be there."

"Then we have to be there too," Bex agreed quickly, and some of the tension tightening Ava's shoulders in the lead-up to her arrival eased. Bex hadn't so much as hesitated at any of the offered plans, and she clearly didn't intend to turn up her nose at anything without due cause.

"That afternoon, I hope to pull out another little surprise for you."

"Weather permitting?"

"Always. But to be honest, the weather actually permits a lot more than it precludes this time of year if you know how to handle it."

"Which you apparently do." Bex shot a nervous look at the steep slope on the other side of the road. "Are you in four-wheel drive?"

"Yes, but I hardly need it. We're almost to my place." She pointed to a light ahead marking the gravel drive to her cabin.

"Wow," Bex said as she got the first full view of the house. "You love Christmas lights."

"Doesn't everybody?"

"Maybe not to this level." Bex laughed as they wound between strings of multicolor bulbs lining the route to her door like runway lights. At the end, they turned and spiraled up the steps to the large porch, which was completely strung with garlands hanging from every beam. The upper levels of

116

the trim dripped in white icicle lights, and in the highest reaches hung a huge star glowing golden as if to encourage all weary travelers forward, or in their case, to signify the end of the night's journey.

"It's beautiful."

"Thanks. It's not nearly as polished as your apartment, but it's home." She killed the engine, but before she could get out, Bex caught her hand.

"It looks really warm and inviting, and I especially love the star. It exudes welcome and a deeper peace. Even if I didn't know who lived here, I'd feel like maybe I could stop in and feel at home."

Her heart swelled. "That's exactly what I was going for when I decorated."

"Then come show me around the rest of the place. I can't wait to see what other touches you used to make it your own."

They carried the bags up the snowy stairs and stomped off their boots on the covered porch before she pushed open the door, where a wave of warmth hit them both.

She'd left a few lights on as well as the heat, which made it all the easier to ease inside. Kicking off her shoes, she shrugged out of her jacket before turning to take Bex's coat, only to find her still standing in the doorway with a quirk of a smile and wandering eyes.

"It's like something out of a holiday movie," she marveled. "If you tell me you built this place with your bare hands, I'm going to start looking around for the camera crew."

She laughed. "No, my great-grandfather was on the crew that built the original frame and foundation, but it's been added onto a lot. The place was pretty run-down when I bought it about ten years ago, which is how I could afford it. My dad helped rebuild the porch right away, and we took the kitchen down to the studs the next summer."

"So, what you're saying is you *re*built it with your bare hands?"

"No. I'm more of a decorative woodworker. I don't mess with structural issues. All my other touches have taken place through the slow, steady slog of home ownership." She took one of Bex's bags. "Here, I'll show you around."

The open kitchen was divided from the living room and dining room by a breakfast bar, but she pointed out a half bath off to the side. "Everything else is up on the second floor."

She led the way, listening to Bex's feet fall on the stairs behind her.

"I love the exposed wood everywhere. It feels rustic but cozy."

"I think you summed up my style rather concisely. Maybe my personality too." She flipped on a light in the hallway, then pushed open the first door they came to. "Here's your home away from home."

Bex peeked around her. "What a beautiful quilt."

"Thanks. Gram made it."

"I'm beginning to see a theme here. Maybe your whole family specializes in cozy."

"Wait until you see the tub."

"Wait? Why wait? Where is it?"

Ava stepped across the narrow hall and pushed on another door to reveal a bathroom with a stall shower, a vanity, and toilet, but the showpiece was clearly the large, white clawfoot soaking tub.

Bex groaned, and the sound sent a little shiver up Ava's spine.

"My apartment just has a shower, no bathtub."

"Then you'll have to make good use of this one while you're here."

"I intend to. Preferably sometime when we've come in from the snow and cold."

"You'll have ample opportunity, but not tonight. Go get settled into some more comfortable clothes and come on down. I've got beef stew in the Crock-Pot, and I made biscuits earlier. You can tell me all about your trip before we get started on those cookies." She edged back toward the stairs before she felt a hand on her shoulder.

She turned to see Bex grinning sheepishly at her.

"What?"

"Did you really make biscuits from scratch at home, so they'd be ready when I got here?"

She shrugged. "Yes."

"I've never known anyone who could do such a thing, much less go to that kind of trouble on my account."

Her chest tightened, and it took her a second to find her voice, "Well, now you do."

Chapter Ten

Bex changed into flannel pants and a long-sleeve T-shirt featuring a reindeer with a wreath around her neck. It was probably the silliest item of clothing she owned, but when Ava stayed with her, she'd worn a different set of Christmas jammies each night, and they all looked as comfortable as this cabin full of personal touches and family heirlooms.

She checked her hair in a large mirror over an antique washstand to make sure the stocking cap hadn't done irreparable damage, but when she leaned closer, she noticed a photo framed in what appeared to be popsicle sticks. She picked it up to inspect the image of a much younger Ava, her mother, and Gram. They were sitting around a table, covered up to their elbows in flour, with rolling pins and cookie cutters all around. Ava was looking up at the camera with a big cheesy grin on her face, but the other two women were smiling at her. The love emanating from the snapshot made Bex's heart ache. How many times had those women made cookies together over the years?

More pictures caught her eye on the way downstairs, and she paused to examine several as she went. Many of the candid shots featured snow or ice activities, which she supposed shouldn't surprise her in a place where winter lasted the better part of a year, but it drove home how much this environment served as Ava's natural habitat. There was a picture of a young Ava, Howie, and some other children all piled into a toboggan, one of her ice skating with some other girls as a teen, and another of her tiniest form staring up in awe at a snowman with her parents on either side of her. So many memories filled these frames, each one steeped in love and place and joy.

She came around the corner into the open living area and smiled. There were two steaming bowls atop the bar, and between them a basket full of golden biscuits, like a buffer of comfort and care between her and the rest of the kitchen, where Ava scurried around setting out an array of cookie baking and decorating supplies.

Bex watched her work for a few seconds, enjoying the sight of her in all her glory. Her long brown hair in a loose ponytail spilled down her back but stayed clear of the flour and sugar. She'd put on some soft Christmas music and hummed along as she moved with intent, stretching to grab a bag of chocolate chips from an upper cabinet or bending to retrieve another bowl. She'd been utterly breathtaking in her dress at the ballet, but here was where she revealed the grace of a dancer.

The thought warmed Bex's chest, but the longer she watched, the more the warmth spread to other parts of her body, and her mind began to wander. She had a building urge to close the distance between them, to place a hand on the curve of her hip and ease her nearer.

"You're assembling quite an operation," she said in a quick attempt to interrupt her own train of thought.

Ava startled slightly as if she'd forgotten she was there. "Yeah, we don't do cookie baking halfway in this family. Every year, we set aside several baking days or nights, and even though we know we're going to get several cracks at it, we never skimp on any one session. All the cookies, all the time. That's how Gram does it, and that's how my mom does it, so that's how I do it."

Bex remembered the photo back in the bedroom and the sense of tradition it projected, even to an outsider. Seeing Ava take up the mantle and wear it as her own only deepened the connection passed down from generation to generation. Bex didn't have any such family traditions, and under other circumstances that may've made her sad, but tonight, she could only summon a sense of gratitude and eagerness to be included in Ava's.

The two of them ate side by side, chatting amicably the way two people who've grown comfortable with each other do. She relayed the story of how the snowy landscape captivated her attention on the train ride up, then heavily complimented the dinner, which seemed entirely too flavorful to have come out of something called a Crock-Pot. Ava told her little bits about the local ski areas and nearby towns, each with their own holiday activities to enthrall locals and tourists alike, but all the while Bex couldn't stop surveying the multitude of confectionary wonders spread out before her.

"How many kinds of cookies will we make tonight?" she finally asked. "I mean, you said 'all the cookies,' but I'm getting the sense you know a lot more varieties than I do."

"Probably," Ava admitted as she snagged a pad of Christmas tree stationery and a pen shaped like a candy cane. "And I didn't mean we'd make every single kind I know, but we have to cover the holiday favorites, which begs the super-important question. Which cookie is your Christmas favorite?"

"Oh wow." Bex felt suddenly put on the spot. "Why do I feel like this might be a test?"

"It totally is. I'm going to judge you a lot based on how you answer."

"Okay, the pressure was fully intended there. Good to know. Do I get a minute to think?"

"Sure, but the longer you take, the more I'll suspect your answer is performative instead of genuine. I recommend you go with your gut."

"Jeez, this escalated quickly, but I'm up for any and all holiday challenges." Bex closed her eyes and tried to rapidly flip through a mental cookie catalogue. There were so many great options, but as she sifted through them, she hit on one that caused her to smile.

"You have it, don't you?" Ava asked softly.

She allowed her eyes to flutter open to find Ava watching her intently. "I have."

"Don't keep me hanging. What does a city mouse crave this time of year?"

"I have to admit I don't know what they're called, but they have the soft, rich cookie dough base and chocolate kisses on the top of them, and I never find them in stores, but a nurse at my practice brings them in at Christmas time, and I look forward to them each year."

Ava's grin spread. "We call them 'peanut butter blossoms.'"

"Really? Is the peanut butter what makes the cookies so smooth?"

"Yes, peanut butter and sugar. I love the way the chocolate gets soft and satisfying when they're fresh out of the oven."

Excitement rose inside her. "You know how to make them?"

"Of course."

"Can we make them tonight?"

"Absolutely. I already bought all the supplies."

"Yes." Bex practically hopped off her stool. "What else? What are your favorites?"

"Actually, those are near the top of the list for me, too, which is why I bought all the stuff, but my tip-top spot has to go to the mini meringues I flavor in different ways."

"Wait a second, you can make meringues at your house?"

Ava cocked her head to the side as if she found the question odd. "I have a stand mixer."

"I don't know what that means, but I assume it's some high-end restaurant-style tool or an implement of magic?"

She bit her lip as if trying not to laugh. "It's a mixer you don't have to hold while it whips sugar into egg whites."

"Seriously, that's all it takes?" she marveled.

"Along with a lot of patience."

"I don't believe you. I've always associated meringues with fancy French bakeries and pastry chefs and astronomical price tags. What are you going to tell me next? Do you intend to wrap truffles in gold leaf or hand paint gingerbread Mona Lisas?"

"Sorry to disappoint. I intend to do some iced sugar cookies, peppermint bark, and bake some pecan meltaway balls for you to take back to Howie, since they're his favorites."

"Of course they are. He's an eighty-year-old trapped in a middle-aged body."

"Truer words were never spoken, but I figure we should throw him a bone since he has to stay in the city this weekend."

Bex opened her mouth on the knee-jerk reaction that New York City was never a hardship or a consolation prize, but this time, the words died on her lips as she glanced from Ava to the cookie supplies and back again. People in New York baked, obviously, but she'd never been one of them, and she suspected Howie wasn't either, and suddenly it did feel like the sort of thing that constituted missing out.

Ava's eyes danced with a hint of a challenge. "What? No argument, city mouse?"

She sighed. "How about a redirect?"

"I'm listening."

"What if we say Howie deserves some cookies for introducing us, because without him dragging me up here, I wouldn't be here again tonight of my own free will."

Ava's smile turned sweet and almost shy as she nodded. "I'll take it."

❧ ❧ ❧

The loud crack of the rolling pin crushing candy canes startled Ava every time, but Bex seemed to relish the job, so she couldn't manage anything other than joy at the peal of laughter bubbling up and out of her guest as she pounded them into crumbles. She was like a kid set loose in a confectioner's shop, and Ava thrilled to see this lighter side of her emerge, so she kept giving her the tasks usually reserved for the youngest helpers.

"Is this good enough?" Bex held up the baggie full of candy cane chunks. "Or do I need to bash them some more?"

Ava took the bundle from her and held it up to the light for inspection. "Those are perfect. We don't want them to turn to dust."

"Great. What do we do now?"

"This is the easy part." She handed them back and gave the white chocolate she'd been melting in the double boiler another stir. "I'll keep this moving while you pour that all in very slowly until we coat it entirely."

"I can handle that."

126

"I have complete faith in those good hands I've heard about."

Bex gave her a little wink as she stepped up beside her at the stove and began to add the candy in a slow, steady stream.

"Nice," Ava said, enjoying the brush of their bodies as they worked.

"Not like this is a test of my dexterity, but I'll take any and all compliments."

"Hey, you're beating the kids, who normally dump the entire thing in at once, so I appreciate an apprentice with a bit of patience."

"Enough patience to be trusted with the magic of the meringues?"

Ava shook her head. "I already told you, you just whip the crap out of them."

Bex glanced over her shoulder at the Kitchen Aid as it whirred steadily on the counter, clearly not buying it.

"Have a little faith. I've done this before, and you're quickly climbing the ladder toward more involved jobs."

"Is there a hierarchy to this process?" Bex shook out the last of the bag into the melted chocolate.

"Duh," Ava said. "Put the metal cookie sheet we haven't used yet on the table in front of your spot."

Bex did as instructed. "I started at the bottom rung unwrapping Hershey's Kisses."

"You hurdled that low bar with ease, which earned you the right to move up to using the cookie cutters on the sugar cookie dough."

"Which I handled like a boss."

"Agreed, which got you to candy cane duty."

"Smashing things doesn't seem like a harder task."

"No, but now you get to spread this mixture in a nice, thin, even layer across the pan. It's going to want to clump

127

and firm up fast. You need to work steadily so it doesn't seize."

"Look, I'm a doctor. I understand the seriousness of seizures, and I know how to stay cool under pressure. I feel confident in my ability to handle the task."

Ava moved the pan to the table and handed her an oven mitt. "I believe in you."

And she did. Bex clearly had never even been in the same room with other people while they baked before. She didn't know what half the utensils were called, but she'd jumped right in with the same level of gusto she brought to every activity they'd shared in New York and with the enthusiasm and competitive spirit she brought to every encounter. Ava enjoyed watching her work, stealing glances at her even while checking the mixer where the meringue began to glisten.

Eventually, Bex turned to catch her. "How am I doing, boss?"

She moved to stand behind her and surveyed the perfect layer of peppermint-laden chocolate. "Ten out of ten. You're in the running for Star Baker for sure."

"No, you haven't even given me a technical challenge yet. Come on, let me at those meringues."

"Whoa, rookie." She held up a hand. "How can I explain this in a way you understand? You cannot jump right from med school to your own practice. You're going to need a residency first."

"Ah, I see Howie's taught you the lingo." Bex nodded seriously. "I understand. What's my next test?"

"We need to shell pecans."

"They have shells? Seriously?"

She laughed. "Yes, and it's a mildly tedious job, but that's not why I saved it for you. I figured since you took me to see *The Nutcracker*, you should get to use one."

"Use one what?"

"A nutcracker!"

Bex's eyes went almost comically wide as she made a little level movement with her hand. "Like put it in some wooden guy's mouth and make him chomp chomp?"

"Yes, and you have to make the chomping sound now while you do it, because that was adorable."

"Fair enough. This sounds fun."

"I already boiled the pecans and shelled half of them earlier, so I won't let it go on long enough to cramp your hands since I know they're the tools of your trade."

"Where's the nutcracker?"

"Everywhere." She gestured around the living room. "I have about thirty of them. Look around."

Bex's eyes scanned the large, open space before she pointed to the top of the cabinet. "There's one, oh, and over by the flour jar. And look, they're little bookends."

Ava nodded as she glanced at the two holding up her stash of favorite cookbooks. "Check the living room."

"Hey, they're all over," Bex called as she wandered around the bar. "I love these twins standing sentinel over your china hutch."

"Those were from my parents the first Christmas I lived here."

"Here's another matching set holding up the garland on your fireplace mantel," Bex said as if getting into the game. "It's like playing the Christmas version of *Where's Waldo*."

"Yes, except instead of one Waldo, there's a ton of them."

"No kidding." Bex pointed to a couple more on either side of the TV. "You have a whole army to protect you here. They're tucked away on all the windowsills."

"I try to spread them out so it's not overwhelming. I don't want it to get creepy like people who collect all those Victorian dolls."

"Good call." Bex nodded, then her eyes went wide. "But wait a second, now that I'm looking around, you don't have a tree! How does Ms. Christmas Country Mouse not have a tree making her house smell of pine by the second Wednesday in December?"

Ava did her best to hide a grin and tapped the side of her nose. "My mother used to have a saying when I was little: 'Don't ask questions this close to Christmas.'"

"Why? Because the tree's one of my surprises?"

She shook her head. "If it is, you don't want to ruin it by playing guessing games. Go back to the nutcrackers. It shouldn't be hard with so many to choose from."

"No, you're right. I didn't even notice them at first, and that's saying a lot, but you've got quite an impressive collection. I mean, I knew you liked them from how you reacted to the show, but I honestly had no idea of the extent."

"Which makes it even more impressive for you to give me such an amazing gift, and all the more reason for me to trust you with one of my prized possessions."

"Thank you," Bex said sincerely, "but which one should I use?"

"You pick."

Bex nodded gravely and looked around as if weighing her options carefully. She turned toward a midsize nutcracker in a red military coat and a black cap.

Ava's heart tightened as Bex picked it up and smiled. "This guy is my favorite. What's his name?"

"Lawrence," she managed to choke out through the emotion tightening her throat.

Bex arched an eyebrow.

130

"After my grandpa. He's the one who made it for me."

"Wow. Maybe I shouldn't use it."

She shook her head. "No, you should. It's the best, and I think Granddad would approve."

❧ ❧ ❧

"Are you sure they're not done yet?" Bex hovered near the door to the oven, soaking up the warmth and watching the first batch of mini meringues bake.

"Not yet," Ava said without looking.

"But how do you know?"

"I can sense it."

"Like magic? I knew it."

"No, because they haven't been in there long enough. What happened to patience?"

"I had patience while they were a fluffy soup in a metal bowl, but now they're the cutest things I've ever seen in my entire life, like little whipped clouds of warm sugary goodness. I am apparently a very rash human. Look what you've done to me."

Ava laughed, the sound even warmer than the air around the oven. "Come on, you've done a great job so far. I guess I could let you take on the biggest artistic challenge of the evening."

That got her attention. "What?"

"I need to pipe the last batch of meringues."

"The peppermint ones?" she asked, as they'd recently completed the lemon and raspberry batches.

Ava nodded and patted the chair next to her. "You should do the honors."

Bex sat down and rubbed her hands together. "I feel like this is a rather huge promotion. I better fortify myself."

131

Ava rolled her eyes playfully. "Is that your way of asking for another peanut butter blossom?"

"From a medical standpoint, you cannot overstate the steadying effect of protein laced with a good sugar spike, plus the flour is a complex carb to sustain me. This is practically health food."

Ava relented and passed her one of the fresh-baked balls of goodness. "Are you sure you're not a lawyer?"

"Positive, but I'd have been a good one, right?"

"I suspect you'd excel at almost anything you set your mind to, which is why I'm letting you do this next part." She scooped the last of the meringue mixture out of the bowl and into a pastry bag before passing it to Bex. "You're going to use your right hand to basically draw little circles while you twist the top part with your left one to force a steady stream through the metal tip."

"Got it." Bex held things exactly the way Ava indicated, but when she squeezed, a little dollop of white goop sprang formlessly from both ends.

"Whoops." Ava scooped them up with a rubber spatula and spooned it back in. "This time start higher on the bag, and work down, while you do the reverse with the tip, starting low and circling up a bit as you go."

She tried again with only slightly better results. Nothing spewed out the wrong part of the sack, but the part that hit the pan looked more like a melted marshmallow than the perfectly proportioned cloud pyramids Ava had made. "Hey, I have an idea. What if I squirt this stuff right into my mouth and then the presentation doesn't matter?"

"I don't know, Dr. Leone. What's your professional medical advice on piping raw egg whites right into your body?"

She shrugged. "We all gotta go sometime."

Ava shook her head. "Let's not either of us go this weekend. I have too much fun planned to spend any time in the hospital with salmonella. Want my help?"

"Help away." Bex tried to hand back the entire job, but instead of accepting any of the instruments, Ava rose and came to stand behind her. Leaning over her shoulder, she reached around as if about to offer a bear hug, but instead, she placed her hands around Bex's. Her fingers were warm, soft, and sure as she guided her to the cookie sheet once more. Bex held still as Ava's body brushed against her back and warm breath fell along the skin of her neck. She wasn't sure how she managed to keep from tensing and spilling everything, other than Ava's gentle guidance overriding her own misfiring synapses.

"Small circles," she whispered next to her ear.

The hair on her arms stood on end. "Like that?" Her own voice sounded lower than normal.

"Perfect."

She glanced down to see she had indeed sculpted the flawless little meringue, but somehow the thrill of success paled in comparison to the other sensations flooding her brain and body.

Ava was so close, and so tender in her touch, but also insistent in her guidance. "Again?"

She tried to reassert her intentions on mastering the task at hand, but she couldn't quite pull her attention away from the sweeter press of Ava's body in all the places it touched her own. If only she could lean back into her arms even a little, they'd be in an embrace, and if she were to turn her head …

The mere thought of doing so cued her muscles, and as they finished a second meringue, she shifted until she looked over her shoulder and right into Ava's eyes. She saw herself reflected in their depths, and noticed so many other things she hadn't before. The catch of a breath, the hint of pink blossoming on smooth cheeks, the fullness of her lips, the subtle brush of long lashes all combined to overwhelm her good sense. She leaned forward across the two inches separating them, and in the half second it took to do so, the oven timer sounded shrilly, causing both of them to jump back like guilty teenagers.

She'd never felt so betrayed by an appliance. Until this moment, she wouldn't have believed such a thing possible, but she couldn't shake the unreasonable resentment at the universe conspiring against what she felt certain was bound to be an extremely good kiss.

Ava sighed out a heavy breath as she turned off the timer and peeked through the little window Bex had been stupidly obsessed with a few minutes ago. "I think they're done."

Bex kicked herself internally for wanting to hear that statement so much earlier, and made a silent vow to be a lot more careful about what she wished for during the rest of the weekend.

Chapter Eleven

Ava sat wrapped in a blanket on her couch, a cup of coffee in her hands and shrouded in silence, save for the occasional crackle from the fireplace or creak of the wooden house warming up. She'd been awoken by the late sunrise peeking through the mountains and glittering off the snow. She knew several people who hated the winter darkness, and she could understand the sentiment from an emotional perspective, but she relished mornings like this when she got to watch dawn break at a reasonable hour. It filtered across her little valley in streaks, with shadows receding slowly as a gentle breeze stirred snow from heavy branches until even the air sparkled.

Anticipation had seeped into the chaos rustling her dreams. Images of Bex, shining and bright but out of reach, unable to hear her or see her in return. Searching, reaching, struggling through waist-deep snow or against a cacophony of discordant sounds without much of a cohesive plot, none of it took a master's in psychology or prophetic tendencies to decipher. The near kiss last night set her on edge even more than the narrow miss in Central Park. She'd done her best to push the first one to the recesses of her mind, but two was too many to write off as a momentary lapse. She and Bex seemed intent on dancing ever closer to a flame, and as much as she didn't want to get burned, neither could she deny the warmth.

The ceiling overhead groaned as footsteps fell across the floorboards of the guest room, and she pulled the blanket tighter around her shoulders, refusing to think about Bex sleepy and snuggly in the moments when she rubbed the sleep from her blue eyes or ran her fingers through her mussed hair.

She wouldn't do herself any favors by imagining things she shouldn't want to experience. Obviously, she was attracted to Bex. She was human, which excused her such emotions, and she could even let herself marvel at the fact that the attraction appeared mutual. She might find the fact surprising, but she wasn't blind or stupid. She'd watched Bex's pupils expand and felt her breath hitch, giving every indication she'd anticipated a kiss with the same delicious sort of tension Ava had. She also wasn't naive enough to deceive herself into pretending either of them would've possessed the wherewithal to stop if the oven hadn't played chaperone. No, the facts were indisputable.

What she felt increasingly less certain about was what she should do now. She clearly couldn't keep relying on the influence of others or inanimate objects to keep her from doing something rash, and a part of her didn't want to be stopped. Deep in her gut she ached to feel Bex's lips against her own, but that part of her was bad, or at least traitorous enough to get her heart broken. She wasn't the kind of woman who had flings. She'd never been good about doing anything halfway, as evidenced by the sounds of a beautiful woman padding around upstairs, for what? Because she had to prove to some stranger she could offer them a superior Christmas? Who cared what someone she didn't know thought about her holiday traditions? Only now she did know Bex, and she couldn't use that excuse any longer because she did care more than she should've let herself. How much worse would it be if she let herself be kissed or held or seduced, and then woke up alone on Christmas morning with Bex back in her city high-rise?

136

She didn't know whether it was a good thing or a bad one, but she didn't have the chance to ponder the possibility for long, as the footsteps worked their way down the stairs. She glanced up in time for Bex to pop around the corner looking ridiculously delectable in dark jeans and a maroon Henley with all the buttons still undone. Her eyes sparkled and her smile made even the sunlight outside seem dim by comparison. "Good morning."

Ava lifted her coffee as all the warnings she'd been trying to give herself evaporated like a fine mist. "Good morning indeed."

Bex dropped onto the couch beside her and stared out the front window for a few seconds before saying, "I thought I was going to win in the expansive view category, given all you can see from my apartment, but you've got a contender here."

"Yeah?"

"The road that seemed a little scary last night is a small price to pay for such a winter wonderland."

Ava followed her line of sight out under the overhang of the porch roof and down a gentle slope into the valley and up again, the rise steeper on the other side.

"Is there a river in the gully?"

She nodded. "It was just a little stream over Thanksgiving, but it's been catching runoff from the snow this week, and it'll swell more in the spring."

"The entire area transformed in a few weeks. I wouldn't have believed such a change possible in such a short time."

Ava turned to look at her once more, wondering if there might be something deeper behind the sentiment, but the serenity of her expression suggested she might be falling prey to wishful thinking. People weren't nearly as subject to changing seasons as the Vermont landscape. Still, she couldn't help but wonder as she watched Bex survey the surroundings Ava held so dear, if maybe they were susceptible to other influences.

❧ ❧ ❧

"Okay, what you're saying is this is a full-on winter attire activity?"

"I'm still not telling you what we're doing until we get there."

Bex laughed. "I can respect your boundaries, but you're dressing up as if we're going to need to ride tauntauns, so I want to make sure I'm adequately prepared. Should I strap a little barrel of bourbon around my neck?"

Ava shrugged into her ski coat and tugged the bottom down until it completely covered the waistband of gray, waterproof pants, then stepped into tall boots. "I've got the drinks taken care of, but you definitely want to break out all your layers."

"How many do you have on?"

"I've got thicker blood than you. Do as I say, not as I do. Are you wearing long undies?"

"I have tights on under my jeans under my snow pants."

"And I saw the Henley under your flannel."

"Howie told me flannel was the fabric of our people here."

Ava snorted. "Of course he did."

"Is he wrong?"

"No, but don't tell him I said so. You'll want to bring glove liners and mittens, but you don't need to wear them on the way. Oh, and also a cap to cover your ears."

"I bought two of them," she said excitedly. "One's fleece-lined."

"Wear that one then. I promise I won't let you turn into a Bex-sicle. Your boots look good. Actually, it all looks good. You might be a natural."

"Thanks." She didn't even try to hide her pride at having nailed this winter wear thing.

"We don't have too far to go, but it's a bit of a winding road."

"As long as you're driving, I'm happy to ride shotgun."

They climbed into the Subaru Forester, and Bex did a double take at the sight of a saw and pile of rope in the back seat. She felt relatively certain neither had been there the night before. "Um, I'm a little less sure I want to see the surprise you're planning. You don't have a plastic tarp back there, too, do you?"

Ava hit the locks on the car door. "Now that you mention it, I do. Still trust me?"

She waited long enough to fake apprehension. "In for a penny, in for a pound, but you should know I told all my colleagues I was coming up here this week and to expect me back in the office on Monday."

"A lot can happen to a person in four days, but just so you know, I don't have murder on the agenda, or at least I don't plan to kill any humans."

"I was feeling better until you added the little caveat at the end."

Ava offered exactly zero more explanations as she backed the car expertly down the driveway, tires crunching the snow as they went. She turned up the Christmas station on the radio, and before long, they were listening to "Winter Wonderland" as they wound from a state road to a country lane, and eventually down to what Bex suspected was usually a dirt driveway, but she couldn't tell for sure, as everything was coated in snow. Honestly, the only way she could tell they were on a designated path at all was Ava steering them in the only places the trees weren't.

They bumped along far enough into the forest for Bex to remember the saw and rope in the back seat before a clearing opened up, revealing a classic farmhouse. To one side stood a large clapboard barn accompanied by several other long buildings Bex couldn't begin to guess at, and an oval pen surrounded by a wooden fence. As they drove closer, a black horse in a plaid blanket glanced up, then seemingly found them lacking in any practical appeal as he quickly returned to trying to pull a chunk of grass out from under the fresh snow.

"What is this place?"

"It's my friend Fletcher's horse farm."

"He farms horses?"

Ava pulled up between the house and the barn. "*She* raises them, trains them, boards them, and rides them. She does grow a couple of other things though."

Before Bex could ask, her cryptic guide killed the engine and hopped out. She scrambled to join Ava as she strode into the barn like she owned the place. The space was dim, but warm. It smelled of a wonderful mix of dirt and something sweeter making Bex lean closer to the bales of hay stacked by the door. She'd never smelled hay before, but she liked it.

Ava whistled a high sound that swung low and back up again, causing Bex to pause, but didn't give her enough time to process before a big black wolf bounded into the barn and charged at Ava.

Bex froze in terror for two seconds that might as well have been years before her pounding heart pumped enough adrenaline into her veins to kick her shocked body into gear, but before she could spring more than two steps forward, she was too late. The animal leapt onto Ava, giant paws hitting her small shoulders with such force she staggered back. She wobbled from one foot to the other trying to regain her balance as Bex reached forward on raw instinct, but she wasn't close enough to stop the large, pink tongue as it swiped across Ava's face.

"Ew, Bear, not the mouth. God, you're a sloppy kisser." Ava laughed, and the sound cracked the icy dread around Bex's heart with such force she nearly buckled under the relief.

Ava glanced over her shoulder and must've registered the remnants of her panic. "What's wrong?"

"That's a d-d-d-dog?" Not her finest oration, but it was all she could summon.

"Yes, do they not have dogs in the city?"

"We do, I mean, I don't, but other city people do have dogs." She shook her head. "Pet-sized dogs. They fit in cars and houses and purses."

"Oh." Ava laughed and scratched behind the wolf's ears. "His size threw you off?"

"He charged at you, and I was too far away, and he jumped up on your whole body."

"I'm sorry, and I appreciate you even thinking about trying to save me when this big lug pounced." She ruffled the wolf dog's fur. "That was not the best manners, but it's our thing. Bear doesn't know he's a German shepherd-Newfie mix. He's a big kid who likes to prove he's grown taller than his mom now. Plus, he got overexcited because he misses me."

"She makes excuses for his bad manners," someone said from the doorway.

They both turned to see a woman leaning against the frame with her arms folded across her chest. She wore light brown overalls and a gray stocking cap, which didn't quite cover the dark curls spilling down around her neck.

"Hiya, Fletcher." Ava greeted her with fondness. "And I'm allowed to parent my dog how I see fit."

"*Our* dog," Fletcher corrected, "still has to follow the rules on the farm, which means no jumping."

"He didn't jump. He just sort of stood up and leaned on me."

Fletcher turned to Bex. "Did he jump?"

He totally jumped, a long, lunging bound that nearly made Bex faint as she misread him as going for Ava's jugular, but she didn't want to say so out of loyalty. She shrugged. "I was distracted. Didn't really notice."

Fletcher snorted. "So, she's got you wrapped around her little finger too?"

She didn't deny the charge, which made Ava smile sweetly before saying. "Bex, this is Fletcher. Fletcher, Bex."

"The city mouse." Fletcher stepped forward and extended a gloved hand.

Bex shook it. "Guilty."

"I won't hold it against you, so long as you don't spoil the dog too. I can't have him chasing horses like he's an overgrown puppy."

"He would never," Ava cooed to the dog as she patted his head. "'Cause he's the bestest boy."

Fletcher rolled her eyes. "Fine, then you take him with you. I've already got Winston hitched up."

"You're the best."

"Yeah yeah, don't get lost out there."

"Me?" Ava winked. "Never."

She nodded for Bex to follow her, and Bear trotted along behind them. They stopped first at the car, where Ava collected the murder tools and a large, black backpack she could only assume held the tarp, but she didn't complain when Ava turned and looped an arm through hers.

"Are you ready for your surprise?"

"Since you promised no killing humans, I suppose."

"Good." Ava tugged her back toward the barn, but this time, instead of going in, they went around.

"What?" Bex asked as she turned the corner to find a beautiful horse tethered to a bright red sleigh. It seemed almost too pretty for reality, as if it must be some sort of prop from Macy's or an elaborate holiday lawn decoration. Then the horse moved, just a little stomp of its hooves, which shook jingle bells along its leather harness and rocked the carriage forward a couple of inches.

"Do you like it?" Ava asked quietly.

"It's beautiful, like something out of a movie. It's, it's, it's …"

"A one-horse open sleigh," Ava finished, "and it's all ours for the morning."

Wonder gave way to enthusiasm as Bear hopped into the sleigh and took a seat as if he didn't know what she was waiting for. "We get to ride in it?"

"Yes. When we were in the city, you said you always wanted to go on a carriage ride, and I loved that you wouldn't because you wanted to know the horses were well cared for, so I found you a place where they're well-fed and well-loved. Old Winston here is as spoiled as they come." Ava patted his neck.

"He's beautiful." His dark-brown coat glistened in the morning sun, and his mane gleamed in shimmering black waves. "Can I pet him?"

"Sure. He's used to that. He's a Morgan, which is Vermont's official breed, and quite a handsome specimen, but he knows it."

She placed a hand on his flank and patted gently, feeling flexing muscles and the heat of his body. "Does he mind pulling the sleigh?"

143

"Not at all. It's his job. He gets jealous when Fletcher trains the younger horses in the harness. Won't speak to her for days."

"Seriously?"

Ava nodded. "Plus, he knows as soon as we're out of Fletcher's sight, I'm going to give him treats, because I'm totally the president of his fan club."

"Then, don't let me slow you down." She eyed the candy-apple red sleigh with 90 percent wonder and 10 percent apprehension. "But I have to warn you. I have no frame of reference for sleigh rides through the woods, and I don't want a repeat of the big bad wolf incident. If you need help, you'll have to give me explicit instructions."

"No worries, I'll do all the driving. I've got experience, a solid sense of direction, a thermos full of hot chocolate, and a wide array of the cookies we baked last night. You just need to hop in, snuggle under the blanket, and enjoy the ride."

Bex ran her hand along the smooth wooden railing, noting the leather seat and the down comforter folded neatly atop it, then smiled before swinging up into the sled. "I think I can handle that."

❧ ❧ ❧

"What do you think?" Ava asked as she guided Winston around a cluster of maple trees.

"My mind's still a little blown," Bex admitted. She'd been uncharacteristically quiet on the ride so far, as her eyes darted from the horse to the sleigh to the surroundings.

"By which part?"

"All of them." She laughed. "You may not have noticed, but you're currently driving a rather unusual vehicle through actual Narnia."

144

She smiled. "I hope that doesn't make me the White Witch, because while she loved winter, she never let it be Christmas, and I think I've made my feelings on that particular subject known. Still, I do have one more ace up my sleeve."

"More?" Bex threw back her head and stared skyward. "You have more than fulfilled my childhood dream?"

"Wait. Did you admit I did one better on what you wanted from the city?"

"Ha." Bex shook her fist. "In this specific instance, I may have to admit Central Park pales in comparison to wherever we are right now."

Ava's heart swelled with something stronger than victory at the affirmation. "I love it out here."

"Are we still on Fletcher's land?"

"Yeah."

"How can you tell?"

She pointed to a wooden board hanging from a low tree branch mostly covered in snow, but she could barely make out the outer two concentric circles. "See the target."

Bex squinted up as they passed under it. "What kind of target?"

"Like for arrows. Fletcher's one of the top mounted archery competitors in this entire region or maybe even the country. She runs a course all through these woods at least a couple of times a day when the weather cooperates, and sometimes even when it doesn't."

"You're making that up."

She shook her head. "Nope, you can see all her gear in the building behind the barn. It's full of bows and arrows and a shooting range. She gives lessons there."

"Shut up! You know an archer named Fletcher?" Disbelief dripped from Bex's voice. "She's not real. You made her up."

"When I was younger, I worried maybe I had, but I swear Fletcher's her full, legal, and born-with-it last name. Her dad was an Olympic archer. Her mom was an equestrian. Google them."

"No. I don't want to break the spell, because that's all too good to not be part of some fairy tale. No wonder you love those Hallmark movies. You're living in one."

Ava laughed so hard the sound bounced off the trees and shook some snow to the ground. Winston glanced up for a second before returning to his steady walk through the woods. "If you think that's quaint, wait until you see what we're about to get up to out here."

"We're up to something? I thought we were just on a ride, which was perfectly thrilling for me."

"I'm glad you're loving it, but this is a working farm, and we don't let city mice off the hook when there are important jobs to do."

Bex raised her eyebrows. "Am I going to like this?"

"I think you might, but either way, I've put it off long enough to raise suspicions, yours included."

Bex pressed her lips together and furrowed her brow as if trying to figure out a puzzle before her eyes finally turned brighter once more. "The tree?"

"You guessed it." Ava gave the reins a little slap, and Winston broke into a light trot. "We're on a mission to find the perfect Christmas tree, and Fletcher has a spruce grove up ahead."

"Now I *know* this Fletcher character is fictional. Mounted archer, horse trainer, Narnia resident, and Christmas tree farmer. Are we in a holiday movie right now? Are we the stars? I think we're the leads."

"Yes, we are, and spoiler alert, it's called *Country Mouse Convert*. Subtitle, 'Ava Wins a Big Bet.'"

"I walked right into that one, didn't I?"

146

"You totally did, but don't worry, it's your word against mine, because Winston isn't going to tell anyone."

"What about him?" Bex pointed to Bear, who sat on the floorboard between them.

"Now, he will totally rat you out, but only to Fletcher, and she doesn't care."

"Hmm." Bex's brow creased again, but before she had a chance to give voice to whatever sparked the expression, she caught sight of the Christmas tree grove. "Wow, there they are."

Ava pulled back gently on the reins, and they glided to a stop next to five rows of blue and Norway spruces in varying sizes. Bear jumped out and began sniffing around, but she and Bex sat admiring the neat and orderly assembly of Christmas trees. The smallest ones had been planted the previous spring and still had protective fences around them, but some of the others topped out at over ten feet. She could remember planting a couple of them in high school back when she'd had other hopes and expectations, but it felt good to visit them with Bex in tow.

"They're beautiful. Do they grow all perfectly shaped?"

"Sometimes, but mostly Fletcher comes out and trims them throughout the year. Still, it's a relatively low-maintenance crop. We always replant the ones we cut, to be good stewards of the land." She hopped down out of the sleigh and reached for the backpack and the saw.

"The implements of destruction make a lot more sense now," Bex said as she followed her.

"Right? And as for the not-killing-humans promise, now you see why I couldn't promise not to kill anything."

Bex nodded. "It is a little sad to cut down something so beautiful."

"It's always bittersweet," Ava agreed, "but this way is much better for the earth. Fake trees release a lot of chemicals into the environment, both to produce and dispose of. There are also issues with the carbon footprint of shipping either real or fake ones around the country. Local tree farms designate land for horticulture, and while the trees are growing, they clean the air."

"And you promise you'll replant one in this one's honor?"

Ava used her index finger to draw an "x" over her heart. "I'll do you one better. I'll plant one for you and one for me."

Bex's smile turned wistful. "I kind of feel like I should plant one for me, but I don't know where I'd put it."

"Maybe you could come back in the spring," she said, then quickly caught herself and added, "I know you won't really have much occasion to visit after the holiday, but we're kind of friends now, right?"

"Totally friends. And you can come visit me in the city too. Anytime you want."

She nodded. The offer was nice, but somehow felt small, simple, and far off compared with the very pressing and vibrant plans they'd made easily and excitedly over the last two weeks. Silence fell between them, and for the first time, it didn't feel completely comfortable.

Perhaps that's why Bex rushed to fill it. "How does one go about picking a tree? I've only ever bought them from stores."

"Same concept. I've got ten-foot ceilings, so we can't go any taller. Then you decide if you want a skinny one or a fat one, check to make sure there are no bald spots and the branches are sturdy enough to hold ornaments, which shouldn't be much of a concern with these."

"They do look rather hearty." Bex walked between two rows of trees, inspecting each one of them intently. "I like this one."

Ava circled it slowly. "A strong contender no doubt."

"Where are we going to put it? I want to make sure I can visualize it in the exact spot."

"Good strategy. I usually move the table out from under the front window and set it there. It blocks my view out, but it lets people driving by enjoy it a bit."

"You're such a giver."

"Yeah, and I get to look at the tree when I'm sitting on the couch, at the dining room table, or the bar."

Bex nodded and pointed to another. "What about this one? It's a little fuller."

"You like 'em full-figured?" She waggled her eyebrows playfully.

"I like all kinds. Mine's tall and skinny because that's what I have space for in the city, but were it up to me, I'd be a total size queen."

She chuckled and turned down another row. "Then, may I interest you in one of these beauties?"

Bex peeked between two trees to where Ava indicated. They were each pushing the boundaries of what she could reasonably fit at her house, but she enjoyed the way Bex's eyes lit up at the sight of them.

"Wow, could you even fit something that size in your trunk?"

"Nope, but it's not going in the trunk. We're going to strap it on top." She smirked at her own word choice.

"Ah, the rope." Bex tapped her temple. "Color me impressed. All this time I'd braced for murder, and you were only prepping for some light bondage."

She burst out laughing. "What?"

"Oh, come on, you've got this sweet, naive country-girl thing going for you, but I saw your little grin there. You're enjoying all this talk of size and trunks, and strapping things on or tying them down."

"Actually, I'd missed the first few allusions, but I caught the last one, yes."

"Glad I'm not alone." Bex stepped over to where Ava kept circling the bigger tree. "Besides, it's a mark of true friendship to be able to deal in double entendres and sophomoric jokes."

"Agreed. No one wants to be friends with someone who doesn't at least snicker at an inappropriate word choice every now and then."

Bex bumped her shoulder with her own. "Favorite irreverent Christmas movie?"

"Oh, a good question." She gave it some thought. "I'm going to have to go with *A Christmas Story*."

"Not a bad pick."

"What about you?"

"I'm team Christmas Vacation."

"I almost went with that one!" She punched her shoulder. "It's basically a dead heat for me."

"We're pretty closely aligned, then, because your pick is a close second for me."

"I like that," Ava said, "but here's the big test. Which tree is the right one for this year?"

Bex wrung her hands for a second as she surveyed her options once more. "Are you sure it's my place to pick? It's going in *your* house."

"Yes, but it's *our* tree. You get an equal vote, and don't worry, I'll let you know if you make a terrible decision."

"All right, then drumroll please."

She patted her legs in a gradually increasing beat until the sound rolled together and Bex jumped forward, pointing right at the tree Ava had already decided on as her top choice.

"That's the one," Bex said enthusiastically. "Strong, tall, full-bodied, and beautiful."

Ava grinned as widely as if the description had been pointed at her. "You got it exactly right."

❧ ❧ ❧

"Timber!" Bex yelled as the tree fell, and a sense of triumph surged through her. Bear gave a couple of quick barks to make sure it didn't pose any threats before bouncing off again.

She rolled onto her back and stared up at Ava, who stood over her, smiling brightly. Her breath caught at the sight of her, which was saying even more than usual because she was actually pretty winded from the exertion of sawing. Still, Ava's beauty in that moment, hair streaming, eyes bright, backlit in a haze of gently settling snow, she could've starred on any screen or stage as the perfect picture of holiday delight.

"How does it feel?" Ava asked.

"Really good," she whispered.

"You just toppled your first tree."

"Right, the tree." She rolled over and sat up. "Quite an accomplishment."

Ava held out a hand to pull her to standing. "You always remember your first time."

"Well played." She smirked, then turned back to her trophy as it lay lightly atop a blue tarp. "What do we do now?"

"We'll wrap it up and fasten the tarp to the sleigh, then head back."

"Do we have to? I like it out here."

151

Ava's smile softened. "I didn't want to assume anything, or leave you freezing, but I sort of hoped we could have a hot chocolate and cookie picnic."

"We earned it with our mad tree-hunting skills."

"To the victor go the spoils." Ava started folding the tarp around the spruce and fastened bungee cords, giving Bex directions on how to clip it to their ride. They were back under the blanket on the bench seat of the sleigh within minutes, this time without a wolf dog between them.

"What do you make of your first ride through the winter wonderland?" Ava asked, turning to face her. "Was it everything tiny Bex dreamed of?"

"Much better," she said sincerely. "I didn't even know to dream of something so very near perfection."

"Very near?" Ava shook her head. "I was going for a perfect score."

"It's not too late. I was promised cocoa though."

"Right, way to hold out for the finer details." She grabbed the backpack and fished out a tall, black thermos followed by two mugs. "Hold these."

Ava poured two equal measures of rich, creamy, steaming chocolate, then fastened the lid before producing a couple of marshmallows from another baggie.

"You even packed the toppings?"

She rolled her eyes. "Like I'd go through all the steps of arranging this in detail and then drop the ball on marshmallows."

"No, you never would." Bex took a sip and groaned a little.

"What's the verdict now?"

"Ten out of ten, and an extra bonus star for presentation. No notes."

"Yes!" Ava cheered, "and I haven't even pulled out the cookies yet."

Bex waited patiently as she dug a tin from the bottom of the pack and opened it to reveal an assortment of the treats they'd made together the night before. "Are these all for us?"

"If you can eat that many, knock yourself out, but Fletcher wouldn't hate it if we left a few of them for her."

"It hardly seems fair not to, since she let us use her horse and ride, land and trees, and dog."

"The dog's half mine," Ava correctly quickly, "but yes, the other stuff's all true. Even if she's a bit grumpy, she's honestly one of the most generous people I've ever known."

Bex hesitated, not sure how personal she wanted to get given how close they'd come to crossing lines last night, but in the end, her curiosity got the better of her. "What's the story there?"

"What do you mean 'story'?"

"With you and Fletcher. You don't have to tell me anything you don't want to, but the two of you have an interesting sort of rapport, and there's a dog involved, and you seem to know your way around here pretty well. I just wondered ..."

"If we were together, or friends with benefits?"

She shrugged, sort of regretting the topic. "If it's none of my business—"

"No, it's fine. We used to date. It was sort of a convoluted thing starting when I was in high school."

"And was she in high school?"

Ava shook her head. "She's a few of years older, but she was the first out lesbian I knew, and she seemed to have it all figured out, at least from what I could tell. She was athletic and handsome and experienced and self-assured. She barely realized I existed, but I crushed on her so hard it hurt."

"Ah yes, latching onto the first queer person in our orbit." Bex nodded and took another sip. "I know it well. Ms.

Grant, the art teacher, for me, but please go on. What happened next?"

"I sort of pursued her really hard in my earnest, baby lesbian way. I was always showing up and trying to be helpful and hanging around the barn under the guise of liking the horses while simultaneously trying to trap her into deep conversations, which, let me tell you, isn't easy with that one."

"It must've worked."

"I guess it depends on what constitutes working." Ava shrugged. "I wore her down after about eighteen months of trying. We became a couple in the official sense. She was kind and patient, but her heart wasn't ever really in it."

Bex had a hard time believing all those things could be true. How could anyone be so close to Ava and not lose a little piece of their heart in the process? The thought startled her, but Ava continued, clearly lost in her own reminiscence.

"We were together for about three years and she was the best first girlfriend a budding queer could ask for. I loved being on the farm with her. Even though I never actually lived here, I might as well have. I totally immersed my life into hers, and she never asked me to, but I think I believed if I made our relationship exactly what she wanted, she'd want me more. I'm a little embarrassed to admit it took entirely too long for me to realize relationships don't work that way."

"I'm sorry."

Ava shrugged. "As far as heartbreaks go, my trauma isn't as bad as most people's. More of a slow realization I couldn't love her enough or work hard enough or become someone else enough for both of us. You can't force these things. If it's meant to be, it will be, and if it's not, no amount of good can force it."

Bex wasn't sure if she believed that. She wasn't a cynic or anything, but nothing in her experience suggested great things fell into place without cultivation. She didn't have any right to argue with Ava's lived experience though. If Fletcher hadn't been won over by the love and adoration of a woman like her, maybe the problem was Fletcher. However, she had no intention of saying so, because whatever the issue, she was reaping the benefits of it. If some other woman had been smart enough to snatch Ava off the market, Bex probably wouldn't be here right now.

"Plus, I got to keep joint custody of Bear." Ava brightened. "He lives with me all summer when Fletcher's competing and on weekends when she's busy, or when I miss him. Plus, I get visitation rights here at the farm whenever I want, along with consultation on any major decisions at vet visits or whatnot."

"That may be the gayest thing I've ever heard." Bex laughed. "A congenial co-parenting arrangement of a dog, post amicable breakup."

Ava smiled. "What can I say? Just because it didn't work out with his other mom doesn't mean we can't still do what's best for the kid."

The sentiment inspired a mix of amusement and admiration, and the words jumped out of her mouth before she took the chance to think them through. "I really like you."

Ava's eyebrows shot up, followed by the corner of her mouth.

"I mean, I like the way you think, and how you look at the world and people, and I didn't mean 'like' as in 'like,' but actually, I do, but I didn't want to—" She rubbed her face. *I like you?* What a dumb, inarticulate, and insufficient thing to say to a woman talking about her first breakup, or anything else.

"Hey," Ava whispered.

She lowered her hands slowly, bracing for a gentle brush-off.

Instead, Ava met her gaze and held it for a few sweet seconds before saying, "I know what you meant, and for what it's worth, I like you, too."

She bit her lip, trying to keep her entire expression from conveying how schmoopy she felt or how wrong she'd just been. Apparently, "I like you," was a great thing to say … and to hear.

Chapter Twelve

Ava turned away from the movie to see Bex frozen with a couple of pieces of popcorn right in front of her full lips. For some reason, she couldn't stop noticing them since last night. Bex's lips, not the popcorn, though she chose to latch onto the latter as a welcome diversion. "Your popcorn string isn't filling up nearly as fast as mine."

Bex feigned offense. "I didn't know it was a competition, size queen."

"It's not, but if I knew you were going to eat half the bowl, I would've put some butter and salt on it."

"Seems like a lack of foresight on your part. You turn on *The Holiday*, then hand me a big bucket of popcorn and don't expect me to eat it?"

"I also handed you a needle and thread."

Bex scoffed playfully. "You might as well have given me an abacus and a forging iron, as I have little sense of what to do with them either. I mean, I get the concept enough, but they aren't exactly the tools of my trade."

"You've never had to sew anyone up in the operating room?"

"Not since med school, and even then, I didn't take any pieces of skin for a decorative souvenir."

"Ew." Ava scrunched up her nose. "Okay, that's fair, if gross, but didn't you ever do this as a kid?"

"We lived in a city known for having rat problems. We never left food out. All our decorations came from stores with the exception of a couple I made in school, but even

157

then, the medium didn't involve needles. I mostly worked within the vaunted mixed media of popsicle sticks and Elmer's glue."

She liked the image of Bex pasting crafts together in a tiny plastic chair at some city school. "I do know that genus of Christmas craft. Almost all of my ornaments are hand-made or passed down for some sentimental reason."

"I'm looking forward to seeing them."

Ava returned to her work believing Bex very much. For all her attraction to flash and spectacle, she hadn't seemed at all bored or snobby about any of Ava's more homespun holiday touches. She honestly seemed downright enthralled with every aspect of picking out and setting up her first real tree. She asked a hundred questions while getting it home and into the stand. She hadn't even balked at the te-dious aspects of making sure it was perfectly level and stable, which was always Ava's least favorite part. Then, true to her detail driven personality, Bex was meticulous when stringing both white and multicolored lights.

"I love this movie," Bex said dreamily as the cast danced and the end credits rolled.

"Me too." Ava sighed. "I'd love to have a little cottage in rural England."

"Of course you would," Bex said without a hint of judgment.

"And you'd rather have the LA Christmas?" Ava asked as she stood and carried her popcorn string to the tree.

"No way." Bex joined her. "I'd hate a hot Christmas. You and I might not agree on the city/country spectrum, but we're at least in line on the climate question. Snow or go home."

Ava nodded. "Right? Can you imagine sweating through your holiday?"

Bex scrunched up her nose as if she found the idea rather distasteful, but before she could follow that line of thought, she spotted the box of ornaments Ava pulled out from behind the table. "Are those all yours?"

"Yes. See why we needed a big tree?"

Bex's eyes widened as Ava opened the plastic tub and began unloading smaller boxes onto the couch. "I apologize for the size joke. You were only being utilitarian."

"I may be a bit of both." Ava grinned. "I need a big tree to hold my collection, but I have a big collection for a reason, right?"

"And I thought the nutcrackers were impressive." Bex held up a glass ball filled with sand. "What's the story here?"

"After I came out, I went to Provincetown with Fletcher and a group of friends. It was my first real grown-up vacation, and also the first time I felt super gay, so I brought a bit of beach home to remember the feeling even back in the snowy mountains."

"I love that, and I love Provincetown. It's one of the few places I regularly visit outside the city."

Ava smiled at another thing they shared. "Maybe we can't find a middle ground of where to spend Christmas, but at least we agree on vacation."

"What about this one?" She held up a tiny photo ornament featuring a bassinet with a fading picture at its center.

"That's me on my first Christmas."

"What?"

"Yup. Wasn't I a supercute baby?"

"Absolutely," Bex said quickly, "though not much has changed."

She raised her eyebrows.

"What? You know you're cute, right? All those hats with the pom-poms and the snuggly sweaters and your rosy cheeks in the snow and your almost unreal eyelashes."

Ava's cheeks warmed. She wasn't sure "cute" was exactly the image she wanted to project, but it wasn't far off either. Mostly, though, she thrilled at the realization Bex took so much notice of her looks at all when it had really seemed the other way around all day. She'd been the one stealing glances and little touches, or noticing how Bex's hair fell across her forehead begging to be stroked back into place so it could fall again.

She shook her head. "Thank you."

"Just stating the obvious." Bex shrugged, seeming a smidge self-conscious. "Tell me about this one."

Ava inspected the angel cookie cutter on a string. "That was Gram's. I loved it when I was little, but after we finished making cookies, I didn't want to put it away. It was too pretty to let go of, so I decided to keep it out all season. She let me put it on a string and hang it from the tree. Then, the next year, she let me take it home. I've had it ever since."

"I love that you saw something too beautiful to be limited to its rightful place, and Gram encouraged you."

"She always has. She lets me see things in my own way."

"You're lucky to have her." Bex sounded wistful, but she turned back to the ornament box. "Do all of these have a story?"

"Some are better than others, but they're all personal, and I could probably give you a mini speech on each of them. Sorry, I'm pretty sentimental."

Bex smiled at her as if she'd said something a little silly. "Why are you apologizing? I was just thinking about how much I look forward to hearing all of them."

160

Ava searched her eyes for any hint of teasing, or even a polite sort of placating, but only found sincerity and genuine interest. Her heart melted a bit. She realized they were still technically talking about the decorations, but no one had looked at her with quite that level of interest for a very long time.

❦ ❦ ❦

"Outside?" Bex asked, not sure she'd heard Ava correctly.

"It's tradition," Ava declared as she held out her coat.

"I don't know this one, but I trust you." She slipped into the jacket and glanced back at the tree they'd just placed a golden star atop. "It's very pretty from in here."

Ava followed her line of sight. "I honestly believe it's the best tree I've had in years."

"You're not saying that to be polite to the city mouse?"

"Not at all. I love everything about this one. The height, the shape, the way it holds up when decorated, the way it filters light. When I do it by myself I get in a little bit of a rut, putting things in the same places each year. You brought a new eye, and I like it."

Bex nodded, more than a little satisfied with the explanation. She'd enjoyed taking turns hanging various family keepsakes from the boughs and watching their styles blend. "Good, now explain to me one more time why placing the star on top means we need to go out into the cold, dark night?"

"Okay, I guess it did come out in a bit of an excited rush the first time," Ava admitted, then began talking just as fast again. "Stars are made for wishing, and Christmas stars are even more powerful because it's such a hopeful time. So, when we put the star on top it's only fitting to send some of our own hopes and dreams out into the world, but that star on the tree isn't a real star—it's a representation of all the things we celebrate."

Bex nodded along. "Which means this star reminds us of the real deal, which is outside?"

"You got it." Ava held open the front door, and Bex's stocking cap. "You're going to need this."

"No kidding." The cold hit her even before she stepped across the threshold. Her breath clouded and hung in the air, and she grew momentarily hypnotized by watching it waft away in the moonlight, but as her gaze followed it skyward, she saw so much more.

"Wow," she whispered softly as the night spread dramatically overhead.

"Worth the trip outside?" Ava stepped up to the railing so close their shoulders brushed together.

"Understatement. I've never seen this many stars in my life." The sky seemed infinite, and she didn't know how someplace so dark could also be so bright. A million pinpricks of light shone small and far away, and yet like some impressionist rendering, they whirled together to create something so expansive she couldn't comprehend its fullness. "It's like there's a cloudy haze of pure iridescence."

"The Milky Way."

"Seriously?" Bex finally tore her eyes off the heavens to meet Ava's.

She nodded. "Have you never seen it before?"

"No. Is it a thing people see all the time?"

"In remote places without light pollution."

"Light pollution." She repeated the strange phrase, tasting its foreign combination. She'd always thought of light as a good thing, not waste, and certainly not a hindrance, but then again, she'd never seen light quite like this before. In the city, light was yellow or red or green, either sickly or painted up. Out here, it shone silver. Had all the manufactured lights in her life choked out the real thing, and she'd never known the difference?

Her chest tightened, and gratitude soaked through her at the chance to see something she'd never even known to look for.

"There's Orion's Belt." Ava pointed up. "See the three stars right in a row there?"

She followed in the direction she indicated. "Yes."

"The faint little ones right down from there are his knife, and the four bigger ones in a sort of rectangle are his hands and feet."

"I see them," she said excitedly. "What else?"

"There's the Big Dipper." She indicated a different spot. "It's upside down, like the cup is pouring into the little dipper, down there."

"Where?"

Ava trailed her hand lower toward the horizon. "This one faces up, like it's dipping soup out from between those two hills."

She shook her head, unable to find it.

Ava took her hand and lifted it level with her own. She tilted her head so close their hair touched, and they shared a line of sight, then drew a light line. "See, the handle bends upward like this."

Bex nodded, unable to speak for a second as her senses filled with the woman beside her, from the softness of her touch to the sweet smell of her shampoo. "Do you, um, know all the constellations?"

"There are hundreds, but I know the big ones. I've always been a bit of a stargazer." Ava kept hold of her. "The last one there in the handle I outlined is Polaris, the North Star."

163

Bex pinpointed it with their joined hands. "There?"

"Yes, I know it's clichéd, but it's my favorite because it's both bright and constant."

She turned to her, this time enjoying the reflection of the light in her eyes as much as she appreciated the unfiltered view. "You and Polaris have a lot in common."

Ava smiled slightly. "For me, it's more aspirational than actual, but that's why I always wish on it."

"Are we allowed to pick the same wishing star, or is it one per person?"

"I like to believe wishes are infinite."

She did, too, though she wasn't sure she'd ever articulated such a thing before, much less with the simple clarity Ava brought to the process. "How does this work?"

"Think of something you want, something inside of you, then focus on the light and let it go."

Closing her eyes, Bex let a wish spin and gather at her core, soaking up the cold of the night and Ava's warmth, picking up pieces of snow and sounds of laughter. She packed on a few sentiments from their time together, and the joy of Christmas that brought them together in the first place, but then she projected out, past this place and this time, and wished with a new fervor that none of the magic surrounding them for the last two weeks would stop in the here and now. She wished that, in some way she couldn't conceive of yet, the peace and happiness of this moment, with this woman, would carry forward, beyond tonight, beyond this holiday, beyond even this season.

Then she opened her eyes, focused on the star, and exhaled softly. She felt the wish leave, pinning itself to Polaris, a light in the darkness, perhaps bright enough she might even be able to see it from the city.

Chapter Thirteen

"Looks fantastic." Ava stood over Bex's shoulder watching her apply an even coat of gold paint to the indent of bold letters.

"Thanks Boss, but it's not like it takes much skill to trace lines you already cut."

"It does to keep it from pooling in the middle and going flat."

Bex sat back and dropped her brush back into a cup. "I still think I could handle the router if you'd let me."

"I'm sure you could." She laughed. "Howie said you had the steadiest hand of any anesthesiologist he's ever worked with."

"You should see me with an epidural."

"As odd as that statement is, I think I might like to, but we're pressed for time, and I'm not going to risk injuring any of those body parts so many people depend on for more important work than sign cutting."

"Fine, I do have a couple of surgeries on Monday. I'm more interested in this time crunch you mentioned. What's on tap?"

"We're going caroling with my family and some friends in town tonight."

"Right, but that's tonight. It's only ..." She lifted her watch to check, then did a double take. "How's it after four o'clock? Have we really been out here for three hours?"

She nodded, finding it a little surprising as well. It wasn't unusual for her to lose track of time in her workshop because she could get so lost in the silence of her own thoughts. But today had been different with Bex there. Even with the radio playing Christmas songs, their conversation never lagged long enough for either of them to need it. They talked easily about childhood memories, favorite presents, school plays, shared rites of passage, and anything else that came to mind. Aside from being fun to do activities with, Bex also proved good company. Always engaged, always thoughtful, and always with something interesting to add to any conversation. "I guess we make a good team."

"We do. Which is why we're going to crush it at caroling."

"Again, not a competition, but we totally will. Everyone will be impressed by our wide repertoire, because there's nothing Christmasy we don't know, right?"

"Right."

"Come on, let's go get changed."

"Let me guess. We need to bundle up?"

"You're starting to get the hang of this Vermont winter business." Ava closed the door to the barn she'd converted into a shop and led the way up a snowy incline to the house.

"Who is everybody?"

"What?"

"You said we would impress people. Who are they?"

"It won't be a huge group, mostly people I'm related to and a few of my friends."

"I don't know much about your friends, except for Fletcher."

"She won't be joining us. Fletch doesn't sing, but my cousin Mel, who you met at Thanksgiving, will be there. Also, my parents and Gram."

"Oh good. I liked her."

The sentiment warmed Ava's heart. "I suspect the feeling's mutual."

"She didn't mind me stealing you away to the city for a weekend?"

"No, she thinks I should get out more."

"Then I like her even more. She's wise and you should listen to your elders."

Ava rolled her eyes as she pushed open the door to the house. "I'll take that under consideration while you get changed. Wear layers because after we make the rounds, we'll go to my parents' house for cocktails."

"Carols and cocktails." Bex laughed as she jogged up the stairs. "I love it."

Ava loved it too. Even though she wasn't a big drinker or partier, she always looked forward to this evening every year. There was something truly special about singing sacred words handed down through generations with the same people who taught them to you. Her family started this tradition well before she was born. Older generations passed on, others moved away, but new people filled the informal choir, and she liked the idea of adding Bex to the mix this year from a purely sentimental perspective. She'd given a lot of thought to inviting someone she'd just met and who likely wouldn't be around for any future events, but in the end, she trusted Bex to understand the importance of being included in a family Christmas event, and that said a lot.

What she hadn't expected, despite all her planning and personal reflection, was the beautiful dulcet tenor coming out of Bex's mouth as the first door opened and their group launched into a rousing rendition of "What Child is This?"

Ava did a double take as her disbelief caused her to stumble over lyrics she had memorized for over twenty years.

Several people in their group shot her curious glances, but she couldn't stop sneaking peeks at Bex. As soon as the carol came to a close and they started their transition to the next house, she slugged her hard in the arm.

"What did I do?" Bex rubbed her shoulder.

"You didn't tell me you could sing."

"You didn't ask."

"I didn't want you to feel obligated if you couldn't. All are welcome, even people who can't carry a tune in a bucket, but that's not what's happening here. You've got the voice of a freaking angel."

Bex laughed. "I wouldn't go that far, but I'm glad I'm not dragging down your average."

Ava opened her mouth, but as she did, the rest of the group struck up "Away in a Manger," and something Pavlovian must've kicked in because both she and Bex began to sing right on cue. Still, she marveled at the sweet, rich voice beside her, which curled into her core and around her heart. What else didn't she know about Bex? Probably a million things. How many of them would surprise her? How many would stir the type of emotions welling in her now? Bex's voice was as beautiful as her eyes and her joy at all things Christmas.

As the song ended and they transitioned once again, she reached for her, this time more tenderly, taking her hand as they strolled.

"You have a lovely voice too," Bex said with a sheepish grin. "Altos and tenors pair well together."

She smiled. "Especially when the tenors don't hold out on us."

"I didn't hold out. We're getting to know each other. That's the fun part." Bex's smile widened. "I mean, there have been lots of fun parts, but getting to share them with you makes them all better."

Ava squeezed her arm as they reached the next door-step. They sang out a refrain of "God Rest Ye Merry Gentlemen," and she couldn't find anything to argue with, either in Bex's assessment or the words they lifted up in unison. Tonight was indeed filled with tidings of comfort and joy.

❧ ❧ ❧

"This is the house you grew up in?" Bex asked as they climbed the steps of a beautiful wraparound porch.

"We moved in when I was in kindergarten, so most of my formative years were spent here on the edge of town." Ava pushed open the front door, spilling warmth and golden light at their feet.

"It's adorable." Bex stepped into a small foyer and began to strip off her snowy outer layers.

"It's not fancy like your apartment. We're not very sleek or fashionable people."

Bex tilted her head to the side. "Did I give you the impression my decorative style was the only kind I could appreciate?"

Ava shook her head. "No, you've been wonderful, the consummate guest. Maybe a small part of me is still waiting for you get bored or find all of this quaint compared with the things you're used to."

"Well, I have found this whole experience almost ridiculously quaint. We did a complete run-through of a small-town main street, and every single person who happened to be home threw open their door to share in song with their neighbors. If that's not quaint, I don't know what is, but you seem to think I'll find quaint trite or laughable, and I do not. I'm here for it."

169

Ava's expression brightened. "I just worried, with how much you hate those holiday movies we shan't mention by name, that you might not like stuff like this."

"I only dislike them because I'm always cast as the villain in need of converting to a romantic charity case."

"No, I'd never cast you as a villain."

"What about a convert?"

Ava pressed her lips together. "Jury's still out on that one, but you agreed to those terms. I won't be held responsible or allow you to blame my beloved movies."

"Fair dues," she agreed. "You know what might help your case?"

"Tell me."

"Show me the room you grew up in that hasn't been changed one little bit since you moved out and has some embarrassing poster on the wall or awkward, preteen photos where you have braces and a side ponytail."

Ava burst out laughing. "There's no such room here."

"Not sure I believe you. It always happens in those movies, and you've done an admirable job of convincing me you're living in one."

"How about I show you the spread of cutesy Christmas-themed finger foods my mom makes?"

"Sold!"

Ava led her into a more formal dining room where the other carolers were already gathered around a long table laden with appetizers. There was a cheese ball shaped like a snowman and wreaths made of crescent-wrapped mini hotdogs, and a Christmas tree made of vegetables. There were red peppers stuffed with cream cheese to look like Santa coats and little slider sandwiches with olives and pretzels strategically placed to make them appear like tiny reindeer. She could hardly take it in. She'd frequented some of the most impressive restaurants in the world and never come across such a visually spectacular presentation.

"Good evening, daughter and Bex," a man in a red Santa hat called from his perch behind a makeshift bar in the corner. "What are you drinking tonight?"

"Depends on what you're pouring." Ava led them through the crowd to greet her dad.

"We've got hot mulled wine, eggnog, Christmastinis, or hot toddies, and nonalcoholic mulled cider for the designated drivers."

"That'll be a cider for me," Ava said, then turned to Bex, "but if you like hot toddies, he makes the best in the business."

"Sounds like a solid recommendation. I'll take one of those please, Mr. Robbins."

"Coming right up." He set to work as a woman turned around and wrapped Ava in a hug.

"Hi, Aunt Charlotte."

"Hello, dear, and hello again, Bex, right?"

"Good memory." She shook her hand.

"I'm Howie's mom. He said you'd be visiting this weekend. Are you enjoying yourself?"

"Very much. Ava's been sharing the holiday charm of your town, and I have to admit, she's making an impressive case for a homespun holiday."

"Wait until tomorrow at the winter festival. It's got charm galore."

"I'm looking forward to it."

"Hi love." Ava's mom bustled by carrying another tray, this one loaded with bits of baked brie shaped like stars. "Don't just stand there. Get Bex some food."

Ava shook her head. "We haven't even gotten our drinks yet."

"Here, let me help." Howie's mom snagged two plates and began piling them with appetizers. "Do you like stuffed peppers?"

"Yes."

"How about stinky cheese?"

"Always."

"And you aren't a vegetarian, are you?"

"Not even a little bit."

"Good," a male voice boomed out from entirely too close to warrant such volume. "We have too many of them in this family already. Load her up on the good stuff. She probably doesn't get to eat like this in the city."

Bex turned her head to the side, trying to make sense of the comment, but since she couldn't do so, she turned to Ava for some context.

"I don't know what you mean, Uncle Clay," she said. "When I was in the city with Bex last weekend, we ate some of the best food I've ever had."

He laughed. "Sure, sure, I know they have cheeseburgers and whatnot everywhere. I just meant stuff like this. She and Howie are probably minorities amid all those immigrants."

She and Ava's shoulders tensed in unison as he steamrolled on.

"Howie told me once there's people from Africa and Thailand and all sorts of places at his office. You probably don't even know what half the stuff they bring to potlucks is even called, much less what's in it, right. Could be goat, could be cat—"

"Actually, I've never had a bad meal from any of my colleagues." Bex found her voice. "Most of them are fantastic cooks, and all of them are even better human beings."

He chortled as if he'd come up with some further response to amuse himself, but Ava cut him off this time. "I

172

hope I get an invite to one of those potlucks next time I visit you, and that my family won't do anything to jeopardize my welcome in the meantime."

"Here are your drinks." Ava's dad stepped from behind the bar. "Why don't you go give Bex a tour and let me handle things here."

Bex accepted the glass, her face still warm from the sense that her response hadn't been strong enough, or that her friends deserved a better defense, while her mere association with them served as fodder for some old codger to make everyone else uncomfortable.

She followed Ava through the kitchen and into a less formal living area with a TV and cozy furniture, but also a brightly lit tree and walls lined with old family photographs.

"I'm so sorry." Ava set her drink on an end table, then turned to her with sincere emotion filling her eyes. "He's awful, and the thing is, I'm not even sure he believes half the things he says or if he does it to get a rise out of people, which might actually be worse. But the older he gets, the more he finds it funny, and it's not."

"No, it's not," Bex agreed. "Ideas like those make my blood boil. I'm sure he finds people like me too sensitive, and maybe I am, but I like that about me. Caring about other people's feelings and dignity is a strength, not a weakness. I believe New York's diversity is one of our greatest strengths. I grew up with people from a hundred different cultures with different worldviews and traditions, and I love that. I'm proudly passionate about how it shaped me."

"You should be, and you won't get any argument from me. Just like you affirmed me when I got overwhelmed in the crowds, I want to make my affirmation clear on this one. New York's diversity is beautiful, and it's not something we have a lot of here. I meant what I said in there. I'd love to see more of what you're talking about next time I visit."

173

Ava took her hand and held it in both of hers for a second before smiling. "I'd love to see any side of your life that sparks this kind of passion in you."

Some of the tension faded from her taut muscles. "Yeah?"

"I like it. Maybe even more than I like your love of Christmas."

She finally cracked a smile. "I'm passionate about New York."

"I know." Ava reached up and ran her fingers lightly through Bex' hair. "I like that, too, even if I don't share that particular passion."

Bex wanted to lean into her touch, so easy, so soothing, so strengthening. Instead, she sighed and glanced up, eager to anchor herself amid the conflicting emotions warring for attention. But when she lifted her eyes, all she could do was laugh.

"What?" Ava asked softly.

"I was trying to find the fortitude not to kiss you, and look at the sign the universe sent me."

Ava followed her line of sight to the sprig of mistletoe hanging from the overhead light.

As their eyes met, all questions disappeared. It was as if the Christmas spirit itself ordained what had to happen next, or, at the very least, blessed the endeavor.

When Ava's lips met her own, the whole world felt right. Gone were the questions and the tension and the near misses. Everything that had happened so far merely served as prelude to this point. Ava was exquisite, as was everything she did, including this kiss. The perfect blend of sweet and sure beckoned Bex forward. Placing her free hand on the curve of Ava's waist, she sought more of her, slowly, steadily, as the remaining hints of tentativeness segued into something stronger.

She wanted to melt into her, and the feeling must've been mutual, because Ava trailed her fingers behind Bex's ear until she cupped the back of her head, gently holding her close as the connection between them blossomed.

Bex didn't want to rush this. She didn't want to reach for more than had been offered, but she did want more, more of the same, and more of what lay behind it. She leaned into Ava, craving her with a building need and the confidence growing from the confirmation of how well they paired.

Ava parted her lips slightly, a tiny gasp, a tightening of her hold on the nape of Bex's neck. Every delicious detail pulled at her core, and she wanted to live in this moment eternally while also eager to see what might come of it. She may've gladly surrendered to either impulse of trying to satisfy them both if not for the sound of laughter rising in the other room.

Ava must've heard it, too, because she loosened her hold and eased back slowly. Bex reluctantly heeded the cue and did likewise. Still, it took several more seconds to break contact completely, and a couple more before she gathered her wits enough to open her eyes. When she did, she found Ava smiling dreamily up at her.

They stared at each other, all the unspoken wonder and uncertainty blending between them before Bex finally managed to nod, accepting the gift of the moment and resolving not to push for more until another moment arrived. "I suppose we should get back to the party before someone comes looking for us."

"Probably," Ava admitted grudgingly. "Are you okay?"

"Yes," she whispered, though okay might not have been exactly the word she would've chosen to describe the electricity coursing through her veins. "You?"

Ava smiled and picked up her drink before taking Bex's hand. "Shall we?"

They strode back into the dining room, casually collecting their plates and rejoining various conversations as if nothing earth shattering had just occurred. Still, Bex struggled with the cognitive dissonance between the way the kiss altered all her senses and how the world continued to turn as if any cocktail could possibly compare to the taste of Ava's lips on her own.

She scanned the room, fruitlessly attempting to anchor herself to any mundane detail, but they all whirred worthlessly until she locked eyes with Gram, who stood in the doorway to the kitchen watching her with an almost conspiratorial grin. Bex raised her glass in a greeting, but in return, Gram glanced pointedly at Ava, then gave Bex a mischievous little wink.

Her heart fluttered in her chest, and she sighed contentedly. She didn't really know what was happening or what any of it meant, but between the power of the kiss and the small vote of confidence, she did feel certain whatever sensation was taking root inside her wasn't off base, and she wasn't alone.

Chapter Fourteen

Ava woke with a smile on her face Saturday morning, and she didn't have a hard time figuring out why. She'd gone to bed happy, all warm and snug after the most wonderful evening surrounded by people she loved, and with the thrilling press of Bex's lips still tingling through her mind. The anticipation and fulfillment of their kiss had kept her walking on air for the rest of the evening, and while Bex seemed eager to talk about it after the party, Ava held off, choosing instead to rely on the late hour and the big day ahead to justify a quick goodnight.

It wasn't that she was afraid to discuss what happened so much as she wanted to live in it. She couldn't remember the last time she'd let herself feel the giddy little flutter of butterflies when someone stepped close, and she wanted to relish that as long as she could. She didn't need to have it explained or convert these feelings into plans. She didn't harbor any illusions about them being a couple, but the sheer perfection of Bex kissing her under the mistletoe would keep her in a dreamy state for as long as she let it.

And what a kiss. If she'd been standing up now, she would've swooned at the memory of Bex's mouth building from gentle caresses to something more confident, almost possessive in the way she'd taken hold of her waist and eased their bodies flush. Her lips were soft but tinged with a commanding presence, creating the most compelling juxtaposition.

A part of her wanted to pull the covers over her head and relive the excruciating flawlessness of the memory over and over all morning. She might've done so at least a bit longer if not for the dueling excitement of the day ahead.

Today was festival day, and she didn't want to miss a minute, so she tossed back the duvet and slid her feet into fuzzy slippers to protect them from the cold floors. After a quick pit stop to brush her teeth and run a comb through her hair, she padded downstairs to turn on the coffeepot, but as she came around the corner, she started at the sight of Bex sitting on the couch with a photo album on her lap and warm fire already blazing.

"Good morning." Bex smiled up at her.

"Morning."

"I heard you moving around and started some coffee for you, but I don't know how you take it, so you'll have to handle things from here."

"Sweet and light," she offered for future reference as she went in to pour herself a mug. "Why are you up early?"

"I'm usually up before the sun, thanks to my job. Yesterday was an anomaly because your guest bed is so comfy." Bex stretched as if to prove she still needed to shake some remnants of a deep sleep from her long limbs, but as she lifted her arms over her head, the old, gray sweatshirt she wore revealed a hint of bare skin at her flat midriff. "I conk out as soon as my head hits the pillow in there."

"Good to know. I've never slept in it. I should give it a try," Ava said in a rush.

Bex arched an eyebrow.

She quickly added, "After you go home, of course."

"Right, hey, about last night ..."

Her shoulders tensed. "It's okay."

"What is?"

178

"You don't have to dissect the kiss. I mean, I know we're lesbians, but I don't need to hash anything out. I promise I won't let it be precedent-setting if you don't want it to."

"Okay." Bex drew out the word. "I was going to say I had a great time caroling, and I appreciated you letting me be a part of your family traditions."

"Oh."

"And as far as the kiss goes, I'm fine with not overthinking it, but I enjoyed it. I enjoy everything about spending time with you, and I wouldn't want any part of us to change into something awkward."

"Whatever do you mean?" She cracked a smile. "What would make it awkward? Me banging on about labels and precedents or overgeneralizations about lesbians as a whole?"

Bex laughed. "You're right. I don't know whatever gave me such a silly idea. And I'm really glad you're still up for mocking me."

"See, I thought I was mocking myself there, but don't worry, I'm sure you'll get your turn as soon as I'm caffeinated."

"Something to look forward to."

She brightened as they fell back into more comfortable topics. "We have so many things to look forward to today."

"Winter festival, right?"

"You got it." She sipped her coffee and enjoyed the warmth spreading through her core even more than the hints of heat that came from stealing peeks of Bex's bare skin, though maybe not quite as hot.

"Let me guess, should I perhaps bundle up?"

She laughed. "You're getting the hang of things, but actually, jeans, a good hat, and gloves with your wool coat will probably do the job."

"What? No need for four layers, waterproof boots, and a St. Bernard?"

"I mean, you can if you want, but this is an indoor/outdoor thing. All the vendor huts will be in the park, but there are plenty of local businesses and warming stations along the way. Plus, there's lots of food and drinks aimed at defrosting folks."

"So, what you're saying is, I don't need a big breakfast before we go?"

"Not even a little bit, and you'll understand why once we get to our first stop."

"Well, in that case." Bex walked close enough for Ava to smell her cologne. "I'd better go get dressed so we can get to where we're headed."

"Sounds like a plan." Ava stared up at her for a second, wondering how such a mundane topic like schedules suddenly felt mildly sensual. She let her eyes wander from Bex's lips to her dark lashes, to her perfect hair, and up a little farther to the exposed beams in her ceiling, suffering a small pang of regret she hadn't hung any mistletoe from them.

Bex followed her gaze, and seeing nothing but bare space gave a little shrug. "And this is all in the same part of town we were in last night?"

"Yes."

"Good. If I end up getting cold, we could stop back by your parents' house and find a way to warm up."

A tiny rush of air left her lungs at the comment and all the ideas it sparked. Despite her earlier comments about not wanting to overthink anything, she couldn't deny the thrill of anticipation in the subtle allusion. "Yeah, let's maybe leave that option on the table."

180

"That cinnamon roll is as big as my whole face." Bex marveled at the mammoth pastry Gram slid across the counter in front of the booth for the Presbyterian Women's Group. "Where did you get it?"

"Get it?" the woman tutted. "We made all these. I've been kneading dough for days."

"It's true," Ava said. "I've seen her do it. She makes them in huge sheets and goes through butter like it's her job."

"Normally, she helps," Gram cut in, "but this year, something's kept her a little too busy."

Bex frowned. "Did I keep her from your kitchen?"

"No," Ava said quickly. "We could've gone over yesterday, but I had too many signs to finish. That's the delivery I mentioned, but we needed to fortify ourselves first. Besides, Mom and Mel were supposed to help you this year."

"They did, but you know two of them equals one of you when it comes to cooking."

"She's an exceptionally good cook." Bex cut back in, eager to pile more compliments on these women. "And she tells me she learned everything from you."

"No lies there," Gram said without a hint of modesty. "Do you cook?"

She laughed. "No ma'am. The only thing I know how to make is reservations."

"Then you'll have to come visit more often so we can teach you a thing or two."

"Your granddaughter already started that process."

Gram's grin turned mischievous. "I bet she has."

"Good Lord." Ava grabbed Bex's arm. "Come on, we're going. I can't take you two together."

"What?" She laughed. "I was talking about cookies."

"Is that what they call it in the city?" Gram called as they walked off.

"You did teach me how to bake cookies," she defended weakly.

"I know. She's just a busybody, and you're just too good looking to be trusted with anything approaching innuendo."

Her cheeks warmed. "Um, thank you?"

"I'm not sure it's a compliment." Ava wound between a few other booths, each one trimmed in holly with homemade treats spread across every available surface. The market sprawled all over the small town. There were foods and crafts, Christmas trees and sweaters. Kids ran around them as holiday standards blared from overhead speakers. Ava directed them to a freshly cleared picnic table in the middle of the town square and pulled off her gloves before tearing into the giant cinnamon bun.

"This place is amazing, but can we pause for a moment to talk more about how you find me good looking?"

"Doesn't everyone?" Ava asked without a hint of sarcasm.

"Not to my knowledge. I'm not generally—" She tore off some buttery goodness and popped it into her mouth. Anything else she'd intended to say dissolved into yummy noises.

"Not generally what?"

She held up a hand until she finished chewing, then opened her mouth again, but only to shove more of the amazing delicacy in. It took her another few solid chews before she could manage to say, "I'm not generally capable of finishing my thoughts when people put things like this in front of me. Holy Mother, does everything your family cooks taste like it descended from heaven on a cloud?"

Ava burst out laughing. "Pretty much all the desserts."

"I'm going to have to up my sugary game next time you visit. I went way too haute cuisine last time."

"No, everything we ate there was amazing."

"Good to know, but that was before I realized you're part elf, which means your four food groups are candy, candy canes—"

"Candy corn, and maple syrup." Ava finished the *Elf* reference with a grin.

"And you even make maple syrup!" She made a motion like an explosion next to her head. "Why did I miss this until now? You're undeniably cute, your winter fashion is always on point, and you know how to drive a sleigh."

"You were asleep at the wheel, really. I mean, we whittled away all morning yesterday in my workshop, and then spent the evening spreading Christmas cheer by ..."

"Singing loud for all to hear." Bex continued the game enthusiastically. "I must've missed all the clues because you're up here in the boonies, and Buddy the Elf lives in, wait for it, New York!"

"Damn, I walked right into that one, didn't I?"

"How could you not? New York is destined to be your home away from home. Think about it. Just like Buddy, you're a little too tall for the North Pole, and while the signs you make are truly works of art, you're not fast enough to produce enough of them for a whole world's worth of chimneys. What if we used my connections to get you a job at Santaland?"

"Wait," Ava held up a hand while she took another bite. "Are you trying to turn this bet into me *moving* to the city? If so, I'll have to take you into Burlington to the hospital and get you a CT scan, since you seem to have lost your mind."

Bex laughed. "I thought maybe we could use one of our favorite Christmas movies as a sort of guide for your transition if you were inclined."

"I am not."

"Okay." She backed off, or perhaps she just cared more about getting her half of breakfast, because even as she let the conversation drop, the idea lingered in the background. She did want to see Ava more often, and while that seemed like a fantasy given all their differences, opposites did clearly attract in their case.

"Besides." Ava finished one more bite and licked the icing from her thumb before pushing the rest across the table for Bex to polish off. "In all your movies-as-a-roadmap plan, your forgot one most salient point."

"What?"

"I love movies about converting city dwellers to country mice."

She groaned. "Talk about walking right into things."

"Yup." Ava grinned. "And today's my day to make my case, so finish up and prepare to have your socks charmed right off."

She shrugged and did as instructed, not really worried about having her world rearranged, but she'd promised to at least keep her mind open to the possibility. As Ava took her hand and they strolled across a snow-covered park, she didn't find it hard to keep her word.

❧ ❧ ❧

"Hi Ava," someone called as she and Bex carried a load of small signs through the crowd.

"Hi Hannah." She did her best to wave with her hands full.

"Who's that?" Bex asked.

184

"My parents' next-door neighbor. She works at the post office and knows the whole town."

A little boy ran by, then skidded to a stop before backing up and throwing his arms around her briefly, then bolting again. "Merry Christmas, Ava."

"Thanks for the drive-by hug," she called after him.

"Another fan of yours?"

"Fletcher's nephew." She leaned closer and whispered. "Don't spoil the secret, but he's getting a handmade sled this year. I built the frame, and Fletch welded it to the rails. It's going to fly."

"Santa's secret's safe with me, Madam Elf."

"There you are," a man called as they approached his booth, which was decorated more than the others, dripping with garland and lined in multicolored lights. "I'd started to worry you forgot about us."

"Never." Ava set her pile of signs on his table and reached across to hug him tightly before turning to Bex. "This is my cousin Isaac."

"You must be Bex." He extended his hand.

"I am indeed." She greeted him with a bemused smile. "Does my reputation precede me?"

Isaac laughed. "Pretty much. Sorry I didn't get to meet you at Thanksgiving. I had to give the holiday to the wife's family so we could spend Christmas here."

"I actually made a similar trade," Bex said. "I spent Thanksgiving here so Ava will be in the city for Christmas."

"What?" She scoffed. "That's not even remotely true."

"If you're going to razz her, I fully support the endeavor," Isaac said, "but you'll have to find a more believable ruse. No one who's met this one would ever buy the idea of her in a city on Christmas morning."

Bex sighed. "It's a tough sell, but I like a challenge."

185

"You two are doing the long-distance thing?" His wife Alana asked as she walked up carrying a three-foot artificial Christmas tree.

"No." Ava glanced to Bex, embarrassed. "We're friends, in a bit of competition."

Alana and Isaac exchanged glances.

"Seriously, we just met a few weeks ago, and decided to spend the holidays proving our own superiority."

"Sure," Isaac said with a hint of sarcasm. "Sounds like a thing new friends do."

"Totally normal," Alana agreed, tongue in cheek. "Who's winning?"

"I am," both she and Bex said in unison, then laughed.

The married couple did that knowing glance thing married couples always do.

"All right." Ava took the box from Bex's arms and dropped it in front of her cousin. "Enough chatting. You two have to get to work, and we have to get to shopping. I'm way behind this year."

"'Cause you've been busy?" Alana asked.

She shook her head and took hold of Bex's arm. "Bye."

"Nice to meet you," Bex called over her shoulder, then turned back to Ava. "They seem fun."

"They are, but you are not winning the Christmas bet."

"Aren't I though?"

"No." She tightened her hold on Bex' arm and turned her in a slow circle. "I had a great time in the city, but you didn't show me anything as adorable as this."

"I'll grant that this whole ensemble is super charming." She pointed to a man stirring popcorn in a massive

186

copper kettle. "And impressive, but we do have holiday markets in the city."

"Are the gifts made by local craftspeople?"

"At some of them."

"And is your grandma there cooking you warm treats?"

"Sadly, no."

Ava grimaced. "I'm sorry, that was supposed to be sass, but it came out as insensitive."

"It's okay," Bex said. "You're right. Vermont has one thing my city can never give you."

"What?"

"Your family. These people here, they know and love you. You share connections with them that are deeply personal. I'm not sure any of that has to do with Vermont, though. I think it has to do with you."

"Ava!" someone shouted from a booth they passed. "Come give me a hug!"

Bex arched her eyebrows like, "see what I mean"?

She wanted to stay in the moment, the two of them going deeper than all the fun activities and jokes and witty retorts. She wanted to admit Bex had just hit on something that might render their bet null and void. She wanted to engage the bigger connection and explicitly invite Bex into it so she could soothe the hint of loneliness behind Bex's reaction, but they didn't have the time or space.

"And bring your handsome city friend too."

She finally turned to Ella, one of her high school friends working in a booth full of curling gear. She smiled in spite of the interruption before returning her attention back to Bex, who grinned.

"Yeah, Ava, introduce her to your handsome city friend."

She laughed. "I'm never going to live this down. Am I?"

"Not even a little bit."

"Hi, Ella," she said as they walked over to the booth. "This is my friend, Bex."

"Nice to meet you, Bex. You two have been the talk of the town today."

"Great," Ava mumbled.

Bex leaned on the booth looking rather smug. "How come?"

"Well," Ella angled closer, "we don't get a lot of people up from New York outside of the skiers, so everyone knew the morning after you got off the train and went straight to Ava's house. Don't get me wrong, people aren't gossiping or anything. We're just happy for one of our favorite people here, and I suppose you got Fletcher's blessing, not that you need it, because Ava's a strong, independent woman, but it's nice she gave you a Christmas tree from the farm."

"Wow, news travels fast."

"You have no idea." Ella buzzed. "What with the whole town coming together for the festival, we needed something good to talk about, and then of course we all saw you caroling with the family last night."

Ava smacked her head with the palm of her hand. "The caroling. I should've known the town would notice."

"What do you expect? We haven't seen you with anyone in, like, two years. Then you bring someone who looks like this," Ella indicated Bex, "and act surprised when people take note?"

"Yeah, Ava." Bex played along. "Are you sure you weren't trying to show me off?"

She rolled her eyes. "I was taking pity on the poor city mouse by including her in some genuine, heartfelt holiday traditions."

"It's because I'm an orphan," Bex said conspiratorially.

Ella frowned. "Are you really?"

"No," Ava shook her head. "I mean, maybe a little, but that's not why she's here. I'm showing her a real homespun Christmas."

"Why? Are you Jewish or something?"

"Nope, I'm just a soulless city doctor. Ava's trying to get me to wake up on Christmas morning and shout 'God bless us everyone.'"

"Stop." Ava slapped her shoulder.

Ella looked back and forth between them. "I don't even know what to believe."

"We're friends. We're both obsessed with Christmas, so Bex took me to New York to show me her holiday traditions, and now I'm showing her mine."

Ella eyed Bex skeptically. "So, you're not a doctor?"

"No, I totally am." Bex flashed her toothiest grin. "Will that impress the rumor mill?"

"Very much so," Ella admitted gleefully.

"Lord." Ava sighed. By the time they made a full lap around the park, the town would have them married off with Bex set to open a new practice on the square. "She's leaving to go back to the city tomorrow, so we do need to run."

"Ava's going to come visit me next weekend," Bex added as she tugged her away.

"I can't believe you." Ava shook her head but couldn't manage to hold in a chuckle. "Do you have any idea how fast that's going to spread?"

"One can only hope."

"Why?"

189

"Because I've seen a few of those movies you've been going on about, and the whole town knowing everyone's business always seems to be a thing. It's part of the charm."

"No. Not true. You like everyone thinking you're some dashing city doctor here to sweep me off my feet."

"Can you blame me?" Bex wrapped an arm around her waist. "No one I pass on the street back home ever knows who I am. I've been here three days, and I've already been cast as some sort of debonair romantic lead. What should I do next?"

"Probably you should stop talking to my friends and neighbors altogether," she said, but she doubted Bex heard her as she'd begun to scan the surrounding booths with new intent.

"I know. I need to buy you something sweet."

"We had a cinnamon roll an hour ago. Isn't that sweet enough?"

"Think bigger, Boo."

"I think you're nuts. Isn't that big enough?"

Bex laughed. "Come on. I've never been the center of town gossip, and what better place than this? It's perfect."

She couldn't argue, not on any level. They were in the center of one of the area's best traditions. Everyone she knew was likely in the general vicinity, along with about every type of sentimental gift anyone could imagine. "It is, but we're not really dating."

"No," Bex admitted, "but we did admit we liked each other, and we have a lot in common, and we had our first kiss last night, so even if it was also our last kiss, being here with you and having you with me in New York has sparked something sentimental in me."

Her heart kicked along her ribs at the sincerity in Bex's eyes. "Really?"

She placed a palm over her heart. "I swear. All joking aside, weren't we just talking about how your relationships make the season special, the same way my memories tie me to the city? Why shouldn't we celebrate our budding friendship and the new memories we're making together?"

She softened. Of course Bex would take something silly and manage to make it meaningful. She'd never considered what they were doing in quite those terms, but she was right. They were building a relationship and making memories to add to all her other cherished reminiscences. She appreciated Bex's not pressuring her to think about a future they'd probably never have, but this moment was worth memorializing right here and right now. "What did you have in mind?"

Bex shrugged. "That's the fun part. I didn't have anything in mind, just the spark of an idea for something we can figure out together, not competing, but cooperating. Something to capture a hint of the whimsy we've shared, so each time we see it or use it, we'll remember this Christmas and the fun we shared together."

She took Bex's hand and tugged her closer. "And I may have an idea that actually blends into what I had planned next."

Chapter Fifteen

"They're perfect!" Bex grinned down at the ice skates on her feet. They were a rich tanned and treated leather on the outside, and fleece-lined with blades so polished and sharp they glinted in the afternoon sun.

"I'm glad you think so. It's a shame you had to rent them last weekend when you clearly love going. Now, every time you pull them on, you'll remember me while you weave in and out of traffic."

"I certainly will. I didn't even know people made ice skates. I thought it was all done by machines."

"It's a lost art," Ava said with a hint of reverence in her voice as she held up her own pair.

"Sort of like your signs." She pointed to the painted wooden moniker over the booth reading "Lacey's Lace-Ups: Skates and More" accompanied by a hand-painted replica of the skates on her feet. "Don't think I haven't noticed them on half of the booths we've passed."

Ava's grin turned a little shy. "You don't know they're all mine."

"They're all hers," the woman who'd fitted her with the skates said. "She's the best in the business, which is why I'm going to give you two those at 25 percent off."

"Lacey, you don't have to," Ava said at the same time Bex asked, "Wait, your name's really Lacey?"

"Yes," the woman laughed, "and I've wanted to do something nice for Ava ever since you dropped the sign off and I noticed all the personal touches you added for free."

"An archer named Fletcher and a skate-maker named Lacey." Bex shook her head. "Seriously, you're making me doubt my whole Hallmark cynicism. This place is too cute to be real."

Lacey laughed. "And any friend of Ava's gets the friends and family discount too. Do you even have a place to use them in the city?"

"So many places. I try to hit most of them every year. I already took Ava to Central Park, and then there's Rockefeller Plaza, the Winter Village, Pier 17, and … wait. How did you know I was from the city? Was it the rumor mill?"

"You know it," Lacey said. "I'm glad you'll get good use out of them. Are you going to try them out before you head back?"

She lifted her eyes to Ava. "What do you say, Boss?"

"We have to. You can't head back onto those busy rinks without testing them first."

"Somewhere here in the park? We've spent the last few hours wandering all over the place, and I didn't see a rink anywhere."

"Nope. Go ahead and take them off because we've got a bit of a hike."

"How much of a hike?"

"Enough that you'll want to put your boots on, but not far enough to call in the St. Bernards."

She nodded, surprised to find herself adapting to the local scales for both temperature and distance, and slipped back into her sturdy footwear before trying to pass her credit card to Lacey. "These are on me."

"No." Ava blocked her arm. "They're Christmas gifts from both of us, to both of us."

"Fair enough."

Lacey arched her eyebrows. "You going dutch with the doctor?"

194

"How about I buy her pair for her?"

"And I buy the other pair for Bex," Ava offered.

They both smiled at each other for a second before nodding in unison, and turned back to Lacey, who shook her head and mumbled, "Yeah, just friends."

Bex was glad Ava didn't argue this time. It wasn't that she didn't think they were friends, so much as she didn't find the term reductive. People always said "just friends" as if it signified some lesser designation, when she believed friendship was the basis of all good and meaningful relationships. She was friends with her colleagues, who she respected tremendously. She was friends with people she also considered family. And yes, she'd been friends with a great many of the people she'd dated. She didn't know if Ava would fit into any of those categories someday, and maybe a part of her did feel a flutter of something more every time she took her hand, but that didn't make the bonds they'd already forged less meaningful. In fact, as they strolled out of the festival together, skates slung over their shoulders, she suspected the opposite might be true.

They reached Ava's Subaru and headed out of town without running into anyone else, which was kind of a miracle. They'd hardly made it ten steps all day without bumping into a friend or family member, and while a part of her genuinely enjoyed getting to meet them all and teasing Ava about being low-key famous, Bex looked forward to it just being the two of them again.

They sang along to "The Most Wonderful Time of Year" on the radio as they drove out of the little mountain hamlet, but then they turned right instead of left toward Ava's house, and she sat up a little straighter.

The road rose steeply as they wound around a few bends growing increasingly narrower. The terrain got steadily more forested until Ava took another right and the street

195

disappeared in front of them. Bex had a moment of confusion, wondering if they'd inadvertently hit a dead end, but her driver didn't seem the least bit flummoxed as she killed the engine and grabbed her skates before asking, "You ready?"

Bex gave a fleeting thought to asking "for what," but in the end, it didn't matter. She was game for whatever Ava had planned.

She followed her up what could only be called a path in the most liberal sense of the word. Ava wove between trees, her feet crunching the snow with such purpose Bex never doubted her internal compass, and true to her word, they didn't climb nearly far enough for her to worry before they crested a lightly frosted ridge and stared down into a stunning vista.

"Wow," Bex said. "You know how to save the best for last."

Below them, a crook in the joining point of two mountain slopes sheltered a frozen pond. Snow had been pushed to all sides, creating an angled bank up to the line of pine and fir trees around the edge. Opposite where they stood, late afternoon sun streaked between two peaks, covering them in a rich light on the blurring edge between gold and orange. Bex had never seen any postcards from the Green Mountain State, but she suspected many of them featured idyllic scenes like this one.

"You like it?"

"'Like' seems a bit of an understatement. I'm not sure I've ever seen a more picturesque nature scene in real life. How'd you ever find it?"

"This is where I learned to skate. My dad used to bring me here all the time. It's sort of a local treasure."

"I can't believe a spot like this isn't crowded."

"Mornings are more popular with the little ones, but with the festival on in town, we might have it to ourselves for a while. Not bad, huh?"

Bex shook her head, still completely taken by the view for a few more seconds before finally tearing her eyes away to look at the woman who'd so generously shared it with her.

When she did, her breath caught anew. Ava stood there on the forested ridge, looking remarkably like some sort of winter angel, or at least a cover model for some outdoor publication extolling the benefits of fresh mountain air. She was every bit as stunning as their surroundings with her flawless skin, and the ends of her long hair stirring on a soft breeze. The depths of her dark eyes reflected the magnificence all around while hinting at something even more expansive inside.

She must've stared too long because Ava finally shifted under her gaze. "What do you think?"

"This is beautiful." Bex gestured around them without breaking eye contact. "But then again, so are you."

Ava's lips parted in surprise, and Bex might've surrendered to the overpowering urge to kiss them again if Ava hadn't reached out for her hand instead. "Come on. Let's go try our new skates."

Bex smiled as she allowed herself to be pulled toward the pond. It might not have been exactly the response she wanted, but she wasn't capable of feeling anything remotely close to disappointment in such a gorgeous place with such an exceptional woman.

Ava's heart hammered in her chest, sending a low bass beat through her ears. They'd been skating for quite a while, but no matter how much they tried to ease the conversation toward more neutral topics like this magical spot or their new skates or childhood memories, she couldn't shake the echo of Bex's words from her brain.

Bex thought she was beautiful.

It didn't make sense. Cute, yes, maybe. She got that a lot, even "adorable" sometimes, but beautiful enough to be on par with such stunning surroundings? She would've laughed if not for the sincerity of Bex's voice. The words came out in sort of a half whisper, raw and breathy. Ava felt their impact to her core, and she hadn't known what to do. She wanted to be seen the way Bex so clearly saw her in that moment. She ached for it, but in the moment, she froze.

No, actually, she'd run. She'd dragged them to the pond as if she could wrestle her emotions back into place by forcing them back onto schedule with preapproved activities. She'd planned for the skating. She hadn't planned for any of the feelings Bex sparked in her back on the ridge.

Bex, for her part, hadn't pushed the issue. She'd gone along with her usual, amiable excitement, lacing up and taking a lap around the ice while Ava's fingers fumbled with a task she should've been able to execute in her sleep. By the time she finally stepped out onto the slick surface, she wasn't even sure she felt stable enough to walk, much less skate, but thankfully, muscle memory took hold and she began to glide.

"I love my new skates." Bex came to take her hand the way she had so many times, only now, the touch carried more warmth.

"I'm glad," she managed. "I like to think of you in them zipping around stumbling kids."

Bex laughed in her rich tenor, and the sound echoed off the hillsides. "If you're used to skating in places like this, I can totally understand why Central Park frazzled you. I

198

didn't even consider it crowded because I had no frame of reference for frozen mountain ponds."

The corners of her mouth curled up, glad to offer Bex something outside her realm of experiences.

"Seriously," Bex said, "I thought I'd won this bet when I saw how much you loved *The Nutcracker*."

Ava swooned a little at the memory of the lush theater, the rich music, the thrill of childhood longing fulfilled, the sight of Bex in her suit, the press of their palms. "That was such a glorious night."

"Right?" Bex laughed. "So perfect, but then there's this."

Ava followed her gaze as it swept in a wide circle before settling on her again with the same intensity as earlier.

"I just don't know if I can be quite as certain about my winning bid anymore."

"No," Ava admitted. "I don't know if I've reached any conclusive verdict either. I'm sure I won the tree-getting category, but then I think about that massive spectacle in Rockefeller Plaza and the way I felt when the lights came on and the choir sang while the whole city spun around that spot."

Bex's smile spread. "I have to admit I did good there."

"You did."

"But you gave me a snowy sleigh ride. How surreal was that?" She laughed. "I can't believe I'm suggesting this, but we might have to have to call it a draw."

Ava scrunched up her face, finding the idea unsavory. "Shake hands and settle on a tie?"

Bex groaned. "I'm not ready to concede. You gave me a hint last night that I want to follow up on."

Her interest piqued. "What?"

"Not going to tell you." Bex did a little spin on her skates, seemingly in an attempt to contain her excitement, then went on. "How about instead of ending at even, we went into extra innings."

Her heart rate revved again at the prospect. "I didn't expect to need them, but honestly, I don't hate the idea of more time in the presence of a true Christmas aficionado."

"The feeling's mutual, surprisingly." Bex bumped her shoulder with her own. "I can't believe I'm saying this, but I'd be willing to give up one of the two remaining weekends left in my city Christmas season to come here if you'd do the same."

"I would, only it'll have to be a shorter visit because I have several orders on backlog."

"That actually works out well. I might have to fly up next time instead of taking the train, but if we can make it work, I'd love for you to be my date next Friday night."

Her chest tightened at the idea of an official date with Bex, and she nodded, afraid if she spoke, it might come out weak.

"Are you sure you don't mind? I know it's a lot to ask this time of year."

"I really don't." She sounded a little surprised, and Bex must've picked up on the tone, because she cocked her head slightly to the side with an expression of mixed confusion and amusement.

"I didn't expect to feel this way," she admitted without a hint of reluctance. "You caught me off guard. I know we hinted at the possibility of using the extra weekends, but I didn't think there was any chance I'd even consider leaving home for a second time in December, but honestly, I want to."

"Good." Bex accepted the explanation easily, but as soon as the words left Ava's mouth, the full impact of them hit her chest.

She'd rather see Bex again in the city than spend a weekend doing things she loved at home.

"For what it's worth, I'm with you," Bex said softly, either reading her discomfort or perhaps experiencing a bit of her own. "I didn't anticipate having such a good time here, but you're making me think about things differently, and as much as I still feel like a city mouse to my core, I like visiting your world. I appreciate you including me in, not just the adventures, but the connections and community, so thank you."

They slid to a stop as Ava turned to face her. "Bex, you don't have to thank me. I love having you here. Even if you couldn't sing like an angel, I still would've wanted to share my holiday traditions with you. It's the sharing them that makes them special."

She nodded, leaning a little closer. "I'm inclined to agree, but perhaps with one addendum."

"Of course." Ava chuckled. "What is it?"

"It's not just sharing traditions that makes Christmas special, it's who you share them with." Then Bex leaned in and kissed her.

This time without the buildup or the guise of the mistletoe, there was no blaming the moment or holiday spirit or elevated emotions. This kiss was all Bex, and Ava melted into it.

No, she melted into *her*. And as they picked up speed, it was a wonder they didn't manage to melt the ice beneath them. Gone were the tentative brushes that marked their first try, replaced by the rush into a full press of both mouths and bodies.

Bex's lips were soft and intent, sweet and skilled. Ava opened up, tasting a hint of sugar and something smoother as she teased her tongue along the corner of Bex's smile. Strong, certain hands at her waist held her close and steady, but despite balancing on narrow blades atop a frozen pond, she wasn't actually wobbly or unstable. Everything about this kiss felt right, and a sense of certainty surged through her.

Still, what little bit of self-awareness hadn't been vanquished by Bex screamed at her not to lose her head. She didn't know where this was going. She didn't want to start something that couldn't possibly end well, and yet as Bex gently bit her bottom lip, she simply didn't care.

Chapter Sixteen

"So," Howie asked the minute he walked into the changing room at work on Monday morning. "How'd it go?"

"Pre-op check looks good. Solid vitals, no history of heart problems, and no adverse reactions to any meds." Bex ran through her mental checklist on the patient she'd just met with for a presurgery consult.

"Good." He drew out the word, then smiled. "Glad to see you've got your work zone blinders on already, but I was actually asking about your weekend."

Bex melted, right there at work. Her insides turned into a puddle of goo at one simple question and the myriad of memories it sent spinning through her brain. She could barely think, much less form coherent thoughts, so she only managed to gush, "Amazing."

Howie laughed. "Seriously? Not fine? Not okay? Amazing?"

"Yeah." She shrugged. "I'm impressed. I went in expecting to have a pleasant time, but she exceeded all my expectations."

"She," he repeated. "Interesting pronoun choice."

She froze. "Does Ava use they/them pronouns?"

"No, I asked about the weekend, but instead of saying 'it,' you said 'she,' so I'm wondering if when you said 'amazing,' you weren't referencing the activities so much as talking about my cousin."

"Ah." Bex forced her mind to slow as she pulled on her scrub cap and tightened the strings. "I guess both. I

mean, she planned some amazing stuff for us. I had my first
sleigh ride and cut down my first tree and skated on a real
pond. Oh, and did you know people can make meringues at
home?"

"Of course."

"Right. Same family." She nodded as she shoved a
few things into her storage locker. "I didn't, though. I was
impressed with the weekend in that sense, but also with Ava.
She's good at everything, and she knows everyone. She's kind
and thoughtful, and she let me help in her workshop, and we
went caroling, and then we went to this festival where, like,
the whole town knows her and uses her signs."

"I heard."

She stopped. "What do you mean, you heard?"

"I talked to my mom Sunday and then had a message
from a childhood friend about my holiday schedule. Both of
them told me about meeting Ava's new city friend."

She grinned, silly-happy to find out the local rumor
mill wasn't even that local and gossip about her presence had
made it all the way to the city. "My mind's blown. I don't
think anyone has ever found my arrival anywhere more interesting than they did this weekend. I'm looking forward to
Ava coming back next weekend, but will anyone in the city
other than maybe us even notice she's here?"

"She's coming back?"

"Yeah." She shut the door to her locker. "No one won
the bet yet. We both had compelling arguments, but neither
took a clear lead, so we're each doing one more weekend on
the other's home turf. Isn't that awesome?"

Howie pondered the question longer than it warranted. "Surprising."

"How so?"

He laughed. "Don't get me wrong. I absolutely love that the two of you hit it off, but you must've formed a pretty strong connection."

She nodded, a little more pensively this time, not sure she wanted to go into detail about the extent of their connection to Ava's cousin, but she felt safe in saying it went deeper than either of them expected. She'd replayed their last kiss nonstop. She couldn't remember any time a woman seeped into her senses so thoroughly. "We seem to mesh well interest-wise. We have an easy sort of rapport, and we like to do some of the same stuff. Which reminds me, she's actually going to be my plus one for the office holiday party on Friday."

"As in, like, a date?" Howie asked. "'Cause mom said kind of the same thing about her bringing you caroling, but I wasn't sure."

"Yeah, I mean, no, but like ... sort of."

He stared at her expectantly as if waiting for more explanation she didn't quite know how to give.

"We're taking things as they come."

"Sure." He shrugged. "I'm a feminist, and I'd never tell two women anything about their own lives and relationships. I just care about you both, and I don't want either of you to get hurt."

"I don't want that either, and I'm not pushing or anything. Obviously, we lead wildly different lives, but we enjoy spending time together. I guess that's where we're at, having a good time."

Howie laughed, and the sound came out a little nervous. "What do I know? I never considered Ava a good-time girl. I don't think she's dated anyone very seriously since Fletcher, and even that didn't seem like a good time, what with all the work she had to put into it."

Bex's shoulders tensed. "I did meet the archer named Fletcher briefly. There didn't appear to be much spark between them, except for the shared custody of the dog."

He snorted softly. "Right? I always sort of suspected Ava exhausted a lot of her emotional resources by being the only one fighting for that relationship. Fletcher's a good person, and she treated her well, but they clearly had major differences in personality and the kind of lives they wanted, and Ava … I don't know. It's none of my business, but if it takes endless work and compromise to keep something together, maybe it's not meant to be."

Her stomach tightened at the memory of Ava saying something similar, something about how all the work of keeping the relationship together ended up actually dooming the relationship.

She shook her head and closed the door on any comparisons between her and Ava's vast differences. She didn't need to worry about those things now, or at all. "I'm not planning to propose this weekend or anything. We talked about the diversity of the city, and I thought she might like to come to the party with me."

"I'm sure she'll love it," he said quickly and enthusiastically. "That stuff's right up her alley, and I hope I didn't overstep. You're both good, smart, caring adults. I trust you both to know what you want in any given situation, not that I get a vote on such things anyway."

Both his sincerity and his concern warmed her. "I knew what you meant, you big softie. You're such a sweet old man, both at heart and in your fashion sense."

He shook his head. "Come on, let's get to work."

"Sure, give me a minute, and I'll meet you in there."

He clasped her on the shoulder briefly, then walked out the door, and she took a few steady breaths to bring herself back into work mode. She didn't need to worry about

206

the future, or Ava's past, or even their weekend plans. She had a surgery, and then another. Then, she'd take what came, like she always did, only this time as she focused on the next few tasks and ran through a mental list of things she'd need to be aware of during the procedure, she couldn't quite shake the disquieting sense she might be missing something bigger than what the day ahead might bring.

❧ ❧ ❧

"I like the mistletoe in there." Ava's mom leaned over her shoulder to inspect the leaves in the wreath as she added the finishing touches.

"Me too," Mel agreed. "Much softer than the holly."

She sat back and looked at her creation with a hint of pride, not just at how pretty it turned out, but at the hint of sentimentality it sparked. She'd snagged some mistletoe from her mom's house, likely from the same stash that had hung over her head the first time Bex kissed her. Then, for a sturdier base, she'd woven in a backing made from the trimmings of the Christmas tree they'd cut down together.

"It's very pretty." Gram nodded approvingly. "And sturdy enough to last until Christmas, if that's what you're after."

She tensed slightly at the undertone of warning there. Pretty and short-lived. She tried not to read too much into the comment or what it might represent.

Mel pointed to the spruce. "Is that from your tree this year?"

"Yes, Bex and I had to trim the lower branches to get it into the stand, and I didn't want to let it go to waste."

"Because you're into using every part of the tree, or because it reminds you of Bex?" her mom teased.

"What?"

207

"Come on." Mel laughed. "How many wreaths do we have to make before we get to good gossip?"

"I don't have any good gossip."

All three of the other women burst into exclamations simultaneously, causing her to laugh. "Have you all been sitting here for the last hour waiting for me to spill about my weekend?"

"Not the weekend," Mel corrected, "the stupidly attractive woman you spent it with."

She tried to appear offended, but couldn't quite hide her smile.

"There it is." Gram pointed at her face. "There's the same silly grin she gets on her face anytime the subject comes up."

"It's only been three days. How often does the subject come up?"

"A lot," the others said in unison.

"You wandered all over town with her," Gram said. "Did you really think people wouldn't notice how she looks or how you look at her? Don't for one second believe everyone within a ten-mile radius doesn't know you two got all smoochie."

"Did you?" her mom asked.

Her face flamed.

"Oh my God, you did." Mel slapped her shoulder. "How was it?"

She fought the urge to go all swoony. "Good. I mean, absurdly good. She's a shockingly good kisser."

"I'm not surprised." Gram stuck a sprig of greenery in her wreath emphatically. "A woman who looks like her probably has ample opportunity to practice such things."

Everyone laughed, even Ava. "I'm not sure that bodes as well for my own abilities because I haven't had any practice for quite a while."

208

"Right? You're always so picky and cautious," Mel said. "Does the fact that Bex broke the seal mean you're getting serious?"

"How could we possibly? Our lives are totally different, and I learned my lesson with Fletcher when it comes to forcing square pegs into round holes. You can't will a relationship into working." She sighed, her mood dropping, but also mingling with a bit of relief to finally give voice to the warnings whirring around her brain ever since Bex kissed her on the pond. In that moment, everything felt wonderfully right, but she couldn't freeze a single instance and live in it forever, as evidenced by Bex getting on a train the next morning to return to her real life.

"You don't have to figure out your entire future with someone in one weekend," her mom said in her kind, soothing way. "You always put too much pressure on yourself. There's nothing wrong with taking time to enjoy your holiday with a new friend without it turning into something more."

"Agreed." Mel slapped the table. "There's nothing wrong with having a little fun now and then. It is cuffing season after all."

"What season?" Gram leaned in as if maybe her hearing let her down.

"Cuffing, like handcuffs, 'cause this time of year everyone wants to be tethered to someone else so they can do all the fun, cute stuff together, like Ava and Bex are doing. You bond over the holiday, and then in January, you realize you liked the fun more than you like each other."

She tried to hide a grimace at the description. She hadn't thought that's what they were doing at all. She couldn't imagine not liking Bex at the end of this, but then again, they'd gone all in on the holiday activities, and she couldn't deny she'd relished the chance to share them with someone special this year. "It is more fun to have a Christmas buddy."

"A hot Christmas buddy," Mel amended. "You need to relax and enjoy every minute of that one while you can."

"I fully intend to." She forced a smile in the interest of playing along. She didn't hate the idea in theory. Who wouldn't want to have a smart, funny, sexy friend to sip hot chocolate with and kiss under the mistletoe? A part of her ached to believe herself capable of leaving things at that, but as she turned to find Gram watching her with intent eyes, she saw all of her own concern reflected there. "What do you think of all this?"

Gram reached for her hand under the table and gave it a supportive squeeze before saying, "I think you just need to be you, and have faith that'll be enough when the time and person are right."

❦ ❦ ❦

"Blood pressure's dropping," Bex called before the warning bells sounded, and everyone jumped into high gear. Some people stepped back while others surged forward. She had no reason to suspect hypovolemic shock in this case, so she mentally catalogued drug reactions as a nurse began to recite numbers in a rapidly descending fashion. Her colleagues ceded right-of-way around the table as Bex worked to make adjustments quickly.

"Shit," she mumbled as she administered another set of counteractions rapidly. She'd prepared for this since the patient had low blood pressure presurgery, but she still hated having to employ contingency plans. She forced a new set of anesthesia through the IV and clenched her jaw, counting the seconds until the nurse reversed course and reported numbers on the rise.

The whole thing took less than two minutes, but it was enough to ratchet the tension in the room up several notches, and what's more, with the entire team on high alert, they'd slowed the procedure in the hopes of avoiding a repeat. Due to both the increased sedative interactions and the risk of postoperative delirium, this was going to be a later night than she'd anticipated.

Bex waited long enough to be absolutely certain they'd fully stabilized the patient before leaning over to one of the residents and saying, "Can you check and see if Dr. Robbins is still in the building?"

The surgeon and several nurses glanced up at her, concern evident in their eyes. "We're fine. It's not business. It's personal."

"She's got a hot date with his cousin," the surgical tech piped up.

She wasn't sure she would've categorized it quite that way, but this was neither the time nor the place to split hairs. Besides, the fact the tech knew her plan made her smile behind her mask as she remembered the way everyone in Vermont had been eager to get the details on her visit with Ava. No one had cared who she dated or how she spent her holiday for a long time. She kept her eye on her patient's vitals and the grin on her face until Howie stuck his head in the door.

"What's up?" he asked.

"I'm not going to be done in time to meet Ava's train. I hate this, but I'm already suspecting a rough recovery here. I feel like a heel for having her come all the way down here and not even—"

"Hey." He held up a hand. "I understand, and I'm sure she will too."

211

"Yeah." Ava would get it, but she felt genuine sadness at the prospect of missing any of the few hours they had left together. "Do you mind picking her up?"

"Not at all. I'm happy to hang with her until you're free."

She nodded, grateful to have him at the ready. At least Ava wouldn't be alone, or worse, with a stranger. "Thanks."

"Happy to do it." He headed out, and she settled back into her surgical routine, but even though she managed to keep the patient's blood pressure up, she couldn't say the same for her mood. A subtle sense of unease hovered over her more than it should have for a couple of hours' delay.

She wasn't someone who believed in bad energy or omens, but something about thinking of her time with Ava as finite and waning unsettled her, or perhaps that was merely the reminder of their real lives and responsibilities creeping in. No matter how much they liked to pretend they were living in the magic of a holiday snow globe, they couldn't completely deny their realities. She lived and worked in the city, and Ava would always be a commuter into her world.

She sighed and shook her head, causing a few of her coworkers to glance nervously in her direction, so she pulled it back together. She didn't need to start overthinking. This temporary blip didn't have to herald anything ominous. She and Ava could still have a great weekend together, and they'd start as soon as she got off work today. She didn't need to worry about anything beyond that ... at least, not yet.

❧ ❧ ❧

Ava stepped off the train with her roller bag in tow and headed for the escalators. Her heart beat faster as her excitement built. After nearly a week of downplaying her emotions and trying to pretend she was merely looking forward to a weekend getaway with a friend, she'd finally surrendered to the thrill of anticipation. She was going to see Bex, the woman who'd set her holidays alight, the woman who'd made her see cherished traditions with new eyes, the woman who'd kissed her in ways that made her toes curl even thinking about it. As she reached the grandiose Moynihan Train Hall this time, she wasn't looking at the ceiling or the crowds. She was searching for one set of eyes in particular.

Instead, she heard her name called in a voice that carried a different kind of familiarity. "Ava! Hey, Ava."

She turned, and her shoulders fell at the sight of Howie rushing against the grain of foot traffic. "Whew, I barely made it."

She hugged him quickly, but didn't manage to keep the disappointment from her voice. "Where's Bex?"

"Nice to see you, too." He laughed. "Mom said you seemed smitten with her, but I didn't quite believe it."

"I'm not smitten." She punched his arm lightly. "I was just expecting her."

"I suspect she felt the same way. I couldn't see her face completely, but when she told me she was stuck in surgery, she had these sad puppy-dog eyes I've never seen on her before."

Her heart melted. "Is everything okay?"

He shrugged. "The patient seemed stable when I poked my head in the room, and we don't do trauma work at the surgical center, so we don't lose people often, but there are always risks associated with the job."

She reached out and squeezed his hand. "I guess I never gave much thought to the things you see at work."

He nodded. "I don't want to be a downer. I'm sure everything's fine, but the anesthesiologist is always the last one to leave the recovery room, and she indicated this one might be more involved than usual. She's going to be late and probably worn out by the time she wraps up."

"Of course." The idea of what it must cost someone emotionally to hold another person's life in their hands overwhelmed her.

"I can take you back to my place, or we could go out somewhere if you don't want to miss your city scenes before the party. Whatever you want is fine with me."

She weighed her options. She didn't want to impose on anyone, and it might be nice to relax at Howie's for a bit before her whirlwind weekend got underway, but she couldn't keep her mind from wandering to Bex leaving an operating room tired and spent. She wanted, more than she cared to admit, to be the person who met her on the other side of that door. "Actually, I'd love to see where you two work if I'm allowed."

"Great idea." Howie smiled. "No one in our family has any real sense of what I do here. It'd be nice to show you around."

She didn't have the heart to tell him visiting her cousin's workplace hadn't been her primary motivation, so she merely said, "Lead the way."

He hailed a cab, and they headed south through the teeming heart of Manhattan. She tried to orient herself to some of the sights she remembered from her trip earlier in the month, but only really cared about the destination, so when the cab pulled up in front of an unassuming brick building, she hopped out eagerly and followed Howie inside.

They were buzzed quickly through a security checkpoint, then into a reception area. The African American woman behind the desk welcomed Howie warmly before turning to Ava and saying, "You must be the cousin."

"Guilty."

"Ava, this is Pamela," Howie said.

"Why's she with you?" Pamela asked. "I thought she was Dr. Leone's plus one tonight."

Howie laughed. "Does the whole office know Bex's date is my cousin?"

"I told them all personally." Pamela grinned. "I deal in information, Dr. Robbins."

"You do it well," he said, "and don't worry, she's killing time with me while Bex wraps up in recovery."

"They've been back there for a bit now." Pamela glanced at her computer. "Suite B. Dr. Benning already spoke to the family. That's all I can tell ya."

"I appreciate it." He nodded, then turned to Ava. "HIPAA concern for you, not me."

"Got it, big shot. I don't want to get in anyone's way."

"No, I can give you a little tour."

Pamela checked her computer one more time. "All the surgery suites are done for the weekend, and we've only got two more people waiting to be discharged. You're free to roam otherwise."

"Thanks." Howie tapped the desk. "See you tonight?"

"You better believe it. I'm saving you a spot on my dance card."

Ava shot him an amused smile as they pushed through the double doors bearing a sign for "authorized personnel only."

"What?"

"Were you flirting with your secretary?"

He shook his head. "No, I was flirting with our patient manager."

"Seriously? You have a thing for her?"

215

"Who doesn't have a thing for statuesque women with a sense of humor and an almost militaristic propensity for order and ethics?"

She burst out laughing as they strode down a long hallway. "When you put it that way, I guess it begs the question, does she have a thing for nerdy surgeons with an awkward wit and questionable fashion sense?"

He sighed. "I don't know. I've never gotten up the courage to ask. We work together. I don't want to make things awkward or run afoul of HR, or you know, get my heart stomped on. Seems like a lot to overcome."

She didn't argue. She didn't have any moral high ground on such matters. She'd never been great at deciding what was too much to overcome.

"So, this is our orthopedic surgery suite." He threw open a door and changed the subject.

"Impressive," she said, not because she had anything to judge it on, but because it seemed the appropriate response.

"Yeah." He straightened his shoulders proudly. "It's state-of-the-art for a free-standing center. We also do our own imaging."

"Nice."

He walked on a few more paces and opened a door on the other side of the hall. "This is where we do most of our plastic surgeries. A lot of reconstructions after mastectomies, but we're also getting more top surgery contouring for gender-affirming procedures."

She smiled both at the idea of him helping with such things and his need to inform her anytime he came near anything remotely queer. "That's very cool."

He kept on walking her through medical suites until they reached a more open area reminiscent of an emergency room with beds arranged around a central nurse's station and separated only by curtains instead of walls. "This is our out-patient recovery area."

"How many patients do you have in here most days?"

"It's always a revolving door. We don't do any surgeries with the expectation of long-term aftercare. Most folks come in here for a couple of hours at most, but we have space for twelve people at a time if you include the two private rooms for people experiencing complications."

"This is quite an operation. I know I like to bust your chops, but you're doing good work here, Howie. I'm proud of you."

"Even if I had to become a city guy to chase the dream?"

"Eh." She shrugged. "I guess you can be forgiven."

"What about me?" Bex called from somewhere farther back. "Am I forgiven, too?"

She laughed and wandered toward the sound of her voice. "For what? Standing me up or for being a city mouse?"

"Either?"

She turned to see Bex sitting on a stool next to a middle-aged man reclining in a hospital bed. "Sorry, didn't mean to barge in."

"No worries," the man said, then nodded to Bex. "She asked first. Told me you'd be pretty."

Her face warmed.

"Well, did I lie?" Bex nodded.

"Nope, you're good on your word, Doc." He grinned at Ava. "Are you the girlfriend?"

Her heart kicked extra hard at the idea and the bluntness of the inquiry, but Bex cut in. "Hey now, privacy regulations are still in effect."

The man laughed gingerly as if letting it fly might cause him pain. "I'm no expert but aren't those meant to protect my information, not yours?"

217

"In that case, she's supposed to be my date for a party tonight if she forgives me for both offenses she just mentioned." Bex finally smiled in the unencumbered way that made Ava's knees feel a little wobbly. "What do you say?"

She tried to sound at least a little grudging, but it only came out wistful. "I suppose you have a very good excuse for not meeting me at the station, so you're off the hook there, but the jury's still on the second count of being an unrepentant city mouse."

"Guilty as charged. What's the sentence?"

"Community service. Probably you'll have to take me to the social event of the season and ply me with foods from around the world."

Bex bit her lip as if fighting to keep her cool for a second before turning back to the man beside her. "You heard the woman. We've got a party to go to, so you'll have to keep it together from here on out. Okay?"

He chuckled lightly, then winked at Ava. "I plan on going home tonight, too, so I'll do my part."

Bex flipped open her iPad and checked a few things against the monitors next to the bed before clasping him on the shoulder. "Your vitals are good. I'll have the nurses monitor you a bit longer. Then, if you can go for a short walk later without the blood pressure dipping below where it is right now, I'll tell them they can spring you."

"Please don't rush on my account," Ava said quickly.

Bex turned to her, expression serious. "I never would."

"I know *you* wouldn't," she said with the same gravity, then smiled at the man. "I was talking to him."

He returned her grin. "I feel great. If this one can't dance, you call me and we'll meet up later."

Ava and Howie both laughed, but Bex just shook her head and grumbled, "Show-off."

Chapter Seventeen

"Thanks for being so understanding," Bex said as she met Ava and Howie in the locker room after finishing her end-of-shift paperwork.

"Are you kidding?" Ava threw her arms around her and squeezed tightly. "You're amazing."

"Amazing?" She laughed lightly, but when Ava didn't let go, she settled into the hug, resting her head on her shoulder and breathing in the soothing scent of her shampoo. "I'm glad you think so."

"You saved a man's life today."

"That might be an overstatement."

"Would he have died if you hadn't been there?"

She thought back to the moment when his blood pressure dipped drastically without any sign of stopping. "He probably would've died without an anesthesiologist."

"And you were his anesthesiologist, right?"

She nodded, her cheek brushing lightly against Ava's. "I guess."

"You guess?" Ava stood back and stared into her eyes. "I don't know what happened, and I probably wouldn't understand the details even if you could tell me, but clearly something didn't go to plan, so your colleagues turned to you and your skills to make it okay again. Then they trusted you to keep him stable until his body could take back over on its own."

She smiled at such a lovely summary. "Thank you. I work hard not to get a God complex, you know? Any good specialist could've done what I did today, but it's nice to be reminded I do get to make a difference."

"Of course you do." Ava clutched the lapels of her white coat and pulled her in for a quick kiss. Her lips smoothed the remaining rough edges from Bex's jangled nerves, and she might've leaned in to prolong or deepen the contact if not for the sound of Howie clearing his throat.

Ava stepped back sheepishly. "Sorry."

Bex returned her expression. "No apologies needed."

"I could leave you two alone if you want," Howie offered, "but I've got your suitcase in my office, Ava, so you could change for the party here, and we could split a cab, or if you need to call it a night—"

"No," Bex said quickly. "If I go home, I'll crash, and I want to celebrate tonight. I'm in my favorite city with my favorite people at my favorite time of year."

"When you put it that way," Ava said with a grin, "what's not to celebrate?"

"Celebrate all the things," Howie agreed. "Come on, let's go."

They were all changed and headed for the door within twenty minutes. Bex and Howie both wore suits and ties, which would've felt rather formal if not for the show-stopping ensemble Ava emerged in. She managed to exude warmth, class, and sensuality in equal measure in the red-velvet, knee-length dress with lace sleeves. And while the scoop neck seemed almost sweetly conservative in front, it dipped to something a little more daring across the back.

Bex let out a low whistle as Ava gave them a slow twirl. "What do you think? Too much? Not enough?"

"Just right," she managed around the knot of attraction clogging her throat.

"I've never been to a formal city party. I mean, I know it's a work thing, so maybe it's more businessy attire, but I

220

also suspected the people you work with are classier than the people I work with."

"Because you work in a shed?" Howie asked.

"Workshop, but yes, I didn't want to bring down your average."

"I don't think there's anything to worry about there," Bex said, not quite able to take her eyes off the creamy hint of exposed skin where shoulder met neck.

"Yeah, you clean up nice," Howie said. "Didn't know you had it in you, you little ragamuffin."

Bex shot him a look ending in an eye roll. "You wonder why you're still single?"

"What?"

Bex ignored him and extended her arm to Ava. "You're stunning. I would've been proud to have you with me even if you'd worn jeans and one of your hats with the pom-poms, but now I won't have to regale all my colleagues with endless stories about how special you are because you'll turn every head the moment you walk through the door."

Ava pressed her lips together as if trying to contain a smile, but the soft rise of blush in her cheeks gave away her pleasure. Bex had to physically fight the urge to lean in for another kiss, but thankfully and annoyingly, Howie seemed content to play the role of awkward chaperone.

"All right, all right," he said. "You're better at compliments, but two things come to mind here. One, she's my cousin, so what you said wouldn't work for me, and two, unless something's changed since she arrived, you are also still single."

While the first item made Bex smile, the second hit her like a punch to the gut.

She was still single. She had a date for the evening, but beyond next weekend, she had no claim whatsoever on Ava, and she hadn't asked for one. She hadn't even given serious thought to something more than a few more days together, but she hadn't thought about saying goodbye either. The two of them had been swept up in the moment or a series of moments filled with light, joy, laughter, and a shared love of the season. It should've been enough. It was certainly more than she'd expected or even hoped for, and yet with Ava dressed to the nines and smiling expectantly at her, for the first time since she was a kid, she started to feel a little greedy about what she wanted for Christmas.

🧦 🧦 🧦

The surgical center staff had rented and decorated a small hotel ballroom a few blocks from the office, turning what was likely a drab multipurpose space into a bit of a holiday wonderland. There was a Christmas tree strung with lights, an eight-foot-tall electric menorah, and a large, black, red, and green kinara. Chinese lanterns hung from the ceiling, and tables decorated with flowers and clay oil lamps gave the room a warm glow while a sweet scent mingled with the richer aromas of food. A small dance floor occupied the center of the space, and a photo booth stood in one corner, but the real attraction seemed to be the multiple tables along the far wall overflowing with treats of every kind. The majority of people gathered around them, so that's where Bex and Howie headed as soon as they walked through the door.

Ava followed along, both excited and nervous. She'd never been anyone's date to an office function, as she'd never dated anyone who worked in an office. Which wasn't to say she was dating Bex. She honestly wasn't sure what they were doing, other than perhaps playing with fire. The two kisses they'd shared back in Vermont had been dangerous enough, both in their buildup and execution. The romance of those moments had overtaken her, and she'd let herself be swept

222

away, but today's kiss felt different. There was no grand setting or great anticipation. She'd merely seen Bex, tired and heroic and beautiful in her natural element, and couldn't resist the urge to connect with her.

Something had shifted between them, and she didn't know what to expect in the evening ahead, especially when she saw Bex looking like some living work of art in the charcoal suit she'd chosen for this evening. Every time Ava stole a sideways glance at her on the way over, her heart did a little tap number across her ribs that would've put the Rockettes to shame. It was almost criminal for someone to be so sexy and yet seemingly unaware of the effect they had on nearly everyone they passed along the way.

Ava had to constantly remind herself to take in the details of her surroundings rather than staring unabashedly at Bex. A big part of her welcomed the chance to return to the roots of their little experiment by focusing on the holidays, but this event felt different from the others, somehow both more expansive and more intimate. What was happening between them hadn't felt like a bet for a while, but tonight more than ever, she was keenly aware it felt different in a deeper way.

"I'm going to hit the bar," Howie said, "Can I get you two anything?"

"You know, my usual," Ava said.

"And I ..." Bex paused, then grinned. "You actually know my standard too."

"Right." He split off and veered left when they kept their course toward the food.

"He's kind of handy to have around," Bex said, "sometimes."

"Sometimes," she agreed, then looked at the food, "but I'm glad you and I are of the same mind on where to head first."

223

"Food. Always food." Bex picked up two plates and handed one to her. "Besides, I promised to show you the ropes, city style."

The first two tables appeared to be catered, with formal trays of roast turkey, sweet potatoes, green beans, and stuffed mushrooms, but as they moved down the line, the setup shifted drastically to mismatched platters and unevenly stacked trays loaded with dishes she didn't recognize.

"This is the good stuff," Bex explained, picking up basically one of each as she went. "Latkes for Hanukkah, okra and greens for Kwanzaa, oh, and don't forget the peanut stew."

Ava pointed to what appeared to be a soft dough around bits of meat. "That looks amazing."

"Short rib bao."

"Don't miss the puri and samosas."

She raised her eyebrows. "Samosas I know, but you'll have to point to the puri."

Bex did one better and dropped a piece of fried bread onto her plate.

"What holiday does this holy helping of amazeballs come from?"

"Diwali," Bex explained as she dished up a few more things Ava didn't recognize but liked the rich aromatic smell of it. "It's a Hindu festival of lights, and it's delicious."

"I believe you, but I still can't wait to verify for myself."

"We need multiple rounds, so we'll come back for dessert later. Let's start with what we have here." Bex steered her toward a table.

"Hey there, Tribeca," an African American man welcomed her in a deep, rich baritone. "And you must be the famous Ava."

"Famous?" she asked as she took her seat.

224

"Any woman who gets this one to leave the city multiple times in December must be a miracle worker."

"Plus, she brought a date to a work function," the woman next to him said, her eyes sparkling with mirth. "I'm glad you have impeccable taste in food, as well as women."

"Amara makes the samosas," Bex said, "and she's one of the best orthopedists in the business. For some unknown reason, she's also married to this lug, Eli."

Eli rolled his eyes "I'm also a surgeon, but to be honest, I don't know why she's married to me either."

"No one does, Eli." Another man came up behind them and placed a hand on Bex's shoulder. He had kind, gray eyes under bushy brows and a permanently furrowed forehead.

"Dr. Benning." Bex started to rise, but he pushed her back down.

"Don't let me interrupt. I've already taken enough time out of your evening. I merely wanted to thank you for handling things so well this afternoon."

"It's the job." Bex clearly tried to brush off the compliment.

"It is, but that doesn't make it any less appreciated." He turned to Ava. "And you must be the Ava who has the office buzzing."

She blushed again. "I am Ava. I don't know about buzzing."

"Trust me, if an old, self-involved surgeon like me knows who you are, there must be considerable buzz. I'm sorry to have kept Bex from meeting you at the station today, but she's the best we have."

"I understand completely." Ava looked at him but placed a hand on Bex's knee to include her in the sentiment. "It's been special to see her at work and with her colleagues.

Up until this point, I wasn't even sure she had a real job, other than perhaps professional Christmas aficionado."

The others laughed, and Dr. Benning shook his head. "Correction, *New York* Christmas aficionado."

"Has she mentioned it's the greatest city in the world?" Amara asked, tongue planted firmly in cheek.

"The greatest city in the world," Eli echoed in song.

Bex pretend pouted. "Go ahead and tease, but answer me this, am I wrong?"

Ava had never cared for cities enough to even have an opinion on such things, so she merely shrugged, which led Bex to turn her intense gaze to the others.

Eli held up his hands. "I'm a Brooklyn boy. I'm not going anywhere else when I've got the best right here."

Bex gave one perfunctory nod, as if she found the answer acceptable before turning to Amara, who at least pretended to give the question some serious thought. "My mother would disown me for not at least mentioning Mumbai, so there I mentioned it, but New York is way better."

Bex's expression was one of pure victory as she returned her focus to Ava, as Howie arrived with their drinks and the office manager she'd met earlier.

"Uh-oh." Howie set a peppermint martini in front of her. "Why does Bex look smug?"

"Because she's taking your cousin home tonight." Pamela dropped into the chair beside Ava, then covered her mouth. "Oops, did I say that out loud? I've already had a couple of mugs of eggnog."

Everyone laughed.

"I mean, you're not totally wrong. I'm happy to have Ava back in the city with me." Bex steered the conversation deftly into a more polite sphere. "But I also won a decisive battle regarding the supremacy of New York City."

Pamela and Howie both groaned.

"Do you want to argue—"

"No!" they said in unison.

"It's not a real fight," Pamela said. "We all agree. Now, for the love of God, give her the drink, Howard, so she has something more productive to do with her mouth."

He obliged, setting the drink in front of her. Bex took the hint and raised it in a toast. "Happy holidays, to the best of colleagues and friends who are family, and who also admit I am right."

They all rolled their eyes or shook their heads, but they lifted their own glasses and drank along, all except for Ava, who eyed the beautiful creature beside her as she pressed her lips to the rim of her glass. "Wait a second. Is your standard drink a Manhattan?"

Bex shrugged.

"Oh my God, are you a walking cliché? You drink something named after where you live?"

"I drink something named after what I love. Don't pretend you wouldn't do the same if anyone ever made a drink called a Vermont."

She threw back her head and laughed. "First of all, it would probably be delicious, but all this time you've spent teasing me about living in a Hallmark movie, and you're trying to tell me a New York, suit-wearing, lesbian, Manhattan-drinking doctor, isn't a living trope if you've ever seen one?"

Everyone else's jaws dropped seconds before they fell over each other in fits of giggles.

"Dude, where did you find this girl?" Eli asked.

"We're keeping her," Amara added.

"Also, your name is Tribeca," Pamela pointed out. "I'm honest to God not sure why we didn't see the trope thing coming."

227

"Fair, fair," Bex managed to grin with the good-natured amiability she brought to every situation. "If I'm a stereotype of a modern, queer New Yorker, I'll wear the mantle proudly, but you have to admit one caveat, Ms. Made-For-TV-Movie-Lover."

"What's that?"

"Look at me, look at my friends, look at the holiday cheer, the food, the light and love, and tell me: Where's the heartless corporate raider or the greedy workaholic, or the grumpy Scrooge lost and alone without the true meaning of Christmas or community?"

Ava shook her head. "No city villains here. You've all made a beautiful holiday celebration, and what's more, you've offered me a welcome to rival even the most endearing small-town hospitality."

"So then, the only city stereotypes I'm being pinned with are the sexy ones?" Bex leaned in and kissed her cheek. "I'll take them and wear them well."

She laughed and then shrugged, because like the others who'd folded easily under Bex's confident assertions earlier, she couldn't find a single thing to argue with in that statement.

🧦 🧦 🧦

Bex led Ava to the center of the room, and only dropped her hand in the hopes of finding more contact in the trade-off. Opening her arms slightly, she let Ava come to her in whatever way she felt most comfortable. "What do you think?"

"I think you throw a great party, and even more importantly, you work with good people." Ava stepped lightly into the circle of Bex's arms, and they began to sway to the music pulsing from one giant speaker near the edge of the dance floor.

The sincerity of the assessment helped Bex release the last of the breath she'd been holding as she melted a little more into the woman pushing against her. "I wish people like your uncle could see what we have here."

Ava circled her arms around Bex's neck. "He probably wouldn't see even if he were standing beside us, but I do. You're right to call out the stereotypes of city people as aloof or disconnected or superficial. I've enjoyed every minute of seeing you in your natural habitat today, first at work, then with your friends. You have more than a sense of place. You have so many people who clearly adore you."

Her chest tightened uncomfortably. "I don't know if I'd go all the way to 'adore.' It's not quite the same thing I saw on display last weekend where the entire town stopped what they were doing to check in with you."

"Maybe not the whole town," Ava admitted, "but these people know you and appreciate what you bring to work, but they also like you enough to rib you about your obsessions and take note of what brings you joy. Their interest is playful, but it's not gossipy or shallow."

"No. I can honestly say no one here is either of those things."

"It's because you all have a shared purpose and commitment. Your values are aligned, and you respect the work you share in ways people on the outside would never fully understand. You all save lives and offer healing together. You've built your community not based on proximity, but on purpose. You created a sort of family based on a shared sense of commitment."

A lump of emotion formed in Bex's throat, and she fought the urge to tighten her hold on Ava's waist. It had been a long time since anyone had made her feel seen, secure, and vulnerable all at once.

"We're a family," she finally managed to say, a little shakily, "and even though we may not share the same last name or skin color or even the same holiday traditions, I've always believed it made us stronger because we choose each other."

Ava seemed to ponder the point. "You may be right. You didn't get thrown together by happenstance or some accident of your genetics. You built something deliberate on a shared foundation. Seems like that would stand up better over time and trials."

"I hope so." She managed a small laugh. "I sort of put all my eggs into one basket. Family of choice is the only family I have left."

Ava gasped softly, and Bex felt the intake of air both against her skin and where she rested her hand on the small of Ava's back. Had she just admitted something sad or hard, or perhaps simply more vulnerable than she'd intended?

She was about to back away from the statement when Ava whispered, "I want to be part of it."

The words were so soft she wasn't sure she'd actually heard them. "What?"

Ava rested her chin on her shoulder and ran her fingers through the hair at the back of Bex's head. "I like the idea of building families by choice, and I like the way you do it."

Her touch was so soothing and intimate, Bex nearly lost her train of thought, choosing to sway a few seconds before speaking. The extra time should've allowed her to come up with something more profound or eloquent, but the press of Ava's body and the sentimentality of the moment rendered her capacity for cohesive thought nearly nonexistent. Had Ava really hinted at being interested in something more between them? They'd been tiptoeing up to the admission for quite some time, but up until this point, they'd steadfastly refused to talk about anything beyond December 25.

She leaned back enough to look Ava in the eyes without breaking any more contact than necessary. She briefly let herself get lost in the depth of their beauty, but in them, she somehow found the nerve to broach subjects previously too daunting. Only, in the same moment she opened her mouth, a heavy hand fell on her shoulder, startling them both. They stepped back quickly as if they were teenagers whose vice principal caught them canoodling during the high school dance.

"Sorry," a deep voice rumbled with laughter, "didn't mean to interrupt your moment there." She turned slowly to see Dr. Benning grinning. "I just wanted to say Merry Christmas before heading out."

"Oh, thanks, but I'm scheduled in orthopedics Monday and Tuesday, so I'll see you then."

He shook his head. "I'm off until the twenty-eighth. I'm skipping town on an early flight tomorrow."

"What? You're not only taking a multiweek vacation, you're leaving the city?"

"Yeah, you should try it sometime. A little rest and relaxation is good for you."

"I take time off all the time."

"I know, but do you ever relax?"

Bex turned to Ava. "I relax, right? You've seen me relax."

Ava pursed her lips and squinted as if trying to flip through some catalogue of memories in her mind. "I think you have fun a lot. I guess relaxing is sort of subjective."

"Astute observation," Dr. Benning said. "For me, relaxing involves a house in the Berkshires with my wife, a good book, and a roaring fire. So, I hope you both have a wonderful rest of the holidays, and I'll see you on the flip side."

Bex shrugged. "To each their own, but I thought of you as a city guy. You're always seeing Broadway plays and giving me recommendations on restaurants, and aren't you a member at MoMA?"

He laughed. "I love the city, but getting away from it every now and then makes me love it even more when I come back. Balance is good for a person."

"Wait, first rest and relaxation are good for a person, and then you say balance is good for me too? What kind of doctor are you?"

"The kind who's not taking any calls for two weeks." He gave them a little bow and began to back away. "Merry Christmas to you both."

"Merry Christmas," they both answered, but Bex didn't quite manage a smile as she tried to process the encounter.

"Hey." Ava tugged her back. "Are we dancing, or is your mind too blown that someone you admire might want to spend Christmas somewhere else?"

"Can it be both? I think the answer is both." She wrapped her arms around Ava's waist once more, snuggling close enough to breathe in nothing but the scent of her, even as the conversation pulled at her brain. The interruption seemed too fortuitous to be ignored completely. What had she and Ava been on the brink of before he cut in? "The Berkshires?"

"They're a mountain range not too far south of, wait for it, Vermont."

"Yeah, but, why?"

Ava shook her head against her shoulders. "Did I do a bad job last weekend?"

"What? No. I mean, you live there. Your family's there. Your friends are there. You, I get. But why would someone from here spend the best day of the year anywhere else?"

"Yeah. I guess you're right." Ava sighed. "I don't know what I was thinking."

"What do you mean? You didn't bring it up. He did."

"No, actually, I did in my own way before he arrived. It doesn't matter now. Do you mind if we go get another drink?"

"Are you sure?" She stepped back to search her eyes again, but this time Ava didn't meet them. Instead, she broke fully away and offered a smile that didn't lift her cheeks. "Yes, and you also promised me dessert."

"Okay." She didn't want to push, and she did want dessert, so when Ava left the dance floor, she followed. It seemed easier and safer than letting her mind wander back to whatever she'd clearly missed.

Chapter Eighteen

"How many Christmas markets?" Ava asked as they sat down on an Uptown-bound subway. She thought Bex had said three as they were coming through the turnstiles, but she must've misheard over the crowd and the woosh of an arriving train.

"Three."

Ava stared at her, perhaps waiting for some crack in her façade or evidence she was joking, or had forgotten the basics of counting.

Instead, Bex held up three fingers and ticked them off as she said, "Columbus Circle, Union Square, and Winter Village, but not in that order, because that would be silly."

"Right." She nodded as if the order of operations was the absurd part of the itinerary.

"We're going to Union Square first. It's more rustic than the others, but they all have unique personalities, and it's probably the closest to what you're used to. I know you like that sort of thing since you were so excited about the one at your place last week." Bex's excitement seemed to grow as she started to gesture. "And we didn't get to do a ton of shopping last weekend because you were entertaining me, and people kept wanting to stop and talk, but we're going to see hundreds of vendors today. We can pick up Christmas presents along the way."

She opened her mouth to say she didn't need many more Christmas presents, and she didn't need to barnstorm every market in Manhattan either, but she could hardly get a word in edgewise as Bex ran through the virtues of each one.

"Union Square also has some amazing ethnic food, like at the party last night, but also professional grade."

Ava started to yawn but caught herself and hid it by pretending to look out at the station they passed. She hadn't even been in the city for a full day, and already she felt the exhaustion creeping in. The Big Apple seemed bigger and busier this time around. They'd waded through quite a crowd to even get to the train today, and with each stop, more people piled on until they were practically sitting on her lap.

"Only one more to go," Bex said as if reading her mind.

She didn't want to be rude. She wanted to surrender to the enthusiasm radiating from her host, and honestly, she did marvel at her ability to be so upbeat on so little rest. They hadn't left the party until nearly two o'clock in the morning, and she'd needed at least another hour to decompress enough to sleep. While waking up at ten would've felt luxurious any other day, this morning it felt borderline traumatic. The lack of legitimate downtime lately might be starting to take a cumulative toll.

Ava told herself that had to be the explanation for the threatening cloud of crankiness hovering over her. She preferred that reasoning to admitting how close she came to asking Bex for something more last night. Exhaustion was much easier to blame than her own embarrassment, but even a convenient excuse couldn't quite eradicate the shiver she felt every time she remembered how the words had practically been perched on her lips when Dr. Benning interrupted.

She'd been so taken up with the moment and the woman whose arms wrapped wonderfully around her that she might've plowed forward anyway if not for Bex's reaction to the news her colleague willingly chose to visit somewhere else. She wasn't even rude so much as perplexed, almost as if she were having trouble processing an absurdity. Even after having spent a weekend in Vermont with Ava and her community, it became crystal clear over the course of that short conversation that Bex had never given any serious consideration to returning on a regular basis. And if she hadn't even considered the possibility, she couldn't have given a minute's thought to how a relationship with Ava might work.

Shouldn't the prospect have at least occurred to her by now? Ava didn't need a marriage proposal or a five-year plan, but if there was any chance of them working as a couple, they'd both have to commit to compromise and creative thinking. She'd learned her lesson with Fletcher about being the only one bringing any dedicated interest to the table, and she couldn't let herself fall into another lopsided romantic equation.

"Here we are." Bex patted her knee lightly before hopping up as if she were light as a feather while doubt weighed Ava down.

She shook her head slightly as she stood and chided herself internally as Bex bounded up the stairs ahead of her. She was in the midst of a beautiful holiday experiment at her favorite time of year with a wonderful person who was becoming a good friend. How many times in her life would she get to experience a day like today?

She took a deep breath and tried to recommit to her original intentions as she took the last few steps with renewed purpose, then emerged from the underground station right into the middle of a bustling market.

Bex turned to flash her one of those knee-buckling grins, as if checking to see if Ava shared in her vast happiness at the magnificent joy pulsing around them, and in that moment, she did.

All the remaining tension fell back into the station behind them as she waded into the teeming mass of people weaving slowly through concentric semicircles of little wooden huts. There was no prospect of moving quickly in such a crowd. She allowed herself to slow, taking Bex's hand so they stayed close as they shuffled from booth to covered booth. Vendors displayed everything from socks featuring various dog breeds to handcrafted wine stoppers.

"Look at the stained glass." She pointed out the beautiful window hangers as they caught little flecks of light.

"I love the colors," Bex said genuinely, then spotting something else ahead added, "But I love black and white too."

Ava followed her eyes to the next booth showcasing classic photos of the city. Her heart swelled as she now recognized several spots she wouldn't have if not for her time spent with Bex, a street corner at the entrance to Central Park, the Lincoln Center, Penn Station.

"I love art," Bex said, "all of it. Anytime someone can make something beautiful from the mundane or from nothing at all, I'm so envious."

She smiled at the thought of this amazing, beloved, rich, and insanely good-looking doctor being envious of anyone, much less someone who tinkered in tiny Christmas market huts.

"Look at the journals." Bex practically hopped into the next hut.

Ava followed her and lifted one of the leather-bound notebooks off the shelf. It was smooth and supple in her hands, and the paper she thumbed through had a nice weight. There were a multitude of different varieties, tanned and dyed in various hues. She ran her fingers across several

238

until she found a rich maroon suede that spoke to her. "I'm going to get this one for Mel."

"Do you think Howie might like one?" Bex picked up a tan journal with an almost corduroy-type finish. "It matches his elbow patches."

Ava laughed. "He'd probably love it."

"Then, I'll take one too."

They made their purchases, and the little bit of retail therapy sparked an equal amount of energy she'd been lacking. Not enough to sustain her for long, but enough to help her drive forward as they turned a corner and entered a section dominated by food stalls.

Bex didn't even hesitate before buying a helping of short rib pierogies and a cardboard carton filled with ricotta pasta coated in fresh parmesan and balsamic glaze. Another set of Ava's senses came to life as they ate and strolled together.

"Does anything in this city taste bad?" she asked around a moan and a mouthful of goodness.

Bex laughed. "A great many things. This is not your mom's dining room spread, which is why you need to stick with me. I've made all the mistakes over the years, so you don't have to."

"Thanks for your sacrifice because I've not had a bad meal here."

"I know I've mentioned this city is the best in the world, but it's only because the rest of the world brought their best with them when they came. None of this food is from New York. Look at the signs." Ava scanned the tops of the booths, each one with a canvas banner advertising things like Italian food, Cuban sandwiches, Trinidad treats, and more. "We're not the melting pot America pretends to be. Everyone here keeps their uniqueness and brings it fully to the table. We're not homogenizing or blending into sameness. We're making space for all of us to show up in our most authentic form of awesome."

Ava nodded as she chewed on the idea along with her pierogi. She wanted to share the vision Bex was working hard to paint for her this weekend. All the holidays, all the foods, all the cultures, and yet she still didn't quite see a cohesive picture yet. Or perhaps she did, but she couldn't see herself in it.

Bex didn't seem to notice, though, as another vendor caught her attention. "Christmas ornaments!"

She darted into the midst of them like a kid in a toy store while Ava finished her last bite of food and tossed the carton into the trash. In the one minute it took her to follow, Bex already had three ornaments in her skilled hands. "Look at these. Aren't they magnificent?"

She couldn't disagree with the sentiment. Each glass ball was painted with meticulously detailed holiday scenes. One held a cityscape in softly falling snow. Another showcased a forest full of pine trees with frolicking animals, and the third depicted a little village decked out in brightly colored lights. They were beautifully intricate, and she picked up the village scene, holding it to the light with a smile. "I bet Gram would like this one."

"Should I get it for her?" Bex asked earnestly.

"You don't need to buy my grandmother a present. Maybe I'll get it for her." She turned it around in her hand until she saw the price tag. "Or maybe not."

Bex's brow furrowed until she saw her line of sight. Her expression softened. "I can pay for it, and you can give it to her."

She shook her head.

"I don't mind," Bex whispered. "It's nothing to me."

"It's not a huge deal for me either." She hung the ornament carefully back on its hook and stepped outside the hut before continuing as quietly as the crowd would allow. "I can afford the price if I need to, but I can't imagine paying that kind of money for something I could make her myself."

Bex seemed surprised. "Could you really?"

"Of course. Don't get me wrong, the artist is very good and deserves every penny. It's beautiful work done on glass, whereas I usually paint on wood, but I could replicate it, or at least produce my own version with my actual village on it."

Bex' smiled turned a little mystified. "I believe you. It just never occurred to me a person, any person, could make such things. They're too perfect, and there are so many. Surely they came from a machine or maybe elves."

Ava found the latter idea charming, but she couldn't let elves take credit for someone else's artwork, so she leaned back into the hut and made eye contact with the only woman working there. "Do you make these?"

The woman nodded.

"What?" Bex hopped back in, too, mind clearly blown. "All of them? With your own hands?"

The proprietor smiled a little wearily. "I start in May."

"Wow." Bex grabbed an ornament and held it out in her cupped hands. "Could I have this one, please?"

"Of course."

Bex bounced lightly on her toes as the artist wrapped it in tissue paper and then set it gently inside a cardboard box, which she snugged into a little brown bag. "Thank you for shopping here today."

"No, thank you for sharing your talent!" Bex effused. "I'm thrilled to have an original piece of handmade art."

Ava's heart melted at the genuineness of the comment and all the awe behind it. Bex hadn't blanched at the price, and she understood part of that came from living in a city where things were naturally more expensive, but she got the sense Bex would've paid more, even if she had less to spend, because she truly valued people's uniqueness. Ava saw it in the way she jumped into new experiences, the way she talked to her patient, the way she related to her multicultural colleagues by embracing their holidays even though they differed from her own beloved traditions. Bex was open and warm and kind, a person who managed to have so many amazing things going for her, and yet still stayed genuine, authentic, and easily impressed. It made Ava's chest ache to think of someone like her actually existing in the world these days, especially in the heart of a cold, crowded city.

Then again, the way Bex existed in the cold, crowded city also hurt Ava's heart a little bit. She had to take a deep, deliberate breath to get the air back into her lungs at the weight of the realization, and the way it tugged her back to the thoughts that had dragged her mood down earlier. Bex's attachment to this city wasn't a reflection on Vermont or Ava or some blind spot born of stubborn pride. Everything about Bex's affinities stemmed from love.

She loved her life. She loved her home. She loved her job, and the people she worked with loved her in return. Love was a great thing, the best thing, and yet every one of those things Bex loved with all the best parts of herself felt like another sharp shard of ice blocking off any hope of the two of them getting a love story of their own.

She clenched her jaw and her fists, trying as hard as she could to keep her mind from taking the next step. She could not let herself fall for someone whose life and goals and dreams were wildly different from her own. She couldn't hurl herself against that brick wall again.

Chapter Nineteen

"So?" Bex asked excitedly as she pushed through the crowd gathered around the ice rink at the center of Bryant Park's Winter Village to snag two chairs another couple had just vacated. "Which Christmas market do you prefer? Union Square or this one?"

"Wow, that's tough." Ava squished her way up to the tiny metal table as a family edged past her. "I liked how Union Square felt a little less corporate, and those pierogies were to die for, but this one's bigger, and there seems to be a sliver more space, which is good for me because the crowds make me claustrophobic."

Bex glanced around and grimaced at the people pressing in from all sides, then hopped up. "Come on."

"What?" Ava asked, seeming surprised at the abrupt departure.

Bex took her hand and led her past the food platform and wound through rows of translucent vendor spaces. "I wanted you to have a view of the ice, but I didn't notice the crowd."

"How could you not notice the crowd?" Ava laughed.

She shrugged as they brushed past another stream of people to the back side of the last row of shops. There, a few tables sat empty along a low hedge overlooking a city street. She turned to Ava hopefully, "Better?"

Her relieved smile said everything Bex needed to hear. "I didn't mean you had to leave the rink-side seats."

"I don't mind." She settled in. "I love cityscapes. Besides, no ice rink in the city can compare to the views around your mountain pond."

Ava's cheeks colored in the way Bex had grown a little addicted to, and she wondered if she was remembering their kiss the same way she remembered it every time she saw anyone on ice skates. "I'm glad I could show you something new, something worthy of your city eyes."

"So many things," Bex said. "I'm out here today trying to keep up with you, also hoping to split that sandwich."

Ava laughed and held up the raclette cheese baguette they'd waited in line an inordinate amount of time to procure. She tore it in half and passed Bex's portion across the table before biting into her own. It took only about three seconds for her to close her eyes and moan, the combination sending all the blood in Bex's brain further south. She suspected Ava had no idea how sexy she could be in little moments when she surrendered to some simple pleasure.

"Amazing." Her dark eyes flashed open and caught Bex staring, but she didn't seem to mind. "Where has this been my whole life?"

"Probably Switzerland."

"Those bastards are good at everything: chocolate, pocket tools, watches."

"Trains," Bex added, "skiing, political neutrality, and melting cheeses."

Ava chuckled as she took another bite, and this time Bex joined her, enjoying both the food and the shared experience, though really sharing anything with Ava added joy to the encounter.

"I don't think I could choose a favorite market." Ava returned to their previous topic. "You could certainly make an argument for either of them, but I like the contrast of

244

doing both back-to-back. They show you two different sides of the same coin."

"And two different sides of the same city, polished and shiny, or bohemian and artistic."

"But both joyful," Ava added.

She took another bite of cheesy baguette. "So many ways to celebrate. Sort of like us."

"Sort of." Ava's expression turned introspective. "But not quite."

"What do you mean?"

"Don't get me wrong. I'm having a great time, even better than expected, given I could barely pull myself out of bed this morning. I like shopping with you. I love how you see little things with such awe. I like that you appreciate art and you're impressed by creators. It's been a great day, but it still feels very much like your world. Even your versions of rustic and cute are surrounded by eight million people, and prices that make my head spin. I see the difference in the experience, but I still see you on both sides of it."

Bex's chest tightened, not just at the observation, but at the deeper truth beneath it. Still, a part of her refused to accept it, because if she did, she'd have to accept other things she hadn't even let herself think about yet. "I see lots of places for you at these markets. They both had a whole booth of maple syrup, which you also make. How could you find a better fit? And you said yourself you could make handmade ornaments. Plus, you already make signs. All these vendors are using cheap canvas banners. You could make a killing on personalized signs in places like this."

"Only if I didn't have to pay a kidney to rent the space. Those people selling maple syrup for $100 a gallon probably pay thousands of dollars for the right to do so, not to mention the cost of living in the city in the first place."

245

"Yeah, but you wouldn't have to pay. You could move into my place all season. You know you've got free room and board with me as often and as long as you want to stay."

Ava froze, baguette in midair, mouth slightly open, eyes wide, several strong indicators Bex had said something momentous. Still, it took Bex several more seconds for the full impact of her previous statement to register. Had she offered for Ava to move in with her? And not just for a weekend, but for an open-ended or even indefinite period of time? The vast implications of both the offer and the ease with which she made it should've been troubling. She should've been racing to backtrack or qualify her comments, but surprisingly, she didn't have any urge to do either. The idea of Ava becoming a more permanent fixture in her life only sparked warmth and joy.

Which is to say, everything about the idea felt joyful except for Ava's reaction. She set the sandwich back down and managed a tight smile. "I'm full. Do you want to shop some more before we head out?"

"Um, we could. Or there's a hot chocolate stand many people consider the best in the city on the corner up there."

"Sure, we could try some." Ava pushed back from the table.

"Or we could sit and talk for a minute." She tried again. "I don't mind. I like talking to you."

Ava made another attempt at a smile, but it still didn't reach her eyes. "You're sweet, but we probably should keep moving if you want to fit everything in today."

"Okay." She rose, aching to reach for her hand, but before she had the chance, Ava moved away in the direction Bex had indicated.

She watched her take a few steps, pause, then without turning back, take a few more. The sense of

246

abandonment felt entirely too strong for someone who was merely headed for hot chocolate, but it stirred the same sort of creeping disquiet she'd felt when Ava left the dance floor the night before. Did mentioning the future make Ava upset or uncomfortable? She hadn't meant to push or pressure. She'd only spoken out of a genuine happiness and the desire to share it.

Had she pinned the things that made her happy onto someone who wanted something different? The sandwich turned to lead in her stomach as she feared she'd hit her mark. The things that made Bex happy made Ava sad, at least in this moment.

She didn't want to make Ava sad, not now, not ever. Understanding settled over her with a sure certainty. She wanted Ava to be happy more than she wanted anything else. Even winning their bet and the realization of what that meant for the two of them made her heart hurt.

🧦 🧦 🧦

"Wow, this is like a real neighborhood." Ava slid out of the cab they'd been in for at least half an hour and stretched her back as she surveyed their surroundings.

Bex climbed out behind her. "We're in Brooklyn, which is still New York City, but also uniquely different."

"It still feels like a city, with houses instead of the skyscraping apartments."

"And the houses are what we're here for." Bex glanced at her watch, then up again. "Well, the houses and because this place is called Dyker Heights."

"Seriously?"

"Honestly. And it's a major holiday hotspot. I'm not just making an easy pun here, but for two Christmas-loving lesbians, it's impossible to leave Dyker Heights off the itinerary."

"Fair dues." Ava started to reach for Bex's arm the way she had so many other times, but now she caught herself. They'd managed to rebound from the awkwardness of the afternoon, at least conversationally, but as much as she loved resuming a more natural rhythm, it also made it harder to keep her guard up.

"Turn right here." Bex pointed as they came to an intersection, then glanced at her watch again.

"Are we late for something?"

"No, it's just now dark, but I wanted you to see the transformation."

Ava turned slowly, searching for signs of some impending shift, but all she saw was a tiny city street filled with well-kept homes scrunched tightly together. The area seemed nice, pretty even, but ordinary, until lights flickered in the periphery of her vision. She spun toward the sight as bright white sparked to life along every eave and tree branch, but before she had even a second to process the details, another pop of color sprang into the gathering darkness to her left. She rotated to see the splash of red and green climbing a small porch and spilling out onto a postage-stamp-size yard. She smiled as "Deck the Halls" began to play from a speaker behind her, and when she shifted her position to follow the sound, a miniature sleigh and eight tiny reindeer appeared on a roof overhead.

One by one, virtually every house on the street lit up like its own unique Christmas tree. Ava stood rooted in awe and pure joy as it seemed like someone down below was flipping on breakers one by one until each fuse in the box of this neighborhood caught hold and sent brightness into the dark winter's night.

"What do you think?" Bex finally whispered, her voice low and rich, and close enough to her ear to send a shiver down her spine.

She met her eyes, each of them reflecting a thousand points of light around them, and said the only word she could find, "Beautiful."

Bex smiled at her, not the cheeky grin, or the megawatt version, but a sweet, wistful expression. "I'm glad it was worth the trip."

Ava cupped her face in her hands as the alarm bells in the back of her brain warned her to brace for impact, but she didn't care. She needed to make sure she made herself clear as she held Bex close. "Every part of this weekend has been worth the trip."

Bex nodded slightly. "I feel the same way, and I don't need anything more. If you're happy, I'm happy."

Her breath caught sharply in her throat, and she closed her eyes, wishing desperately for that to be true. She wanted the simplicity of believing the two of them only needed to be happy together. It would be such a nice illusion to indulge in. Instead, she lowered her hands and stepped back.

"Are you okay?" Bex asked.

"Yes." And she was. Okay was an accurate description on many levels. There wasn't anything wrong. They'd had a lovely day together, and she had no real complaints in the moment other than perhaps the larger complexities around them and life in general. And yet she couldn't shake the sense there should be more. "I need to stay in this moment. It's a good moment. You've taken me to a new place, one I didn't even know existed, and it's so lovely."

"But?"

"There's no 'but.' Not really. I want to be here right now, with you. I don't know why my mind keeps trying to jump to what's next and where we go from here."

Bex nodded and then tentatively took her hand, raising her eyebrows as if asking permission.

She hated the doubt she saw there, and guardedness be damned, she intertwined their fingers and squeezed tightly.

They strolled down the street, looking at the lights on several more houses before Bex said, "You can do both though, right?"

"What?"

"You can love where you're at in this moment *and* wonder where you're going."

She shook her head. As much as she wanted to believe she could do both of those things at once, and perhaps she could on other occasions, she feared acknowledging their relationship wasn't going anywhere would take a lot of joy out of the moment. Still, she said, "I'm going home tomorrow."

Bex squeezed her hand "I wish you didn't have to, but I understand, and it makes it easier knowing I'll get to see you again next weekend."

She stopped walking and turned to face her. "Do you mean that, or is it just natural for you to say nice things because you're a nice person?"

"You think I'm a nice person?"

"Obviously."

"What?" Bex laughed. "You live in a holiday movie. I like to think we've moved past my being a villain here, but like a nice person at my core? I feel like that's a big step."

She sighed. "I'm sorry. I should've said so sooner. I believe you're a stellar human, the total package."

"I'd feel amazing about that assertion, over the moon even, if not for the sense there's a rather large 'but' coming."

"No."

"Really?" Bex leaned closer, eyebrows raised. "'Cause I worry I've upset you a couple of times this weekend, and I'm not sure why, but you can tell me. I'm not one of those mandatory Christmas-cheer people. My holiday spirit isn't precious enough to mandate forced pleasantries. If something's weighing on you to the point that you worry I'm not looking forward to seeing you again, I'd like to know how I can remedy the issue."

Ava gave her a little shove with her free hand, but then tugged her back with the other. "Ugh, why do you have to be so perfect?"

"I could ask you the same thing."

"No, because I haven't been perfect this weekend. I've been up and down and all over the place in my own head. While you continue to be wonderful at every turn, I've been doing this push-pull thing where I want to kiss you, and I also want to set healthy boundaries around whatever we're doing here."

"Oh." Bex frowned. "Is that what's happening?"

"Obviously not effectively! Tonight's our last night in the city, and we're standing here in the middle of a profusely decorated, urban wonderland discussing heavy topics instead of enjoying everything right in front of us."

"I get it," Bex said softly. "I hadn't thought of things in quite the same terms, but I might've gotten there eventually. I considered next weekend something to look forward to first, though."

Her heart twisted in her chest. "I'm glad to hear you say so."

"Good, because it's true. I don't know what comes after that, but I like you enough to spend the days before

Christmas in your world instead of mine, and I mean, look around at how awesome mine is." Bex gestured at a house loaded with about fifty decorations too many. "I don't know what that means, but it must mean something, right?"

She nodded and pulled Bex in for a hug. "Thank you."

"For what?"

"Being you … and for being right."

"Right?" Bex held her a little tighter. "You admit I'm right?"

"About some things." She laughed. "Not about our bet, mind you, but about how we have next weekend, and that does mean something to me too."

"Good." Bex kissed her forehead and stood back. "Because I already booked my tickets. I have a morning surgery on Friday, but I'm taking an early afternoon flight into Burlington."

"Flights? Aren't you fancy?"

"I am. Also, I have to cover one shift on Monday morning, but I didn't want to miss a minute with you, so I'm flying back Sunday after lunch."

She hugged her again, not because the news changed much about their time together or her discomfort about where they were headed, but it at least confirmed Bex was open to the discussion and looking forward to seeing her, even on her own home turf. Realizing she wasn't alone in whatever came next allowed her to exist a lot happier in this place, in this moment, and with this woman.

Chapter Twenty

Bex sprinted through the terminal in JFK, not even stopping to check the schedule board as she blew past it. Her duffle banged across one side, and her work bag slapped against the other. She'd received a text saying her flight had started boarding several minutes ago, and if she'd already missed her window, she didn't want to know.

She'd spent her whole morning steadfastly refusing to consider the possibility of not making it to Vermont. Her first and only surgery had gone long for no apparent reason, and she had to transfer her patient, which she hated. Then, Pamela tried to corner her about some paperwork for a Monday surgery she hadn't even wanted to take in the first place. Who scheduled a medical procedure on Christmas Eve, and why had she agreed to work it? Of course, at the time, she'd expected to be home all weekend, and a couple of hours in the morning wouldn't impede her plans, but that was before she met Ava. If she'd known she'd have the possibility of being in Vermont—

Her feet faltered and she stumbled, nearly sprawling across the busy concourse as her brain diverted all its resources to not finish that thought. Even if she didn't have to work on Monday, she'd still want to be home on Christmas Eve. She had plans and traditions. She lived for that night in the city. She wasn't coming home for work, she was coming home for her life, the best part of it.

Still, she picked up speed once again with the urgency of someone desperate to flee, weaving between crowds of people pushing toward harried gate agents, all of them clamoring as the dreaded red "canceled" labels appeared next to more and more of their listings.

Bex hadn't even known about the impending snow-storm until she started checking flights in the cab on the way and noticed everything west of Detroit seemed wrecked with disruptions. Her driver tried to explain something about an arctic clipper that had pummeled the Upper Midwest and was currently slamming Toronto, but since it was slated to go north of the city, it hadn't appeared on her radar, literally or figuratively, until she remembered Burlington was also north of the city. She did her best mental geography quickly to ascertain whether anything barreling from Chicago to To-ronto would likely hit Vermont in short order.

She shook her head as she dodged a young couple with twins in a double stroller. She couldn't control the weather. She couldn't control the airlines. She couldn't con-trol where Ava lived. She could only do everything in her power to get to her. She'd promised.

She took a wide corner toward her gate and practi-cally hurled herself at the gate agent, who was reaching for the door.

"Stop," she commanded, then regained a modicum of her manners and added a breathless, "please."

The woman smiled tightly. "Dr. Leone?"

"Yes." She panted and held up her phone to show her ticket. "Sorry I'm late."

"We're all cutting things a little close today." The agent scanned her screen, then nodded for her to head down the jet bridge. "Hope you get to where you're going ... and you plan to stay there for a bit."

She jogged toward the plane, and the flight attendant took her duffle, saying something about overhead storage, but she didn't have any more mental bandwidth to make sense of extraneous details as she crashed into her seat, spent and flooded with relief tinged with a new apprehension.

So much of her body and brain had been consumed by the desire to get to Ava, to see her, to hold her, to live their last moments to the fullest, and to assuage the fears she'd expressed during their conversation at Dyker Heights. She'd been nearly apoplectic at the prospect of not making good on the sincere vow to make it to Vermont. She hadn't even considered the opposite possibility of getting stuck there.

🐾 🐾 🐾

Ava's phone buzzed beside her, and she checked the notification to see Bex's flight had taken off on time. She bit her lip, not wanting to give away that her mind had been elsewhere for the last hour, or the vastness of her relief at the confirmation she'd feared might not come.

"Where are the scissors?" Gram lifted up a pile of red and gold tissue paper to check underneath. "Wrapping presents is the folding laundry of the holiday world."

Ava laughed. "You're not wrong, but I don't mind it so much when we have time to really enjoy it."

"I have all the time in the world," Gram said pointedly.

"Me too," Ava's mom said. "No hot dates for me."

She rolled her eyes at that characterization of her plans.

"Same for me." Mel piled on. "I don't have anything else I'm eager to run off and abandon you all for."

"Come on." Ava glanced at her watch for the tenth time. "I'd love to stay and help more, honestly, but I've got to leave now if I'm going to make it to the airport on time."

"We're teasing." Her mom put a gentle hand on her shoulder. "I'm happy you have something nice to look forward to."

"And we don't want you to have to outrun this storm," Gram added. "I hate the idea of it wrecking your plans."

"Not at all. I built the weather into the weekend. Sledding, snowmen, hot cocoa, movies. The only precarious part is the airport runs."

"You be careful."

"I always am."

Gram leaned over and kissed her cheek. "I know, and I love that about you."

"Wait." Mel held up a hand. "Are we not going to address the fact that she basically admitted she hopes to get snowed in so she can shack up with Bex for a few days?"

She hugged them all quickly. She didn't have time to indulge any more conversation. "I have to go."

Still, as quickly as she dismissed the charge and hopped in her car, she couldn't quite keep her own mind from wandering where Mel's had. The possibility of getting snowed in with Bex had its appeal. She'd already let herself undercut the enjoyment of last weekend by trying, fruitlessly, to erect some sort of emotional barriers. It hadn't worked. She'd still left the city more and more impressed with Bex. She was kind and sensitive and passionate, and all-around amazing. And while Ava still couldn't conceive of any long-term relationship hope for the two of them, maybe she didn't need to. Just because they didn't see a path toward a future didn't mean what they shared right now couldn't be powerful and meaningful. Worrying about things beyond the scope of this weekend wouldn't change anything, and she didn't want to ruin the present based on what might be.

Perhaps she and Bex might find ways to stay friends, or they might drift apart slowly after the holiday ended and their real life took over once more, or maybe without the magic of the holiday to bind them to each other, they would never get another shot at a weekend like this.

There were no guarantees, and somehow, this time, that didn't spark fear so much as a sense of urgency. She and Bex had each other, right here, right now, and the only thing she could control around those truths was what she chose to do with them in these moments.

🦉 🦉 🦉

"Look at these snowflakes. They're huge!" Bex marveled as giant flakes hit the windshield and melted slightly before being whisked away by a wiper blade only to start the process again instantly. She found the mountain drive in such conditions utterly hypnotizing. The storm had picked up mere minutes after Ava pulled onto the interstate, and the large flakes rushed toward the quick-moving car making it look as if they were making the jump to lightspeed, but here on the slower, winding roads, the quickly deepening blanket of snow settling around them carried a more soothing quality. The transition mirrored her own internal workings as her brain and body shifted from the frantic remnants of her departure from the city to a more relaxed state associated with her arrival here in Vermont.

Then again, she wasn't the one driving. She suspected if she'd had to guide the little Subaru through the snowy mountain passes, she might've been considerably less relaxed. Still, if Ava felt any tension, or even relief at pulling safely into her driveway, she didn't let it show. Instead, she turned to Bex as she killed the engine and said, "Home sweet home."

The grin that had settled on her lips the moment they saw each other at the airport spread. Bex saw the trap in admitting Ava's house felt like home, but she didn't completely hate the descriptor. There was something sweet about being welcomed into Ava's space, and the sensation only grew as they pushed inside the house, warm and fragrant with the scent of recently baked treats. Bex began to shed her snow clothes.

"I'm going to head back out and batten down the hatches before I haul in enough firewood to get us through the next twenty-four hours," Ava said.

Bex arched an eyebrow. "Sounds like a lot. Is it a lot?"

"We're supposed to get twelve to eighteen inches of snow."

"Whoa, I don't even have to ask. I know that's a lot."

Ava shook her head. "It's not unusual here. We all know how to hunker down."

A little shiver of excitement ran up Bex's spine, brushing away the fear that tried to push in about her possible exit. She'd deal with those issues if and when they arose. Right now, she wanted to bask in the electricity of an impending storm with this woman. "What can I do to help?"

"You don't have—"

"I want to," she said quickly. "I want to experience all the things with you."

Ava's lips parted and her lashes fluttered closed as she seemed to focus on breathing before the words could come. In the void, Bex realized the far-reaching implications of the statement she'd made with genuine ease.

She should walk it back, put caveats or guardrails on the sentiment, but she couldn't think of any, so instead she plowed forward. "I mean, in New York, more than four or five inches of snow comes with a lot of headaches. It'll be nice to experience blizzard prep with someone who's clearly a pro."

"Right." Ava's features relaxed. "The first step is making sure we have what we need inside. Then, we'll get the temperature up in the living room before we raise our own core temperatures."

"Our core temperature, like body heat?"

"With food or hot cocoa," Ava said quickly. "We don't need strenuous activity or ... anything. You know what? Why don't you get some kindling going in the fireplace. That seems ... well, safe."

She nodded. They were clearly dancing around innuendo if Ava believed having her start an actual fire constituted safety in this situation, but she wasn't sure what to make of their new awkwardness. Two weeks ago, they would've both leaned into the playfulness.

Bex waited until Ava retreated outdoors and then crouched next to the fireplace, wondering what had shifted. Perhaps it was the reminder of their dwindling time together, or maybe the stress of the storm and how it complicated all their plans, but it felt like more.

A gust of wind kicked up, rattling the windows and reminding her she had work to do. Thankfully, they both seemed to use their respective tasks to collect themselves, and by the time they settled into more comfortable clothes before a roaring fire, their natural rapport rebounded.

"What do you think for tonight's movie? Classic or modern? Funny or poignant?" Ava tossed Bex a fleece blanket and curled up on the opposite end of the couch under one of her own.

"How about *Scrooged* or *Elf*?"

"Wrong!" Ava said, then laughed as she picked up the remote.

"What do you mean 'wrong'? It's a preference. You asked for mine."

"It's a test, and you failed."

"I've never failed a test in my life."

Ava eyed her seriously for a second before saying, "I believe you, but there must be a first time for everything, because you're in Vermont less than a week before Christmas in the middle of a snowstorm. There's clearly a right answer to the movie question."

She rolled her eyes so hard her head lolled back. "Damn it, you planned this."

"Of course I did." Ava pressed a button on the remote and the TV flickered to life, revealing the already-cued opening credits to *White Christmas*.

"I suppose all's fair in love and Christmas bets." Bex snuggled a little deeper into her blanket and pulled her steaming mug onto her lap. "Are you going to tell me all the insider Vermonty tips and tidbits as we watch?"

"And talk during the movie? Blasphemy!" Ava's smile curled up from behind her own mug. "I might sing along a time or two."

"I'll play Bing Crosby if you do Rosemary Clooney's parts."

Ava sighed playfully and feigned a swoon. "I've been waiting my whole life for someone to make me that kind of offer."

Bex's heart gave a little tap against her ribs, causing her to wonder if she hadn't been waiting to make such an offer even if she'd never realized it until right this moment. Warmth spread through her stronger than the cocoa warranted as the opening credits gave way to the first number, set not in Vermont but WWII Europe. She'd never been a big one for military-inspired sentimentality, so she kept stealing glances at Ava.

She was beautiful, all curled up and snuggled in, her eyes dancing the way they did when something caught her interest. Her soft lips mouthed along the words to the movie, and Bex shivered as the urge to feel them move against her own overtook her, swift and unexpectedly strong.

She forced her attention back to the TV, but even as the movie scenes shifted back to the States and musical numbers more to her taste, she couldn't keep her mind from wandering to the woman beside her. She was so not the type of person Bex tended to fall for, but she couldn't deny the distinct possibility that she was. How else could she explain the sense of excitement hanging over her during what, by all accounts, should've been a rather mundane holiday evening? Nothing here held the traditional appeal of a full-blown NYC spectacle, so why did she feel so on edge? There was no hustle and bustle to navigate, so why wouldn't her heart rate settle into a more subdued rhythm?

She wasn't dense. She understood that the energy coursing through her, strong enough to rival the types of highs she generally associated with the city, had little to do with what they were doing and everything to do with the woman she was sharing the experience with.

She glanced at Ava once again, not fully trusting herself to look away if she got caught this time, but, apparently, she didn't have to, because no sooner had their eyes met than the world went dark.

For one disconcerting second, she feared the sight of Ava so close and perfect had somehow short-circuited her brain, but then she noticed the fire still flickering on the other side of the room. As her eyes adjusted to the faint orange glow, she realized the power had gone out.

Still, her haze of disorientation wouldn't quite let her consider what that meant. "Should I be nervous?"

Ava reached for her hand. "Not at all."

261

The touch of soft fingers skimming across her palm did little to calm her.

"We've got a good base of heat in the house and the fire's already roaring. We've got plenty more wood to burn, but movie time is probably over for tonight."

"Sorry, I know you were looking forward to that one."

"It's okay. This is exciting. It's not every day a blizzard causes a blackout."

The wind rattled the window harder than before as if to amp up the drama.

"I don't think I've ever had a blizzard blackout before," Bex admitted. "What do we do now?"

"Actually, you've already got the hang of it." Ava squeezed her hand a little tighter. "You must be a prodigy."

"Oh, I most definitely am," she agreed playfully, "but just so we're on the same page, what exactly am I excelling at?"

Ava laughed. "Blizzarding. You snuggle up, you stay where it's warmest, whisper in the dark, and tell each other things you wouldn't say in the daylight."

Bex's breath caught, and she suspected Ava could hear because she scooted closer on the couch.

"Tell me about the best Christmas you ever had as a kid."

It wasn't the type of question she expected, one more in a series of surprises, but this one at least anchored her to something foundational between them.

"Um, wow, tough to say." She tried to clear her brain, which was no small task at the moment, but Ava waited patiently. "Probably when I was five. My parents had split up, and my dad moved out, but he was still coming around occasionally, and on Christmas, he showed up dressed like Santa. Red pants, red coat, hat, but no beard, so he wasn't trying to actually play the role of Santa, and he didn't come to the door."

"How did he get there?"

"I was sitting by the window wishing it would snow, but it was unseasonably warm, and I saw his boots first."

"Out the window?" Ava asked, sounding totally engaged in Bex's memory.

"On the fire escape. He was climbing down from the roof. I didn't even know people could get on the roof of the building, but he climbed down and sort of hopped onto the metal landing with a clank and gave me this Cheshire cat grin."

"What did your mom say?"

"She laughed and shook her head. He always had that effect on her. It didn't make sense or gel with the rest of her personality or life at large. She was so careful and studious all the rest of the time, always gauging risk and reward, always making the sensible decision, but when he showed up, she let all three of us climb back up the fire escape."

"When you were five?"

"I know, right?" Bex laughed at the memory. "She never let me go out there any other time, not even as a teen, but we all scaled the whole thing that evening and opened presents under the stars and waited for real Santa's sleigh to fly over the city skyline. I don't even remember what I got that year. I just remember the three of us stealing magic together one last time."

Ava finally closed the distance between them completely and rested her head on Bex's shoulder. "I think you're good at stealing magic, or making it anyway."

She pressed her cheek to her hair, breathing in the scent of her for a moment before asking, "What about you? What's your most magical childhood Christmas memory?"

Ava didn't hesitate. "Also the Christmas when I was five, but you already know that story."

She arched her eyebrows even though Ava couldn't see her. "I do?"

"Yes, and I still can't figure out how, because it wasn't some random little detail. You know exactly when I got Fuzzy and why he was the best Christmas present in the whole world."

"Oh yeah, your puppy named Fuzzy that Santa put in your stocking. He told me about it when we went to visit, or he told you anyway, and I got to hear."

"No." Ava shook her head and sat back enough to stare up at Bex intently. "You told him. You planted it somehow before I even got there."

"I did no such thing."

Ava searched her eyes in the dim light before shaking her head. "You did, but I don't know how, which goes back to my point about you making magic."

"Even if I had," Bex paused and bit the bottom of her lip before shaking her head against the impulse to give this woman anything she asked for, "and I'm not saying I did, a magician never reveals her secrets. It would spoil the fun. What's the next question, please?"

Ava looked as if she might argue for a second before relenting. "Okay, fine. For the sake of Christmas magic, I'll move on. What was your best Christmas as an adult?"

She smiled immediately, not even having to think to summon her answer. "That's easy."

"Oh?"

She leaned forward so close their noses brushed together lightly before saying, "It's this one."

Chapter Twenty-One

Ava thrilled at the answer, then again as Bex's lips touched hers. She melted against her, as if her body had ached for this moment ever since she'd set eyes on her, looking all golden and glorious. She fought hard not to surrender fully to the pull of Bex's magnetism, but a part of her must've anticipated doing so, because instead of getting her fill and pulling back, she pressed forward.

If Bex backed away, Ava would've been forced to admit this had also been her best Christmas in ages, and so much more. Instead, she conveyed as much as she took Bex's face in her hands and pulled her deeper. Parting her lips, she welcomed more than she ever had. Still, she craved more in a way she hadn't allowed herself to acknowledge until the moment when it overwhelmed her completely. Trailing her fingers down Bex's jaw, her neck, her shoulder, then into the collar of her shirt, she luxuriated in the line of her collarbone.

Bex nibbled lightly at Ava's bottom lip and shifted her body so they faced each other more fully. Resting her hands on Ava's hips, she tightened her grip slowly as she swept her tongue along Ava's.

She gave a little moan of pleasure, and her hips rocked forward as her body took full control of her brain. This woman was too much to resist, and no part of her even wanted to. Any awareness of danger or even good sense fled as Bex's talented hands inched up under the hem of her shirt.

"Yes," she mumbled against the corner of her mouth, granting consent Bex hadn't even requested yet. She wanted her so strongly, she would've granted her anything.

Taking hold of Bex's shoulders, she held their bodies together as she leaned back until she lay on the couch with the glorious weight of a perfect body extended over her.

Bex kissed along her neck even as her hands worked upward as if they intended to meet in some magnificent middle. Ava burned with the awareness that she didn't want any barriers between them. She caught hold of Bex's shirt and pulled up before breaking contact enough to remove it completely. Then, shifting as much as their positions would allow, she arched her back and lifted her head, encouraging Bex to do the same for her.

As they resettled, the sensations Bex's skin induced as it slid against her own set her nerve endings alight. From the softness of her breasts to the ridges of her ribs and the plane of her abs, everything about her screamed perfection. Ava's body was torn between twin desires to push up into the contact and to sink even deeper into the puddle of need gathering at her core.

"You feel amazing," Bex whispered, pulling her mouth away from her lips and lower along her neck, straight down the center of her chest. Ava slipped her hands into the silken hair she'd always found flawless, and reveled in the opportunity to tangle it. Bex took her time kissing along every inch of newly exposed skin, demonstrating the attention to detail Ava had always admired in thrilling and excruciating ways. She'd never let herself imagine this experience, but even if she had, her brain would've struggled to imagine something this wonderful.

As Bex moved slowly, her mouth hot and wet, she inspired the same in Ava, and when she finally closed her lips around a nipple, every other part of her tightened as well.

She'd never reacted to anyone so completely. She felt torn, both wanting to keep doing the same thing forever and palpably needing to go further than even the new paradise they'd found.

Bex, in her usual fashion, managed to somehow do both by replacing her mouth with skilled hands and massaging, even as her lips trailed lower. Ava fought the urge to squirm beneath her or rock up too hard, because even in her mounting need to follow the path Bex was leading her down, she didn't want to rush any part of the journey. Still, when Bex barely nudged at the waistband of Ava's pajama bottoms, she eagerly shimmied out of them, extending the invitation and making sure no barriers remained to inhibit their current trajectory.

Everything about Bex's mouth built anticipation: the press of her lips against her stomach, the sweep of her tongue lower, hot breath against her most sensitive core. When Bex closed around her, the back of Ava's eyelids went white.

She lost the ability to process anything other than Bex doing what Bex did best, showing, sharing, pulling her out of herself and into something more than she'd imagined. She had no idea how long she stayed balanced between existing more fully in her own body than she ever had and rising higher above it all. She bit her lip to keep from crying out, but the effort was as futile as it was warranted.

A single word rose from her throat, encompassing all the others as it spilled forth.

It was a whisper, a prayer, a plea, and most of all, a release.

"Bex."

She shook under the power of it, disintegrating for the woman who wielded it so beautifully.

Bex stayed with her, constant and attentive, always shifting but never relenting until Ava caught hold of her shoulder and dragged her back up along the length of her own aching body.

Every nerve ending still burned for her, but as their lips met again and she tasted herself on Bex, vulnerability gave way to a new kind of agency. "I want you."

"You have me," Bex said in a low voice leaving no room for doubt.

"I want to make you feel—"

"You do." Bex cut her off with another kiss. "All of it, Ava. You have me so—you're like a miracle, I am so— God, I can't even speak. You've completely overwhelmed me."

Ava clutched her, shivering with the strongest desire to give her everything. "What do you need?"

"Only you."

Ava started to shake her head. Surely it couldn't be that easy, but Bex took hold of her hand and guided it between them. She gasped as her fingers slipped into the pool of wetness at the apex of Bex's thighs. Something primal and powerful took hold of her as she stroked that need, then lowered her head, intending to meet it more fully, but Bex caught hold of her chin and gently raised it once more.

"Stay."

The word cut through the haze, or maybe it sharpened her senses, but Ava complied.

"Nothing turns me on more than watching you," Bex said, her voice husky and strained.

Ava's heart clenched in her chest as part of her rebelled against the idea she could offer anything so compelling to this amazing woman who had shaken her foundations, but the sincerity in Bex's gaze left little room for those doubts to take hold. Instead, they were carried away on a tide of arousal as she and Bex moved together.

Slipping her knee between muscled thighs, she increased both access and pressure, causing Bex's body to tighten in every place it met her own. Ava watched in awe as the beautiful form against her rose and fell, flexing and contracting in a magnificent loop.

Flickering firelight cast them both in hues of orange and dancing shadows as their movements grew frantic and she fought to imprint each flawless detail in her mind, her skin, her heart. She'd never even known enough to ache for something as perfect as this moment, this woman, but she knew with utter certainty that now she'd always crave the press of her body, the clutch of her strong hands on her waist, the dig of short fingernails on her back, the flush of hot breath on her neck, the echo of her own name on those parched lips, or the sweet sensation of Bex going slack in her arms.

She would crave her forever.

Chapter Twenty-Two

Light surrounded Bex. She could tell even through her heavy eyelids, but she wasn't ready to try to lift them yet. The warm cocoon created by the combination of blankets and Ava's body offered a type of unparalleled perfection she didn't even have to process. She merely wanted to exist there for eternity.

Oh no. The last part of that thought seeped through the languid sort of floating haze, and she struggled against her own growing awareness. She didn't want to remember anything but the last twelve hours, the completion of a connection as natural as breathing. They'd moved together so beautifully and fit with a precision she'd never experienced in any area of her life. It would be easy to believe in predestination, but nothing beyond this moment was actually a foregone conclusion.

It wasn't even easy.

Perhaps sensing her growing tension, Ava stirred in the crook of her arm, and Bex found the fortitude to face the light, if only for the reward of seeing her here, now, in what might prove to be their last uncomplicated moment.

Her breath caught at the sight of her, dark eyelashes resting peacefully against pale skin, her hair cascading over bare shoulders. She smiled in spite of all the clichés running through her brain about angels and goddesses and magic. Ava was too real, too close to be reduced to simile or metaphor, but for someone like Bex, who spent her life chasing every experience, every thrill, every flash and clamor, she'd

271

never once considered the possibility that quiet contentment might outstrip any adventure.

Ava's eyes fluttered open. "Are you watching me sleep?"

"Maybe. Is that creepy?"

"No." Ava stifled a yawn. "Kind of sweet."

Emotion tightened Bex's throat, so she merely kissed Ava's forehead in response.

"Power's back on."

Bex glanced away from her for the first time since she'd opened her eyes to see a lamp on the table had turned on, as had the blank TV. For the sake of warmth and the prospect of a hot shower, she could've been grateful, but she couldn't shake the sensation the outside world had intruded on their safe haven.

"Do you want some breakfast?" Ava asked, and her own stomach rumbled as if giving Bex a hint as to the correct answer.

"We probably earned some."

Ava smiled against her skin. It was the closest they came to acknowledging the magnitude of what they'd done. There wasn't much use of recapping the events of the last night, as they'd both been fully present, and she doubted either of them would ever forget the details of something so earth-shattering. Neither had it changed anything fundamental about their lives or personalities. How strange that something so powerful could transform so little. And yet, Bex didn't want to simply accept the facts of their reality and move on. What they'd shared meant something to her even if she didn't fully understand what. In the end, she merely managed to whisper her most sincere, "Thank you."

Ava lifted up enough to kiss her cheek, and for a second, it felt as if she might lean in for more, but instead, she stared down at Bex for a heavy second before saying, "Thank you."

She climbed over her and headed up the stairs.

Bex stayed put, looking up at the exposed beams of the little mountain cabin, wondering where they could possibly go from here.

🦉 🦉 🦉

Ava slid a plate piled high with bacon across the breakfast bar as soon as Bex came down the stairs. She was freshly showered, and the ends of still-damp hair stuck to her neck. She wore a simple pair of gray sweatpants and a long-sleeved, red T-shirt with a faux cross-stitch pattern that read, "You'll Shoot Your Eye Out."

Ava smiled at every part of this scenario. She'd woken up in the arms of a stunning, talented, attentive woman, who also had a sense of humor and a childlike joy in Christmas. Every single thing about Bex screamed perfection, except for one. She slammed the door on that part, pushing down an almost desperate need not to let it intrude on today.

Turning away to collect herself, she lifted two pancakes from her griddle and flipped them on top of the stack she'd already started.

"I'm still impressed you can manage to whip up a full breakfast in the time it takes me to shower and change."

"It's not complicated." Ava poured the rest of the batter into the pan. "Pancakes only have like five ingredients."

"That's the first place I'd run into trouble, as I probably don't have most of them in my house, so I'd have to go to the store, find them, bring them home, and then I'd still have no idea what to do with them. It'd be much quicker and probably safer for me to use the time and effort to make reservations somewhere nice."

"Then you'd starve here this morning because we can't go anywhere. We've got probably a foot of snow, and while it's slowed since last night, it hasn't stopped fully yet."

Bex glanced out the window and grimaced. "Are we going to have to dig out?"

"Oh, no. My dad has a snowplow on his truck. Once things calm down this evening, he'll come clear the driveway. We'll be able to drive by tomorrow."

Bex sighed, sounding a little too relieved for Ava's taste. "Whew, that's nice, but does it wreck our plans for today?"

"Actually, it doesn't." Ava flipped the cakes. "I'll admit losing power last night threw me off, not that I'm complaining, mind you."

Bex flashed her a grin. "Glad to hear it."

"But I accounted for the possibility of a snow day today."

"And nothing's, uh," Bex stumbled slightly, "changed those plans?"

She shook her head. "Not unless you want it to."

"I don't."

The quick response calmed her nerves considerably. "Me either. I'd like for us to have fun today, and worry about anything else that might warrant worry later."

Bex nodded. "What did you have in mind?"

Ava killed the gas flame on her stove and collected the pancakes before coming to sit beside her. "Eat up and then I'll show you."

Bex laughed as she nearly stumbled all the way forward, but Ava's mittened hand caught hold of her jacket. "Are you kidding me? You have your own sledding hill?"

"Any hill's a sledding hill when it snows this much." Ava dropped an antique wooden toboggan on the ground between them.

"When you grabbed that thing from the barn, I couldn't figure out how you were going to get us to some park or public slope. It never occurred to me you'd only have to walk out the back door of your workshop." She surveyed the rolling hill and the picturesque countryside blanketed in white. "Is everything here this beautiful all the time?"

Ava shrugged. "I mean, I do live in paradise. Beauty comes with the territory."

Bex snorted softly, but as she turned to Ava once more, any hint of an argument died before it reached her lips. The woman was stunning, breathtaking, and a million other words or sensations she couldn't even articulate.

Ava flashed her a smile that stretched her pink cheeks until they crinkled around her eyes. "You ready for this?"

It took Bex a few extra seconds to realize she was talking about the toboggan, not the emotions swirling inside of her, and still she could only manage to nod.

"You want to ride in the front or the back?"

"I don't know how to drive one of these. You better take the lead."

Ava laughed, then sat down on the toboggan and scooted forward. "There's not much driving involved, but I like the idea of you holding on to me, so I'll go first."

Bex couldn't fault her logic, so she snugged in behind Ava, wrapping her arms around her waist.

"Wrap your legs up over mine too."

"This might be my new favorite winter activity," she said as she entangled herself around Ava in a position similar to the one she'd woken up in. A flood of memories surged up, forcing the air from her lungs until it hung in a translucent cloud around them both. She involuntarily tightened her arms around Ava's waist, the impulse to cling to her stronger than reason, but also fitting for the situation.

As if sensing her cue, or perhaps suffering a swell of emotions herself, Ava chose the opposite path and pushed off with the force of someone eager to outrun them.

They tilted forward until gravity took hold. They picked up speed quickly, and soon the wind whistled in Bex's ears. The hill hadn't seemed this steep or as long from the top, but as the ride went on, clutching to Ava, heart racing, the world blurring around them, Bex didn't want it to end. Not the hill, not the hold they had on each other, or the way everything else faded when the two of them existed purely present with each other. Last night had been the final shift they'd been careening toward with the same force that propelled them toward the bottom of the hill. The only options were to ride it out or wreck them both, the thrill and the danger intermingled as tightly as their bodies.

She managed to squint into the wind long enough to see they were nearing the plain at the bottom and suffered a pang of regret, but it evaporated as they leveled out but continued to glide smoothly through light snow, their combined weight counteracting every force that should've slowed their trajectory. They skimmed across the frozen field, and for a few glorious seconds, it felt as though they might have enough momentum to keep defying the laws of physics, but no sooner had she considered the possibility than they hit a bump and went momentarily airborne. They landed with a discombobulating thump jarring every vertebra in her back and dislodging them from the sled without Bex managing to loosen her hold on Ava. Tumbling, rolling, and sliding, they took each bounce in unison until the cushion of snow cradled them to a stop.

Bex lay on top of Ava. Snowflakes clung to her dark lashes and fluttered against her cheeks, and her chest rose and fell as they tried to catch their breath through the low rumble of laughter shaking through both of them.

"We survived," Ava finally said, her voice light and amused.

"Did we?" She wasn't sure. It seemed as though something inside her might've broken, or perhaps she hadn't managed to stop falling yet. She stared down into those dancing eyes that filled her with a sense of exhilaration every bit as enthralling as the ride they'd shared. Maybe it was the adrenaline still surging through her, or perhaps the magic they'd always believed in finally overtook her senses, but even as she lowered her head, intending only to steal another kiss, the words rushed forth on frozen breath, and she blurted out, "Come back to New York with me."

Chapter Twenty-Three

Ava trudged up the slope, dragging the toboggin behind her. The going wasn't easy. Despite doing her best to stick to the path they'd packed down with the sled, the snow was still deep enough that she sank up to her shins with each step. Only it sort of felt like she was sinking lower emotionally.

"I'm sorry," Bex called as she stumbled along behind her. "I didn't mean to offend you."

"You didn't," Ava said.

"Kind of feels like I did."

She sighed. She wasn't handling this well, but she hadn't prepared herself, not for anything that had happened over the last twenty-four hours. As much as she wanted to pretend she was merely making the most of their remaining time together, she wasn't the kind of person who had flings or fell into bed with someone to kill time during a power outage.

She'd merely been trying to stay calm and follow Bex's lead until she left. She'd been aware enough to realize she might break down when that happened, but she hadn't stopped long enough to let herself consider the possibility of Bex asking for more. And now she was literally running, or at least slogging away, from the prospect as quickly as conditions would allow. She wasn't trying to be petulant or obtuse. She simply needed time to pull herself together, and she couldn't do that out here, in the open, exposed and vulnerable, with nothing to anchor herself to but the intensity of Bex's electric gaze.

"Come on," she finally said as they neared the top of the hill. "Let's get inside and warm up. Then we can talk."

Bex accepted the offer, or perhaps she was too winded from the climb to argue, but either way, Ava appreciated the opportunity to collect herself and face whatever came next within the comfort and emotional safety of the home she loved.

By the time she stomped off her boots on the front porch and opened the door to her sanctuary, she'd nearly convinced herself Bex's question hadn't even been real, or at least not as real as it felt when lying beneath her, their hearts beating rapidly in unison. Maybe she'd been swept up in the magic of the moment, or perhaps Bex had only offered an extension on their bet rather than asking Ava to move in with her. There was one simple way to find out, and as she shook off her snowy outer layers, she feared they'd put off this conversation long enough.

Turning to Bex, she said, "I think we need to talk."

"Sounds ominous." Bex shook out her hair and forced a smile. "Do we need hot cocoa and a warm fire first?"

"Now who's stalling?"

"I think it's me," Bex admitted through chattering teeth, "but if I'm about to be let down gently, I'd really rather not be freezing."

"Fair. Do you want to go take a hot bath while I stoke the fire?"

"I suppose it would be inappropriate to ask you to join me in the bath?"

She snorted softly.

"I'll take that as a yes." Bex flashed her an almost mischievous grin. "Would now be a good time to mention I brought a Christmas present for you?"

Ava softened slightly. "What's happening right now?"

"I don't know." Bex reached for her hand and pulled her toward the couch. "I worry I keep hurting you in these little ways. I watched it happen twice last weekend, and then again this morning. I think things are going great, and I feel so close to you, but then you pull away or shut down, and the discrepancy confuses me."

"It confuses me too," she admitted. "There are times everything seems almost too perfect to be real."

"Like last night?"

"Yes." She sagged against Bex. "Last night was effortlessly amazing and natural and right. It didn't take any grand plans or negotiations, and if we could live like this forever in unison, I'd be all in, but that's not how this works, and the times when you noticed me pulling away were times when reality crashed in to remind me of what we're up against."

Bex nodded thoughtfully. "And that's what happened when I asked you to come back to the city with me?"

"That sort of question brings up a hundred others, and maybe I'm immature, but I didn't want to face them yet."

"That's not immature, it's human. Who wouldn't want to live this happy, easy existence as long as possible? Honestly, I was probably suffering the same rash impulse when I blurted it out. I just didn't want this to end."

"So, you didn't really mean—"

"No, I did. I meant I want you with me." Bex stanched that line of worry. "Ava, you're amazing. I've enjoyed every minute with you, and I want more of them. More kisses, more adventures, more silly thrills, and drinks that turn into dinner that turns into midnight. I might not have thought through what I said in the moment, but it doesn't make the request untrue. I want you to come back to the city with me."

"And see, this is like all those other times you say exactly the right thing, right up until the end."

"The part about the city?"

She nodded. "I love the idea of waking up with you tomorrow and the next day and the next. I love it so much I might even entertain the idea of waking up with you there on Christmas morning, but to what end? What about the days and months and Christmases to follow?"

"What about them?"

"In order to make this Christmas morning a dream come true, I need to know it's actually more than a dream. I'm not asking for a marriage proposal here, but I need to have some hope for down the line, and I haven't gotten that from you."

"Why not? I just told you I want more for us."

Her chest tightened at the sincerity in Bex's voice. "I appreciate that more than you can know. I worried all we could ever be was a Christmas fling, and honestly, I saw the appeal there, but I don't want to be sitting here a year from now, sad and brokenhearted. I don't want to learn to think of Christmas as the time of year when you were mine, or worse, associate my favorite time of year with losing you."

Bex's lips parted, and she blew out a slow breath before saying, "I hadn't thought of that."

"And I don't want you to think about it anymore. I want us to remember each other happily. I want only good memories."

"But what if we could be more than memories? What if we could have a present and future?"

"Does this future involve me moving to the city?"

"Would that be awful?"

"My life is here. My job is here. My family is here."

"And my life and job and the family I've built is in New York." A tinge of frustration crept into Bex's voice.

"I know. I won't lie and say I didn't occasionally harbor some fantasies of you chucking it all away to become a small-town doctor, but not after last weekend. What you've made for yourself matters, and I'd never want to take you away from what you love."

"But isn't there some way to make things work out so no one has to lose anything? People have successful long-distance relationships all the time."

"Is that what you want?"

Bex's shoulders dropped. "I don't know, but I mean there has to be something. Where there's a will, there's a way, right? You have a custody agreement for a dog for crying out loud."

Ava smiled in spite of her rising sense of helplessness. "I do."

"And Howie, he's made a city move work while still maintaining great family ties."

"He has." She pursed her lips together.

"What?" Bex took both her hands and squeezed. "Tell me."

"I don't want to be the one who always has to make it work. I tried for too long. And it's not that you're not worth it. It's that I'm also worth it, and I don't think it makes me a bad person to be proud of the life I have here."

"Of course not, and I'm not a bad person for feeling the same way."

She shook her head, then cupped Bex's face in her hands. "You're not. There's no bad person here. We're past villains and stereotypes. This isn't a Christmas movie. We're real people, and you're one of the best I've ever met."

"You're one of the best too."

"We're just not meant to be the best together, then.

"But don't opposites attract?"

Ava laughed. "There's no lack of attraction here. I'm attracted to you so much I can hardly stand it, but it goes much deeper than the physical. I'm drawn to you mentally, emotionally, and every other way, which is why I don't want to ruin our friendship by trying to change each other or tarnish our connection by straining it to a breaking point. We've had an amazing holiday season together."

Bex leaned into her touch more fully. "The best."

"Then, let's not let it end on a sour note."

"Okay." Bex leaned forward and kissed her softly and for not nearly long enough. "I did get you a present though."

She chuckled softly. "I got you something too."

"Are we going to open them tonight?"

Ava sat back. "What if we didn't? What if we put them under our respective trees, and we open them at the exact same time on Christmas morning?"

Bex smiled. "It'll be like we're spending a small piece of our Christmas together even while we're both in our own spaces."

"A fitting end to a bet that's clearly a draw." Ava extended her hand.

Bex hesitated only a second before taking the peace offering. "I guess it is. Merry Christmas, country mouse."

"Merry Christmas, city mouse."

🦉 🦉 🦉

"We need one more winter activity," Bex declared when the sadness became almost too much to bear.

"What?" Ava looked up from the weather report on her phone. "Now?"

"Why not?" She forced a smile. "We're both up early. You said the storm is over, and we should be able to make it to the airport without any major issues. What else on your list didn't we get to yesterday?" Bex phrased the question as delicately as she could without directly alluding to the fact that they'd both sunk into a bit of a depression after their conversation.

They'd managed to finish watching *White Christmas* and do a bit more baking before calling it an early night, but Bex had barely slept, tortured by the contrast of her empty bed with the memories of the night before. They hadn't spoken about it this morning, but the dark smudges under Ava's eyes suggested she hadn't gotten much rest either.

Bex didn't want it to end like this. They'd shared too much and made too many beautiful memories to let one painful conversation sully them all. Ava had been strong enough to realize she didn't want to associate Christmas with loss or sadness, but Bex didn't want those emotions associated with her either, so she added, "Please, one more activity?"

Ava nodded slowly as if considering options. "I suppose we could build a snowman."

"Yes!" she agreed a little too enthusiastically. "There's tons of snow, and I haven't made one since I was a kid."

"Okay, you know what you need to do, right?"

Bex smiled. "I don't know. Is it perhaps, bundle up?"

Ava managed a little laugh. "You can teach a city mouse new tricks."

Bex tried not to let the comment sink any lower than its surface implications as she pulled on every layer she owned one more time and bounded out into the snow. She sank up to her knees immediately, but this time, she didn't stumble as she worked to pat down a large, circular platform.

Ava came out holding a carrot, some cookies, and a bag of birdseed. "I brought supplies, but I couldn't find any coal or corncob pipes."

"No worries. Our snowman would never smoke. He's much too smart."

"Then, maybe it's a snowwoman."

"I love the way you think. Let's give her a nice curvy figure and a PhD."

"Dr. Snowwoman." Ava grinned as she went to work rolling snow into as big a ball as she could manage before sliding it into the spot Bex had cleared. They worked in tandem to build her torso and then a head they lifted together and reinforced until their new friend stood a smidge taller than even Bex.

"You're the doctor here," Ava said. "You better do the facial construction surgery."

"Will you assist, surgical nurse Ava?"

"I'll do my best."

Bex nodded with fake seriousness, then held out her hand. "Nose."

Ava placed it in her palm, and Bex attached it securely in the middle of the snowwoman's face before extending her hand again.

"Eyeballs?"

Ava handed over the cookies for Bex to press into place.

"Mouth?"

"Um." Ava looked around, but everything was buried in snow.

"What's the birdseed for?" Bex stage-whispered.

"Oh, I always do birdseed for hair to give the winter birds a place to land and get a cold winter snack."

"I love that," Bex exclaimed, genuine warmth moving through her at Ava's ability to exude care even in frivolous activities. "You do the scalp, and I'll carve a little tray to fill up for the mouth too."

They brushed against each other as they worked, and Bex almost didn't want to step back from the easy, casual touch. She didn't know when she'd have such quiet intimacy again, and she struggled against the urge to admit as much, though doing so wouldn't change anything but their mood.

"Lovely." Ava surveyed their work. "Now she needs a name."

The snowwoman smiled at them with a mouth full of seeds and a mop of short, dark hair. She thought of something and opened her mouth to offer a happy reference then came up short.

"What is it?"

She shook her head.

"Looked like you had something there."

Her smile faltered. "I almost said we could name her Parson Brown, but then I worried she'd ask us if we were married, like in the song, and I didn't want to let her down."

Ava pulled Bex into a quick and unexpected hug.

Bex melted into the embrace as much as their puffy coats would allow. "I'm sorry."

"Don't be," Ava whispered. "You're not letting anyone down. You're a good person, Bex, so much better than I anticipated, and you made my holiday even better than I imagined too. You improved on what I'd always thought of as perfect."

She rested her chin on Ava's shoulder. "You did too. I've never met anyone who's better at Christmas alone than we were together."

"That's pretty special." Ava leaned back but didn't let go of her. "Let's have Dr. Parson Brown bless and bind us always in the holiday spirit."

"Okay." Bex took both of Ava's gloved hands in her own and positioned them evenly in front of the snowwoman. "Do you, Ava of the great north country, take me, city mouse

287

and all, to be your partner in the holiday spirit no matter how far apart we are?"

"I do." Ava's smile crinkled her cheeks all the way up to her stocking cap. "And do you, Tribeca of the greatest city in the world, take me, the country mouse, to be your partner in the holiday spirit no matter how far apart we are?"

"I do." Bex said, then leaning forward slightly, asked, "One more kiss isn't going to get us any deeper than we've already gone, right?"

Ava's dark eyes danced with the light reflecting on the snow. "I don't think this is official unless we do."

"In that case ..." Bex closed the distance between them and sealed the new bond in the best way she knew how, by soaking up the perfection of this woman's lips one last time.

Chapter Twenty-Four

"Knock, knock," Ava called without actually knocking as she pushed open Gram's front door. "Happy Christmas Eve!"

"Eve?" Gram shuffled out of her kitchen in a quilted nightgown and a pair of fuzzy slippers. "Is your clock messed up, or have you simply lost all concept of time? It's barely seven o'clock in the morning. Eve happens at night!"

She forced a laugh at the humorous rebuke. "I was up early, so I thought I'd help you get ready for tonight. I couldn't sit around all day at home. I'm too excited."

"Excited," Gram huffed and headed back into the kitchen. "More like lonely."

Ava froze in the entryway, as the charge chilled her veins.

"Don't stand in the door," Gram called. "Come tell me what's wrong."

"Nothing's wrong," she said when she found the co-ordination necessary to walk and talk again. "And I'm not lonely either. I've got you, and we're about to have a full house of people I love on my favorite night of the year."

"Correction, we're going to have a full house in about ten hours. Half the family still has to work, and the other half is cooking or wrapping presents. Howie's flight doesn't even arrive in Burlington until nearly five."

"Doesn't mean we can't start getting ready."

Gram pulled two mugs from a cabinet and set them on the table, then poured each one three-quarters of the way

289

full. "This is my first cup, and I'm going to need at least two to wake up my cold bones. You better sit and tell me what's going on, because even when you were a little girl, you waited at least until after breakfast to start in on the holiday barrage. Is this about your friend leaving yesterday?"

"No." Ava did her best to keep a solid lock on the door Gram seemed intent on prying open. "I'm fine. Better than fine. I'm happy. I've had the best holiday season ever, and I can't wait to continue with my family today."

"It's okay to miss her." Gram sat down and patted her hand. "You two really hit it off. I've never seen you so happy to break out of your routine before."

"Can we talk about something else?" She rose and turned toward the pantry. "I know, let's make a pie."

Gram caught hold of her arm. "No. Sit down and have a chat."

She shook her head. She didn't want to pour her heart out. Not now, not for the next two days. She wanted to be filled with yuletide joy. She wanted childlike excitement and anticipation. She wanted holiday magic to buoy her up the way it always had. "Can't we just enjoy the day together? It's Christmas Eve in Vermont."

Gram clucked. "It's Christmas Eve in New York, too, or are you trying to avoid that idea?"

"Oh Gram." She sighed and sank back into her chair as a hundred memories brought back a thousand emotions. "Why couldn't you let me pretend I didn't know that for a while?"

"Because you wouldn't have enjoyed it." Gram pushed the other mug of coffee toward her. "You don't fake the Christmas spirit, and you can't force yourself to feel blissful. You only overcome problems by working through them."

Ava shook her head. There was no working through this one. She and Bex had already had their hard talks. She'd felt the choking hopelessness of it all and cried the fruitless tears of futility. None of it got her anywhere. "We're both good people who care about each other, but our lives are too different. She's got her roots there, and mine are here. Our goals, our jobs, our families, it's too much to overcome with goodwill and a healthy dose of romantic chemistry."

"Maybe," Gram admitted, "but is it too much for love?"

Ava's chest burned, and the warmth rose all the way to her face. "We don't, I mean, we didn't have enough time to, we never said ..."

"I know," Gram whispered. "It happens fast sometimes. I never thought you'd be the type to get so swept up by someone. You've always been steady and constant, but that's how I knew for sure what it was. You wrecked your entire holiday routine for this woman, and you weren't even bothered."

She shook her head, letting the realization sink in.

"Any other year, you would've been miserable to miss even a tiny smidge of the traditions you spent your whole life refining, but I don't think that's what you felt with Bex."

"No," she whispered. Misery had been the furthest thing from her experience. She'd already admitted this had been her best holiday ever. "I loved almost every minute I let myself be truly present with her."

"Well, that's something."

"Sure, but what?" She hung her head. "We don't celebrate Christmas year-round. Believe me, I've tried. It doesn't work. Everyone returns to their real lives eventually, and we can't do that in two different places."

Gram sighed. "I can't imagine it would be easy, but then again, if I'd asked you on Thanksgiving morning, could you spend your holiday in two different places and still experience everything you wanted, I doubt you would've said yes."

Ava sat back and tried to give the idea genuine consideration. Thanksgiving seemed so very long ago, and the woman she'd been then felt as far away as Bex did right now, but it didn't take too much to imagine how she would've felt about a split Christmas back then. "I probably would've been horrified at the idea."

Gram laughed. "That's what got you into this position in the first place. You were sure you had all the answers. You knew for certain you had the right way. You made a bet with a stranger you couldn't even conceive of losing."

Her chest tightened. "We called the bet a draw. I'm still here. I still love my life and my traditions. I didn't lose the bet."

"No, you just lost a big chunk of your heart."

She gasped, then slowly let her head fall to the table, unable to deny the charge.

Gram's hand rested on her shoulder. "I know it's hard. You're a good woman. You already care so much about so many things, but didn't the last month teach you that you have room for more?"

"I don't know what the last month taught me," she muttered. "Probably a lot of things, too many to process, but I can't make sense of any of them, at least not in some way that doesn't smash up against the realities of our situation."

"You know you have it in you to try something you never tried before. And you know you can be happy doing things differently if you have the right person to do them with."

She sighed, but didn't argue.

"And you know spending Christmas in two different places made it better than you believed it could be."

292

She sat completely still until Gram gave her shoulder a little shake.

"Right?"

"Right."

"If you can spend the most important time of your year split between her life and yours, and make both of those lives better in the process, why can't you do the same in the more mundane parts as well?"

She lifted her head. "It's not as if I didn't think about it. I couldn't stop thinking about it toward the end, but it's daunting. There are so many obstacles. I worry I'd lose myself completely in doing the work of making us work."

Gram smiled. "I understand, but I don't think you're giving this one enough credit. She spent the first month of your relationship meeting you halfway. She didn't make you work for it or earn it or convince her of anything."

"She came here first, didn't she?"

"And last," Gram said.

Why hadn't she realized that until right now? Had she been so afraid of what she might lose, she never stopped to consider what she'd already been given?

"Did you ask her?"

"Ask her what?"

"If she'd be willing to keep meeting you in the middle?"

She shook her head. "I never seriously considered the possibility. I thought we'd have to choose one life or the other. Or I'd end up doing everything to hold onto her. I didn't dare wait to see if she'd try to hold on to me."

Gram stared at her, eyes soft with compassion, as she let Ava wander further down this path for the first time.

"She might've wanted to." She remembered the intensity in those blue eyes as Bex stared down at her. "She asked me to come back with her."

"Did you ask her to stay with you?"

"No. All I could see were the pitfalls and problems. I didn't ask anything of her. I didn't want to risk it. I just knew neither one of us could give up the lives we loved. I didn't want that for her any more than I want it for myself."

"But what if you found a way to merge them? It seems to me like you've already seen some pretty special returns on doing so for the last four weeks."

A new feeling stirred in her chest, and she made one last effort to push it down. It wasn't that she didn't want to believe, but rather she wanted it so much the desire frightened her. "What would that even look like? How could we possibly bend our worlds to our will? I'd end up missing half my time here with the people I love."

Gram shook her head. "I think you're asking the wrong question."

"What's the right one?" Desperation crept into her voice.

"What'll it look like if you don't figure out how to bend? 'Cause it seems to me you'll end up missing *all* your time with the woman you love."

Ava pushed back from the table almost involuntarily.

"You have any answers?" Gram asked hopefully.

She shook her head.

"You going to go try to find one?"

She nodded numbly, overwhelmed by the prospect, but no longer able to avoid it.

Gram leaned forward and cupped her cheek. "I believe in you, Ava. I believe in you more than I believe in the holiday spirit or magic or anything else you need to harness. You'll figure it out if you set your heart to the task."

She wasn't nearly as sure, but she forced herself to stand and say, "Thank you. I'll see you later tonight."

Gram merely smiled up at her. "Whatever you need to do, but just in case, Merry Christmas, Ava."

🐑 🐑 🐑

By the time Bex had dressed in her scrubs and dragged herself through the pre-op ward, she couldn't tell if volunteering to take a surgery on the morning of Christmas Eve was one of her best ideas or one of her worst. When her alarm had gone off, it definitely felt like the latter. All she'd wanted to do was stay in bed, surrendering to the lethargy clinging to her ever since she'd boarded the plane in Burlington. But, once she'd forced her blood to start pumping, she felt grateful for the sense of purpose that always accompanied her arrival at work. Here she had answers. Here she had options. Here she felt useful and the day, meaningful. Only today was Christmas Eve, so she shouldn't have to manufacture any of those feelings in the first place. They should've come baked in, free of charge or effort.

She shook her head, trying to clear it as she pulled back a blue curtain and focused on the patient in front of her. He fit the bill of what she expected from his chart. Early twenties, healthy, good musculature. The only discordant aspect of his appearance was the swell of breasts under his hospital gown, but then again, she'd expected that as well, given that he was here for gender-affirming surgery. "You must be Louie."

The young man smiled up at her. "I'm about to be."

"That's the spirit, but you being here means you've already done the hard work. I'm Dr. Leone, your anesthesiologist, and I'm honored to help you reflect a more accurate version of yourself to the outside world."

"Thanks. I'm like 10 percent nervous and 90 percent excited."

"Seems like a great ratio," Bex admitted, wishing she could summon the same sort of odds for her own day, but she pushed away the thought, or at least pointed it back where her attention belonged. "You must be pretty dedicated, though, if you sign up for a major surgery the day before a major holiday."

He shrugged. "I didn't have anything planned."

"I guess if you don't celebrate Christmas, it's probably a great time to do these things. You get the place to yourself, right?"

He lifted his shoulders again, though this time they seemed heavier. "I get time off work from NYU. I should be through the worst of the pain before the spring semester starts."

"Smart." Bex pulled up a stool. "I'm going to make sure you feel as little pain as possible."

Louie grimaced. "Too bad I didn't meet you sooner in this process."

Bex nodded, understanding he referred to a kind of pain she couldn't numb. "How can I help?"

"You're going to put me under, right?"

She nodded. "And wake you back up again. I assume you've been briefed about the recovery?"

"Yeah, they're going to transfer me to a care facility tonight. Then tomorrow, I'll go home to spend Christmas as a new man."

"And you have someone there to help you with bandages, food, drains?"

He shook his head.

"You don't live with any family?"

"No, for the same reason I don't have plans this Christmas. They only want to celebrate with someone I couldn't ever be."

Her chest tightened. "I'm sorry. It's clearly their loss if they can't celebrate with the real you, but I imagine it's still hard to pass a major milestone all on your own."

"Yeah," he admitted with a little crack in his voice. "My neighbor's a nurse. She agreed to check on me when she gets home from celebrating with her family, and I've been on my own for a while now. I'm pretty resourceful. Besides, the way I look at it is if I'm going to be alone on Christmas morning, I might as well like who I'm with. This surgery is going to make me like who I am more than any other Christmas in my life."

She rose and rested a hand on his shoulder and squeezed, trying to find any adequate response. "That's a perfect mindset."

He stared up at her and managed a little grin. "What about you? Do you have anything special planned?"

She shook her head without thinking.

"Nothing?"

His apparent surprise inspired the same in her. She did have plans. She was going to do all her favorite things, holiday movies, church at St. Patrick's, and she'd secured reservations at a Michelin-starred restaurant and tickets to a Broadway play. She had plenty of plans. Why hadn't she answered the question in the affirmative?

Then it hit her so hard she sank back to her stool. It wasn't that she didn't have enough planned, so much as those plans no longer felt special.

"It's okay, Doc," Louie offered, likely misreading what caused her sudden rush of sadness. "Life isn't about what you do, it's about who you do it with, right?"

Bex bit her lip and nodded until she could present the steady image he deserved from his doctor. "Absolutely, and let me assure you, I'll do all I can to make sure you spend yours as comfortable and content as possible."

A hint of genuine excitement returned to his expression. "I'm really looking forward to Christmas then."

She felt a tinge of his exuberance surge into her with a hint of the clarity she'd lacked over the last couple of days. "You may've helped me feel the same."

"Sudden change of plans?"

"I'm not sure yet. I've got some things to figure out, but I might be going to Vermont."

He wrinkled his nose as if he found the idea distasteful, and she loved him even more. "What's in Vermont?"

She laughed. "I've asked myself the same thing many, many times, but you just helped me remember that a more important question might be, '*Who* is in Vermont?'"

Chapter Twenty-Five

"Ladies and Gentlemen, in preparation for our on-time arrival into JFK Airport, please fasten your seat belts and return your tray tables and seat backs to their full and upright position."

Ava's hands trembled as she slid the magazine she'd been holding in her lap since takeoff back into the pocket in front of her without having read a single article. Her brain had been a blur since she'd left Gram's, and what few cohesive thoughts she could form swung wildly between hope and fear. What kind of person hopped a plane on Christmas Eve with no plan and no warning to a place she knew so little about?

She'd really hoped to have heard back from Howie before she took off, but when she'd called the surgical center, Pamela said he and Bex were both in a procedure and offered to take a message, but Ava hadn't known what to say.

She'd been over and over and over it incessantly, and she still didn't have any more answers than she'd had yesterday. All that had changed was her willingness to live with not knowing. She could've at least said with some certainty she wanted to wake up beside Bex on Christmas morning, and as many mornings as possible, but that didn't seem like the kind of message you had a colleague deliver. Instead, she'd boarded one of the last planes with an open seat, afraid if she didn't act immediately, she'd miss her chance to do so at all.

She glanced out the window as the city glinted in the afternoon sun, a sparkle of silver amid a gray and white landscape. Bex was down there, along with eight million other people, and while Ava managed to feel bold and adventurous ninety minutes ago, now the predominant emotion had become overwhelmed. For someone who'd watched hundreds of holiday movies, she'd never once given any thought to the logistics of how the grand gestures at the end of them actually worked out.

Would she take a cab? Where to? She didn't have Bex's address. She'd never needed it. She could go to the surgical center. She knew the name, which should be enough for a cab driver, but would Bex still be there by the time she arrived? Would anyone? Maybe she should text her and suggest they meet atop the Empire State Building or some other romantic place, but were any of them open on Christmas Eve?

The bump of the landing gear on the tarmac jolted her out of the panic spiral. Another announcement alerted her to what any person could've surmised, that they had arrived and were free to use cellular devices.

She switched her phone out of airplane mode and tapped Howie's number.

"Hello? Ava?" He picked up after only one ring. "What's wrong? Are you okay? Is Gram—?"

"What? Yes. Of course, or she was when I saw her this morning."

He sighed. "Then why do I have five missed calls and no messages. Pamela said you tried the office too."

"I didn't mean to scare you. I didn't know how to explain in a hurry."

"Explain what?"

"I'm in New York."

"Say that again."

"I'm in the city ... or, I don't know the rules about boroughs and such. I'm at the airport."

"Which one? There are at least three."

"JFK."

He laughed.

"What's funny?"

"About a million different things. What's happening right now?"

She shook her head and looked around as other passengers began to unbuckle and collect their belongings. "I don't know. I wanted to get to Bex, to do the big romantic thing, and you'd think I'd be better at it, but it's harder than it looks on TV. I thought maybe since you're in the city, you could at least tell me where I need to go and how to get there."

The plea was met with silence, or maybe not silence so much as the din of crowd noise in the background while Howie seemed to first ponder the request, then choose his words carefully. "Give me the information from your, um, schedule details."

"I don't have a schedule. I just landed."

"Yes, those details should suffice."

"My flight?" *Why hadn't he said so?* "I'm on Delta Flight 527."

"Perfect," he muttered. "Now, wait."

"Wait? Where?"

"Please hold."

"Hold? What the hell, Howie? We're getting off the plane."

"Great. Stay." Then he disconnected.

"Howie, hey, what the—" She stared at the blank screen as someone jostled her from behind. *Stay? What was she, a puppy?*

She should've known better than to trust him with something this big and emotional. She allowed herself to be carried away in the current of people shuffling up the center aisle and off the plane, then stepped out of the stream as soon as they edged into the terminal. She needed a moment to collect herself and try to formulate a new plan that didn't involve putting all her eggs into the Howie basket, so she eased into a chair and waited for the crowd to thin out.

Stay?

That didn't make sense. She could've done that on her own … in Vermont. She pinched the bridge of her nose and tried to stem the suspicion she should have. She could've at least formulated a better plan, or perhaps asked him a few pertinent questions when his flight arrived in—

His flight. She checked her watch. The timing could be close. Was Howie at the airport? The same airport even though there were apparently three of them? She hopped out of her chair. Why wouldn't he have said so?

She scanned the throngs of people, looking for him amid the crowd streaming in both directions. Turning slowly, she tried to home in on any familiar feature even as her brain told her she couldn't possibly be so lucky as to run into someone she knew in a city this big or busy.

She stood frozen to her spot, overwhelmed by the enormity of it all, too afraid to move, too stricken to sink back into her seat, not knowing how much time had passed, until a slow awareness began to seep in with a familiar certainty. She marveled, much as she had the first time in Penn Station, to discern the sensation of a particular set of eyes on her amid such teeming masses of humanity, but this time, she understood the power of their connection. She recognized this feeling beyond all logic and reason. No other gaze had ever made her feel so seen. She turned to meet it, a smile starting in her heart before it reached her lips as the crowd parted enough to reveal Bex standing mere feet from her, still in her work clothes with a backpack slung over one shoulder. She dropped it, and they sprinted toward each other.

Colliding in an instant, Ava clutched her tightly, hands working almost frantically up Bex's hips, her sides, her arms, until she cupped that perfect face in her palms. Then she planted a kiss right on her mouth before realizing they'd probably skipped a hundred steps and even more questions. She stepped back only enough to stare at her, but the words wouldn't come. Instead, she burst out laughing.

Bex did the same, and they might have simply dissolved completely if not for Howie clearing his throat nearby.

She became aware of his presence and the stares of several other passing travelers, but she couldn't quite tear her eyes off of Bex. "How?"

"Why?" Bex shot back.

"You."

"But, you, too."

"Wow." Howie set Bex's backpack at their feet. "I've never seen either of you lost for words. This is going to take all night to sort out, and I have a flight to catch."

"Thank you," Bex managed, without turning fully to him.

"You're welcome, and Merry Christmas to both of you. I hope it's your happiest ever, Bex. And Ava, I hope it's even better than the year you got Fuzzy."

That broke through her disbelief, and she finally looked at him and back to Bex. "Fuzzy? Did you get my cousin to give you inside information?"

Bex bit her lip and shook her head.

Howie must've realized he'd stepped in it because he backed away. "You should talk about other things, like what

303

you're going to do now. Bye!" Then he bolted down the concourse.

She turned back to Bex.

"What? I mean he's awkward, but he got us together, and he's right. You don't want to spend your Christmas here in the airport, do you?"

She tugged her closer. "I want to spend my Christmas with you. That's why I'm here."

"Me too." Bex kissed her. "I have a ticket on the same flight as Howie. I wanted to wake up with you tomorrow and as many other mornings as I can. Anywhere, everywhere. I don't pretend to know how, and I know it'll take a lot of work, which makes you nervous, but I swear you won't be the only one trying this time because I'm all in. I'll do whatever I need to do to make you happy."

She was grateful for Bex's strong arms still around her because she nearly swooned, growing dizzy from such perfection. "I want all of that too. We can do long distance, or we can split time. I know how important this place is to your identity, and your job is amazing. I'm flexible enough to come to the city a lot more than I let myself admit."

"But I won't take you away from your family either," Bex vowed solemnly. "I can arrange my shifts to come to Vermont a lot. I'll become one of those doctors who takes long weekends and vacations, and I don't know, maybe some hospital in Burlington can use extra shifts or rotations. I'll figure something out."

"I believe you." Ava laughed at how easy it all seemed once they both decided none of the details mattered as much as the motivation. "The question is, what do you want to do now?"

"I can still get on the plane right now."

"Oh, I hope you don't."

"Why?"

"Because I don't have a return ticket." She went a little loopy again at the implications of that statement. "I came here with no plan other than to find you. I don't know what I would've done if I'd somehow made it to your place after you'd already boarded a plane to Vermont."

"You planned to spend your entire Christmas in the city?"

"With you." She added the most important part.

"Together." Bex nodded. "We're on the same page. Okay. We can do this. It'll be our first step of many, right? Since we're here, let's go get us both a ticket for tomorrow. We'll spend tonight just the two of us, alone together in my world because I do want to have you to myself for a while."

Ava kissed her again as a shiver ran through her at all the images her decree inspired.

Bex pressed forward until their entire bodies pressed flush, then apparently remembered where they were before easing back. "Then tomorrow, we'll fly back to Vermont in time to have Christmas dinner ... where?"

"My parents' house. Everyone will be there."

"Everyone," Bex said, "including us."

"Yes." Ava hugged her tightly. "Together."

"Let's make decisions like this always," Bex whispered.

She snuggled a little closer, nuzzling the crook of her neck and breathing in the scent of her. "Let's make a whole life like this."

Epilogue

Warmth hit Bex as soon as Ava pushed open the door to her parents' house, and she wondered if this was about to become a constant state in her life, stepping from the crisp cold into a home that felt more like an embrace than a place. She smiled at the idea as she shed her coat and a large portion of the family rushed toward them.

"Merry Christmas," Ava called as hugs commenced, only this time, Bex wasn't standing on the outside.

Gram got to her first, pulling her down to her height before encircling Bex with her arm and whispering, "Merry Christmas, and well done, you."

She grinned. "You're not mad at me for keeping her away last night?"

Gram patted her cheek. "I know you won't do it every time."

"I promise," Bex said, meaning it.

"Good." She stepped back only for Howie to take her place.

"I'm not going to take credit for this, because you are two brilliant women responsible for your own agency, but I am going to take this moment to say, 'I told you so.'"

She laughed. "You did. You were correct about the lesbians in Vermont."

He squared his shoulder proudly. "Forget Vermont. You've doubled the number of lesbians in the family."

"Hey!" Ava cut back in. "Merry Christmas, and thank you for dragging this one to Vermont, also to the airport yesterday, but don't think I've forgotten you traded my cherished childhood memories in the process."

Howie grimaced, then opened his mouth as if he intended to defend himself or perhaps apologize, but Bex held up a hand to stop him, then tapped the side of her nose.

"Nope, not a word," she instructed. "I cop to nothing, because even if I were called upon to keep any of Santa's secrets, and I'm not saying I was, I'd take them to my grave because I'm a true believer."

Ava's entire posture softened. "I respect that. More than respect, I really like it."

Howie clearly took this as a personal pardon and nodded gratefully before backing away.

Ava shook her head as she watched him go, then looping her arm through Bex's, directed her toward the living room where they'd had their first kiss. "I mean it. Your belief in magic is one of the things that drew me to you."

"I'm glad to hear it, because, you know, it's not just Santa I believe in."

"No? I'm looking forward to learning all the other things about you too. Want to give me a preview before we join everybody else?"

Bex pressed her lips together playfully. "I think I already started to last night."

Ava's cheeks flushed, and she closed her eyes with a contented little hum as if her mind were replaying particular memories, so Bex surrendered to the urge as well. They'd spent hours in each other arms, tangled together, breaking apart only long enough to enjoy a luxurious dinner before midnight Mass, then crashed into each other again in a different kind of holy expression.

When the morning light dawned on a new Christmas, they'd opened their presents from each other. Ava seemed delighted with the twin nutcrackers Bex had commissioned in their likenesses. Likewise, Bex had been completely enthralled with the hand-painted glass ornament Ava made for her. It featured, in miniature detail, all the country Christmas experiences the two of them shared in Vermont, from caroling, to sledding, to skating, and even a sprig of mistletoe.

Bex opened her eyes again and glanced overhead to find her new favorite plant still hanging above them, before saying, "Speaking of my beliefs, I feel it's a solemn duty to kiss under mistletoe."

Ava leaned forward and kissed her on the mouth. "Me too. What else?"

"The Christmas spirit."

"Obviously."

She smiled. "Also, hard science, the superiority of New York-style pizza, the transformative power of a good book, the magic of a well-cooked meal, singing in the shower, wishing on stars, and most of all, I believe in true love ... which is what I feel for you."

Ava gasped.

"I mean it," she said with a new pleading in her voice. "I'm not the kind of person who says such things lightly. I am in love with you."

Ava bit her lip and nodded as tears filled her eyes. "I love you, too. And I love that you said it here, today, like this, because it's what I asked Santa for."

"Are you serious?"

"Yes. When you pulled that whole thing at Santaland and made me talk to him, and you apparently moved mountains to make it personal and special and magical just for me, I didn't ask to win the bet. I asked him to find a way to let me keep you, and not for Christmas, but for always."

Bex marveled as she did the math. "You got there a week before I did. I worried I'd rushed in or fallen too fast, but I didn't know how to stop myself. Logic and stubbornness weren't working for me, so I guess it's only fitting I took a similar sort of route you did."

Ava raised her eyebrow in question.

"You're what I wished for when we stood on your porch searching for a Christmas star."

"Are you serious?"

"Absolutely. I wanted to keep you in my life, and I didn't know how, so I took all my hopes and pinned them to Polaris." She shrugged sheepishly, feeling only a little silly that a medical doctor admitted such a thing aloud. "I told you. I'm a believer. Even more than I'm a city mouse. I guess that's especially important to lean into now since I'm only going to be a half-time New Yorker."

"You'll always be a New Yorker," Ava said quickly, "no matter where you go, but I guess I'm a half-time country mouse now too, huh?"

"You know what they say about taking the girl out of the country but not the country out of the girl."

Ava tugged her close once more. "Who would've thought those identities brought us together only to be the undoing of them both."

"I don't know. Getting together was the important part. Maybe we had the right idea, but we lost time by clinging to the wrong aspects of them."

"How so?"

"I think the last month has proven we both have a title more important than 'city mouse' or 'country mouse,' and it's the one that really brought us together."

"Which one?"

Bex smiled down at her. "Christmas mouse."

Ava arched up to kiss her cheek. "Oh, I do like that one. I think we should keep it forever, no matter where we go."

"Which reminds me. What are you doing for New Year's Eve?"

Ava shook her head. "I hadn't even thought about it yet."

"You know there's nowhere in the world like New York City for—"

She laughed, cutting off the speech bubbling up in Bex. "How about if we take things one holiday at a time."

She squeezed her a little tighter. "Fair enough, Christmas Mouse. You've got yourself a new deal."

ACKNOWLEDGEMENTS

I, like so many queer Christmas aficionados, have long wished to see more diverse representation in holiday stories. Like many of you, I crave the chance to see LGBTQ characters get their happy holiday endings in movies, books, and plays, though for me it doesn't just stop there. I also want to see more city-based seasonal classics. As someone who always spent holidays in small towns with big families, I totally understand the charm and comfort of a country Christmas, but as a New York State transplant, I have also come to recognize there is no better place in the world to make the yuletide gay than the Big Apple! I hope that no matter which side of the divide you're on, you will see yourself represented on these pages.

I would like to thank my early readers and fellow NYC Christmas fans, Barb and Tony, for their quick reading skills and contagious enthusiasm for this book, which confirmed that I'm on the right track. Lynda Sandoval made me both laugh and think with her substantive edits, while Avery Brooks took the details and polished them until they shined. Brisk Press once again stepped in with their speed, generosity, and expertise to get this book out in time for Christmas. Kevin from Book Covers Online dazzled me once again with an adorable cover. And my proofreaders, Ann, Moana, Melissa, and Radar caught so many of those pesky typos that managed to slip past us all. I'm so grateful for everyone's time and talent. I also want to thank all the readers who continue to make this work both possible and worth doing. Special shout out to my Patreon folks for providing me with a safe space to work through important details like names for dogs and horses.

On the personal side of things, Georgia Beers and Will Banks have been my Hallmark-movie watching buddies, helping to fuel my love of the genre and my desire to put my own spin on it. Anna, Melissa, and Nikki continually encourage me to keep writing things I love. My therapist, Leah, helped me move from a place where I felt weight around my writing to a place of light and joy. Most of all, my family has inspired such a tremendous sense of fun around this project and life in general. I cannot remember when all three of us had such a great time researching one of my books. Susie and Jackson, from trips to Vermont to dinners at Rolfe's, you two drove home the idea that Christmas isn't about where you spend it, it's about who you spend it with. You two are the wish I make on every Christmas star, come what may.

And to my creator, redeemer, sanctifier, and true reason for the season, *soli deo gloria.*

ALSO BY RACHEL SPANGLER

Learning Curve
Trails Merge
LoveLife
Spanish Heart
Does She Love You
Heart of the Game
Perfect Pairing
Edge of Glory
In Development
Love All
Full English
Spanish Surrender
Fire & Ice
Straight Up
Modern English
Thrust
Plain English
Heartstrings

THE DARLINGTON ROMANCES

The Long Way
Home Timeless
Close to Home

About the Author

Rachel Spangler never set out to be a *New York Times* reviewed author. They were just so poor during seven years of college that they had to come up with creative forms of cheap entertainment. Their debut novel, *Learning Curve*, was born out of one such attempt. Since writing is more fun than a real job and so much cheaper than therapy, they continued to type away, leading to the publication of *Timeless, The Long Way Home, LoveLife, Spanish Heart, Does She Love You, Timeless, Heart of The Game, Perfect Pairing, Close to Home, Edge of Glory, In Development, Love All, Full English, Spanish Surrender, Fire and Ice, Straight Up, Modern English, Thrust, Plain English*, and *Heartstrings*. Now a four-time Lambda Literary Award finalist, an IPPY, Goldie, and Rainbow Award winner, and the 2018 Alice B. Reader recipient, Rachel plans to continue writing as long as anyone, anywhere, will keep reading.

In 2018 Spangler joined the ranks of the Bywater Books substantive editing team. They now hold the title of senior romance editor for the company and love having the opportunity to mentor young authors. Rachel lives in Western New York with wife, Susan and son, Jackson. Their family spends the long winters curling and skiing. In the summer, they love to travel and watch their beloved St. Louis Cardinals. Regardless of the season, Rachel always makes time for a good romance, whether reading it, writing it, or living it.

For more information, visit Rachel on
Instagram, Facebook, Twitter, or Patreon.

You can visit Rachel Spangler on the web at
www.rachelspangler.com